Advance Praise

"Compulsively readable, *Off to Join the Circus*, Deborah Kalb's foray into adult fiction, is a study in human nature and the bonds we form, and sometimes break, within our own families. In this breezy and brilliant novel, three generations in a close-knit family are forced to examine their relationships with each other when a "legendary" member of the family reappears after a sixty-four-year hiatus. Ms. Kalb infuses her story with wry wit, snappy dialogue, and the universal themes of acceptance, betrayal, resentment, secrets, and redemption in this tale that explores the repercussions of a prodigal's return with characters we can all relate to. Perfect for book club discussions."

> — Kathleen M. Rodgers, author of *The Flying Cutterbucks*, a 2021 WILLA Literary Award Finalist in Contemporary Fiction

"In *Off to Join the Circus* novelist Deborah Kalb makes the difficult feat of engaging the reader with good people look almost easy—just like a circus acrobat. Serious and joyful family matters play out, with the requisite tears and laughter. Smoothly shifting point of view between several members of the three-generation Pinsky clan, Kalb's three-ring circus takes place over a jam-packed fortnight. A prodigal octogenarian sister returns after seventy years, a bar mitzvah boy prepares for his big day, infidelity and new love are discovered, and everyone counts down to the arrival of a baby. Readers who enjoy Anne Tyler's Baltimore families and Laurie Colwin's denizens of Manhattan, step right up and meet the Pinsky family of Bethesda."

> — Ellen Prentiss Campbell, author of *Frieda's Song* and *The Bowl with Gold Seams*

"Deborah Kalb's *Off to Join the Circus* is exactly what readers want: a warm, insightful family story that you can't put down. Told fluidly from multiple points of view spanning three generations of the Pinsky family, we get to glimpse inside the mind and heart of each member. These are fully realized people, instantly recognizable, yet uniquely individual, with all their loves, misunderstandings, everyday anxieties, and deep connections to each other. Even the elderly sister, who defined the idea of "being circus" for all of the Pinskys by leaving her family sixty-four years earlier, can't escape the profound ties that pull her back into the fold. From now on, because of this novel, "circus" will mean more to me than the big top; it will resonate with the very essence of being alive."

> — Roselee Blooston, author of IPPY Gold medal winner *Trial by Family*, and *The Chocolate Jar and Other Stories*

"A heartwarming portrait of a multigenerational family. Kalb excels at crafting multiple points-of-view, giving strong and distinct voices to each character, while amping up the drama and intrigue to keep the reader wanting more. I enjoyed every page right up to the satisfying finish."

— Suzanne Simonetti, author of *The Sound of Wings*

"With charm, wit, and heart, Deborah Kalb provides an intimate portrait of the Pinskys, a Washington D.C., Jewish, suburban clan who loves maybe a little too hard. On the eve of a bar mitzvah, milestone birthday, and birth, Aunt Adele turns up after a 64-year absence that has created emotional ripples throughout three generations of Pinskys. *Off the Join the Circus* illuminates how the most estranged relative can both ruin and restore the balance to a family's ecosystem. I devoured the novel in three sittings but reflected on these deeply flawed but loveable characters for days afterwards."

— Michelle Brafman, author of *Washing the Dead* and *Bertrand Court* &
 Swimming with Ghosts

"Readers will meet a charming ensemble cast of characters threaded together in this warm and heartfelt family drama."

— Renee Rosen, author of *The Social Graces*

"Come one. Come all. *Off the Join the Circus* is ready to amaze you. With sly humor and a big heart, Deborah Kalb's debut adult novel takes readers to Washington D.C. to meet the perfectly imperfect Pinsky clan. A high wire act that examines the bonds of enduring family love, this refreshing novel will keep you thinking long after you read the last page."

— Sally Koslow, author of *The Real Mrs. Tobias*

"What a wild ride! Huge thanks to the talented Deborah Kalb for creating the messy and lovable Pinsky family. Fully relatable and entirely unforgettable, they catapulted off the page and into my heart. It's a busy, fast, imaginative book, chock full of plot twists and complicated but endearing family relationships. A great read!"

— Ellen Meister, author of *Take My Husband*

"What a delight of a book! I want the Pinsky family to adopt me; I could have stayed on the page with them forever. Deborah Kalb's multi-faceted cast is remarkably differentiated— each wounded in their own way—while still braided in the ultimate consolation of family. *Off to Join the Circus* brings to life a remarkable tale of family love transcending a sixty-four-year absence of a beloved sister and aunt and the upheaval of her return."

— Randy Susan Meyers, international bestselling author

"The sudden appearance of a long-lost relative challenges three generations of a family to reexamine their choices, aspirations, and regrets, and along the way discover new capacities for expansiveness and adventure. *Off to Join the Circus* is a lively and generous novel filled with humor and grace, reminding us of the dynamic nature of how we see ourselves and those we are most closely bound to."

— Hester Kaplan, author of *Unravished and The Tell*

Off to
Join the Circus

Off to
Join the Circus

A Novel

Deborah Kalb

Apprentice
House Press
Loyola University Maryland

First Edition

Library of Congress Control Number: 2022950481

Hardcover ISBN: 978-1-62720-448-4
Paperback ISBN: 978-1-62720-449-1
Ebook ISBN: 978-1-62720-450-7

Design by Brian Leechow
Editorial Development by Rachel Hoos

Published by Apprentice House Press

Loyola University Maryland
4501 N. Charles Street, Baltimore, MD 21210
410.617.5265
www.ApprenticeHouse.com
info@ApprenticeHouse.com

In memory of my grandparents, Max Kalb (1897-1962), Bella Portnoy Kalb (1899-1976), William P. Green (1901-1997), and Rose Bell Green (1903?-1993), with love and appreciation.

One

Howard

The call came in about five p.m., the afternoon of Howard Pinsky's seventy-fifth birthday. He had retreated to his study. His wife and his oldest daughter were busy in the kitchen, cleaning up after the birthday celebration. His youngest daughter was in the family room with his grandsons, all of them absorbed with their respective phones. His middle daughter was lying, hugely pregnant, on the living room sofa, attended by her husband, who was massaging her feet.

Howard loved them all beyond words, but there were times when he just needed to get away. Being the center of attention was not his thing.

"Gramps, you okay?" Max, the older grandson, had asked, as Howard had left the room. At fifteen, Max could be alarmingly perceptive. He also could be as obtuse as any other kid his age.

"Thanks, Max, I'm just going to take a rest," Howard had said. But he didn't intend to rest. He intended to read. He sat down in his favorite chair, a leather one that had been in his office at the law firm until he retired a few years back. The phone had been ringing nonstop all day. Old friends. Distant relatives. Former colleagues. All calling to wish him a happy birthday. He just needed some peace and quiet. He glanced at the Washington Nationals bobbleheads on his desk. They were out of order. He rearranged them. Probably Will, the younger grandson, had been in here. He was the other big baseball fan in the family.

Howard pulled out a book. A new spy thriller his wife, Marilyn, had given him. He put his feet up on the footstool that accompanied the leather chair. He sighed with satisfaction. The perfect way to conclude the afternoon.

And then the phone rang yet again. He glanced wearily at the caller ID. "Unknown," it said. Probably a crank call. But what the hell. Maybe it was another birthday greeter.

He picked it up. "Hello?"

"Howie?" The intonation. The voice. It was just the same as it had been all those years ago. A wave of dizziness hit him. He felt himself telescoping backward, like in an old movie but in reverse, the images shifting from a seventy-five year old retired lawyer, to a first-time grandfather fifteen years ago, to a young father with his girls, to a senior in college meeting Marilyn for the first time, to a kid sitting on the plastic-covered living room sofa in West Orange, New Jersey. He was eleven. He had just graduated from elementary school.

He was having trouble breathing.

"Hello? Howie? Are you there?"

"Uh," he managed to say. What does one say to a sister one hasn't seen or spoken to in sixty-four years, he thought hazily.

"Howie? I wanted to call. It's your birthday."

Now she wanted to call? After sixty-four years of not calling? After she disappeared at age sixteen, ran off who knows where, and never contacted him again? She had stayed in touch, through occasional phone calls, for decades with their parents. But after their deaths, more than a dozen years ago, nothing.

Of course, he'd tried to track her down. But she was elusive.

The phone calls were hard to trace, and she seemed to move frequently. At one point he'd convinced his parents to hire a detective, but the search had come up empty. And at a certain point, he'd just given up.

"Adele has decided to leave home," his father had told him. They'd been in Howard's bedroom, the day after his elementary school graduation. His mother, hysterical, was in his parents' room, crying. "She left a note."

"Where did she go?" Howard asked from his cross-legged position on the braided circular rug, glancing up at his father. This was the most unexpected thing that had ever happened to Howard. Bobby Slotnick's sister wouldn't do something like this, he knew it. Neither would Stuart Bernstein's sister. Howard looked at the new Erector set he'd been given for his graduation. He wanted to build something. Maybe see if Bobby or Stuart was around to help him.

"Oh, she's run off to join the circus," his father said, waving one hand in the air. "Who knows, Howie, off to join the circus." And he wandered out of Howard's room, a dazed expression on his face.

The circus? Which circus? What would Adele do in the circus, anyway? Howard could hear his mom weeping, and his dad trying to comfort her. But where exactly had Adele gone? He knew some things his parents didn't know. He knew all about how she'd sneak out of the house at night to meet her boyfriend, Chuck. He knew that she took the train into the city to do who knows what when their mom thought she was at her piano lessons. How she really didn't want to go to college, although she'd been accepted to Barnard already for the fall. She'd skipped a grade. Howard knew she was very smart. Probably smarter than he was, even though he was probably the smartest kid in his class at the Gregory School.

Maybe something with animals? She was very fond of their cat, Boots. Or maybe something on a high wire? She'd always been good at gymnastics. He remembered seeing her turning cartwheels in the back yard, over and over, when they were younger. It had made him dizzy.

"Howie!"

He was thrust back into the present. It was 2018, not 1954. He was in Chevy Chase, Maryland, not West Orange.

"Adele."

"He speaks!" Adele's voice was a little raspier than he remembered, but not too far off from how she'd sounded at sixteen. She was eighty, he realized with a shock.

But what the hell?

"You're the one who hasn't spoken in sixty-four years," he burst out.

"True," she said. "But I've decided enough is enough. Estrangement is ridiculous at our ages."

It was ridiculous when they were kids, too. When they were young adults. When they were middle-aged. He remained silent.

"So your family?" Adele said. "Marilyn? The girls? All well?"

She knew about the existence of Marilyn and the girls from his parents. But not the grandsons. They'd come along afterwards.

"Yes," he said.

"Sarah, that's the oldest, right? She's married?"

"Yes," he said again. This was all too overwhelming. He took a deep breath. He felt as if he might pass out.

"What does she do? What does her husband do?"

"Her wife," Howard said. "Sarah's the director of a nonprofit here in D.C., and Vilma works for a Finnish company." Vilma seemed to spend pretty much all her time in Finland lately, which was where she was from. But he was concerned about Sarah. She had way too much going on, especially with Will's bar mitzvah coming up, and Vilma's absence was not helpful.

"Wife, husband, whatever," Adele said.

Well, that was good, Howard thought.

"Finnish? Like, Finland?"

"Yes."

"Any kids?"

"Two. Max is fifteen and Will's almost thirteen."

"And are they her biological kids?"

What? Adele disappeared for sixty-four years and then started asking that kind of question? He ignored her.

"And Diana?"

"She's married to a chef named Philippe. They're expecting their first baby next month."

"A French chef, how wonderful," Adele said. "First baby, at how old?"

"Forty-four," Howard said. And yes, he was worried. But excited. Diana's doctor said she was as healthy as a horse. So he really shouldn't worry. But Diana had always been the most difficult of his daughters. The one most likely to run off to join the circus. The one who reminded him of Adele. Since the advent of Philippe, though, Diana seemed much happier. Calmer. Although Howard and Marilyn found Philippe far too absent-minded. "And he's Belgian."

"Okay," Adele said. "And little Lucy? She's married too?"

"Divorced." Howard sighed. Lucy, a decade younger than her sisters, had been married a year out of college. It was as if she'd been as eager as possible to detach from the other Pinskys and start her own separate life. Which was a positive thing, of course. But then it had all fallen apart.

"Don't you have any questions for me?" Adele asked.

Questions for her? He had a lifetime of questions for her. He'd been waiting for this moment for decades. And now that it was here, he couldn't focus. He couldn't figure out what to say. It was all too much. He felt a surge of anger rising up within him. He started shaking. His heart was pounding. Would she be the death of him, in the end?

"Holy shit," he exploded. "You call me up after all this time and expect me to be coherent? You left me, Adele. You fucking left me. I was eleven years old." And he found himself on the verge of tears. Not something that happened to him often. He took some more deep breaths. The image of Dr. Goldstein, his cardiologist, flashed into his mind. Maybe he should make an appointment.

"Ah, yes," Adele said. "I suppose I did catch you by surprise. Well, here's another thing to think about, Howie. I'd like to come for a visit. I'd like to stay with you. Maybe for a couple of weeks. Get to know each other again."

Two

Marilyn

"And you said yes?" Cat's roundish face was crinkled in confusion, Marilyn noticed. As well it should be.

Marilyn nodded. How could she explain this to her best friend? The reappearance of Howie's prodigal sister, after sixty-four years? The person whose absence, Marilyn was convinced, had influenced the trajectory of his life and, in turn, all of theirs? She and Cat had discussed Adele, ad nauseam, for decades now, and both of them detested her. Or the hole she'd left in the family fabric. That's what Marilyn detested, at least.

"So she calls him on his birthday, and asks to stay?" Cat continued, frowning and putting down her coffee mug, which featured a drawing of a woman wearing a pink pussy hat. "And he said what?"

"I have to ask Marilyn," Marilyn said. Which was a perfect response, she had to admit. She took another sip of her coffee and glanced around Cat's spotless kitchen, filled with souvenirs from the years she and her ex, Skip, had spent in various Foreign Service postings around the world.

"Howard's always been a good guy that way," Cat said. "So then what happened?"

Marilyn told her. The discussion that had gone on for several days. Her own resentment of Adele. Her feeling that a visit from the dreadful, disappearing Adele could only destabilize the entire family. Sometimes Howie seemed to agree with her, and sometimes he seemed transported back to his childhood memories, to a time when Adele was the most important thing in his life, and at those times, he seemed to think a visit was a great idea. Finally, on the fourth day, Marilyn had concluded that a visit might indeed be the best thing for Howie. Exorcise those ghosts. Two weeks? Well, she'd have to see how it went. So in another ten days, Adele would be flying in from Hawaii, where she apparently had been living for years under the name Adelaide Montgomery.

"Adelaide Montgomery?" Cat asked.

"A stage name."

"So she actually did join the circus, then?"

Marilyn sighed. "She hasn't given Howie a straight answer about anything. They've talked a couple of times, but mostly she just asks him questions about the kids." Asking, asking, asking, without revealing anything. And poor Howie seemed too overwhelmed to ask anything coherent of his sister. Once she arrived, Marilyn would sit her down and give her a piece of her mind. What had Adele been thinking, leaving her eleven-year-old brother, who worshipped her, and not contacting him again for sixty-four years? Did she have any idea how it had affected Howie? The repercussions for the entire Pinsky family?

"...told them yet?" Cat was asking.

"Oh, sorry," Marilyn said, returning her attention to Cat. "I was distracted."

"Did you tell the girls yet?"

Marilyn nodded. Once the decision to have Adele visit had been made, they had invited everyone over for a family dinner, last night, where they'd broken the news. Adele was a legend in their family. The mysterious aunt who had possibly joined a circus, or was the type of person who could possibly join a circus, which none of the other Pinskys were. Except Diana. Their reactions had been characteristic. Sarah had fretted over the impact on Howie. Diana had tossed her head and tried to turn the conversation back to her pregnancy. Lucy had withdrawn a little further into herself. Max had frowned thoughtfully and asked a bunch of questions about Howie and Adele's childhood. Will had said, "Cool!," and returned to looking up baseball scores on his phone. Philippe had been working at his restaurant. Vilma, of course, was in Finland.

"Should we walk now?" Marilyn asked. Part of her would rather just sit in Cat's kitchen. The weather, beautiful that morning, had turned windy and chilly. But she needed exercise, she knew. She was nowhere near her step goal for the day. And her knee, which had been troubling her off and on for the past year, was feeling okay, so there were really no excuses.

She and Cat, Catalina Thompson, who lived three houses away, had been friends since they'd met at the playground down the street when Sarah, and Cat's older son, Tim, were babies. They had bonded immediately. Both Marilyn and Cat were teachers— Marilyn taught English at the local community college, and Cat, who was originally from Mexico and had met Skip when he was stationed there in the late '60s, taught Spanish at the high school. She was completely bilingual, an accomplishment Marilyn admired.

Cat stood up and stretched. "Yes, let's do it," she said, heading for the front door and reaching for a coat that was hanging on a coatrack. Marilyn pulled her own jacket on, and they departed.

"The thing I've been wondering about," she told Cat, as they proceeded down their street toward a footpath, which linked to the Capital Crescent Trail—a walk they'd taken thousands of times-- "is why she chose to do this now. After all this time." Marilyn had various theories, but she just didn't know.

"You said she's eighty, right?" Cat said. "So it's a question of mortality." Cat had gone through treatments a couple of years back for stage-two breast cancer. She was doing fine now, but both of them had been shaken by the experience. Marilyn had taken her to most of her appointments, as Cat's boys, though attentive, lived in California and Texas.

Marilyn had wondered about that. Could Adele be sick? Possibly dying? Of course, Adele hadn't said anything about her health, but then she hadn't said much of anything, had she? Except her endless questions of Howie, prying into their lives.

She nodded, and wrapped her scarf more closely about her neck. The wind was whipping around, causing her to shiver.

"Not to change the subject, but I was going to tell you something I heard from Tim about Skip," Cat said. "You won't believe this." And she launched into a story her son had told her about her ex-husband and his much younger second wife. Apparently they had bought a boat and were planning to sail it to various places up and down the East Coast.

Skip had left Cat for this younger woman about twenty years ago now. Marilyn, who hadn't especially liked Skip but hadn't expected this to happen, was shocked. As was Cat. Howie, on the other hand, who had always opined to Marilyn that Skip was an asshole, and that no, he wasn't interested in going to dinner or the movies with the Thompsons, said he wasn't surprised at all.

Marilyn had tried, over the years, to introduce Cat, who she thought was incredibly brilliant and beautiful, to various newly single men of her acquaintance. Nothing had ever worked out, although Marilyn hadn't given up. She had a former colleague in mind whose wife had left him a few months ago.

Just then, Marilyn sensed a buzzing in her jacket pocket, and she pulled her phone out. Sarah. "Sorry, Cat, I have to take this," she said.

"So can you or Dad take Max to the dentist this afternoon?" Sarah asked breathlessly. "I'm so sorry, I totally forgot. I'm really sorry. I scheduled this meeting for the same time, and…"

Marilyn wished Sarah wouldn't sound so apologetic. She, Marilyn, loved taking Max and Will places. And she was grateful that they still talked to her. "Of course," she said. "I'd love to." It was one of the best things about being retired. She and Howie had always helped Sarah a lot with the boys. Sarah, single at the time, had become pregnant twice through donor insemination, and then she'd met Vilma a few years after Will's birth, but by then the pattern was set. And these days, Vilma was hardly around anyway. Marilyn had tried to broach the subject of Vilma's absence with Sarah, but Sarah told her not to worry, that things were fine.

Sarah apologized a few more times and thanked her and hung up.

"Was that Diana?"

"No, Sarah," Marilyn said.

Diana was a whole other situation that sent Marilyn into a frenzy of worry. Granted, Diana was only a few years older—well, okay, five years older—than Marilyn had been when Lucy was born. But this was Diana's first child. Who knows what could happen? Diana seemed to be breezing through the pregnancy with flying colors, and she did have Philippe to help her, but somehow neither Diana nor Philippe inspired the greatest confidence in either Marilyn or Howie. Philippe had to be the most absent-minded person Marilyn had ever met. And Diana, well, she was just like Adele. Or just like how Marilyn imagined Adele, anyway. Except that Marilyn loved Diana beyond words, and had no such feelings toward Adele.

Marilyn's phone buzzed again. A text, from Lucy. "Bringing

Will to your house late afternoon?"

Lucy also helped out with the boys. She taught English—which filled Marilyn with pride--at the middle school Will attended, where Max had also gone, and often spent time with them after school. She would sit in her classroom grading papers, and Will—or, previously, Max—would sit there too, doing his homework. It seemed to work out well. Then she'd drop Will at Marilyn's house until Sarah got back from work.

Lucy, who had been about as problem-free as a child could be, had climbed onto Marilyn's worry list, too, since Lucy and her former husband, Jeff, had parted ways. But Lucy was not one to share her problems. At least, not with Marilyn. Maybe Lucy would have confided in Sarah. Or maybe Diana? She'd need to ask them.

"Yes, Dad will be there, I'm taking Max to dentist," Marilyn texted back.

"Great, thx," Lucy replied.

Just as Cat was gearing back up to tell more about Skip's sailing expedition, the phone rang once more. It was Howie.

"Adele's had a change of plans," he said hesitantly, as if unsure of how she'd respond. "She'd like to come a week early instead."

Three

Diana

Diana sailed into the Starbucks, her stomach jutting in front of her like the prow of a ship. She was wearing her usual outfit, a teal blazer with a black shirt and bright pink tie. Along with black maternity pants. It was difficult to dress like the subject of her latest assignment when she was eight months pregnant. But she was giving it her best shot. Ghostwriting was almost as fun as acting, and she had managed to make it somewhat lucrative. Between her earnings and Philippe's success at the new restaurant, all should be well once the baby finally arrived. She felt a twinge of heartburn, and reached into her bag for a Tums, which she popped into her mouth.

She glanced around. The Starbucks was located in the basement of a hotel near a Metro stop, and it featured a view, upward, of a multi-story set of balconies. The place was half-empty at eight p.m., and she saw no sign of her fellow writing group participants. This was unusual. Generally Marcia was the first to arrive, followed by Gideon. Poppy was often late, and Nick sometimes failed to show up at all.

Diana, as the acknowledged leader of the group—the only one who was actually the author of several published books, although as the ghostwriter her name either did not appear on the book cover or appeared in small print below that of the celebrity she was assisting—loved her writing group. It was an eclectic mix of people, the remnants of a Meetup group that had long since disbanded. Diana had organized them into a small tribe of acolytes that met every Monday night. By this point, five years in, it had become more of a series of therapy sessions than an actual writing group, but she did try to focus them on writing whenever she could.

She bought a bottle of water—no caffeine for her right now—and sat down on a bench, pushing the table away from her stomach. The baby flipped around and started kicking her in the ribs. Diana had been to Dr. Patel again that morning, and she had pronounced Diana and the baby in excellent shape. "Another four weeks to go," Dr. Patel had said. "He or she will be making an appearance shortly." Diana and Philippe had chosen not to know the baby's gender. Dr. Patel, who knew, had been very good about keeping it from them.

"You really need to get the crib," her mother had said over the phone that afternoon. "And the changing table. I'm going to take you this week. Or maybe Sarah or Lucy would like to come along and we could all go this weekend."

Sarah, maybe. Lucy, not a chance. But her mother didn't know that. Diana frowned. She really didn't feel like thinking about Lucy. She decided, instead, to think about Gary M. Blattner, the subject of her latest ghostwriting assignment. Blattner, the inspiration for Diana's outfit, was a ubiquitous presence on cable financial news programs, having made millions in the market. Now he was writing his autobiography, with Diana's assistance. Diana wasn't especially fascinated by the stock market, to be honest. Her previous assignments had featured actors. Her people. But her success with these actors had led one of them to recommend her services to Blattner, and she had accepted the assignment the day before she learned that the IVF cycle had been successful. She and Philippe had gone out to celebrate both accomplishments. In the morning, not the evening, because he had to get to the restaurant by late morning.

Diana liked to dress the way her subjects dressed. It helped her get into character. She had adopted Blattner's gravelly voice and profane speech patterns, which he managed to avoid while on air. The Blattneresque attire had fit much better before she started to show, and then to balloon. But she felt she was still capable of carrying off the look. She had hoped to finish a good draft of the manuscript before the baby arrived, and this was still possible. Unless he or she decided to show up early. Which was also possible.

"Diana!" It was Marcia, hustling toward the table with an iced coffee. "Oh my, you look resplendent!" She hugged Diana and sat down next to her.

Marcia, a retired elementary school teacher, was working on a fantasy book for kids, featuring kindly sea creatures and endangered heroines. She tended to talk the way she wrote. Diana was constantly telling her to tone it down a little. Diana's own fiction writing, on the other hand, was concise to a fault. And, in her opinion, this style had paid off. She'd had two stories published recently in literary journals, much to the amazement of her family, who probably would always think of her as a screwup.

"Thanks," Diana said in her Blattner voice, turning toward Marcia and nodding at her. "As do you." Actually, Marcia didn't look particularly resplendent. She looked the way she usually did, her pale freckled face eagerly smiling, her gray hair frizzing, and her shoulder bag overflowing with papers.

"Oh, here comes Poppy," Marcia said, waving at their fellow group member. Poppy was a perpetually angry twenty-something with bright blue hair and multiple piercings and tattoos. Diana had only one tattoo, a tasteful butterfly near her right ankle. "Poppy, dear, here we are."

"Yeah," Poppy said, waving back. She approached the table, clomping toward them in her black combat boots. "Holy shit, Diana, you look like a whale. A whale in teal and pink." She grinned at Diana and then at Marcia. "Doesn't she?" She turned back to Diana. "So I want to talk about my new story tonight, okay?"

Diana nodded. Poppy, who had first joined the group as a college student and was now working for an animal rights organization, had been writing dystopian short stories for quite a while now. This latest one showed more promise than many of the others, Diana thought.

"Hey, people." A deep voice sounded, and Diana turned around to find Gideon. A fiftyish lawyer, he was writing a novel based on the history of his enslaved ancestors, which he had been researching for years. "Diana, you look great."

This was quite gratifying, Diana thought, as she watched Poppy and Gideon sit down with their lattes. Being noticed was something Diana had never minded. Even if she was being noticed for looking like a beached whale. Maybe she should have gotten pregnant years ago. She nodded graciously. "Thank you."

"So let's get started, okay, Diana?" Poppy asked. "Nick's probably going to be late anyway, so let's not wait for him this time."

Nick, a reporter in his early thirties, covered Congress, which was a nonstop job, and he often was unable to join them.

"Yeah," Diana said. She decided to abandon her Blattner voice for the time being. Staying in character was surprisingly exhausting tonight. She sipped at her water, as the baby kicked her again.

Poppy started reading the opening of her story, which revolved around a young woman fending off loneliness and terror in the ruins of a New York-like city. Diana made some comments, as did Gideon and Marcia, and then Diana noticed Nick rushing towards their table.

"Sorry I'm late," he said breathlessly. "There was this big vote in the House and I had to file something." He sat down and pulled out his phone, and seemed to be texting. He glanced up at the others. "My editor. Just a couple of questions, sorry."

"Fuck it, Nick," Poppy said, glaring at him. "Always late and then too busy to participate. Aren't we important enough for you? I was reading my story."

Nick frowned at Poppy. "Jeez, stop it, Poppy, okay? I want to hear your story, all right? I'll be done in a second."

The two of them bickered constantly, like an older brother and his fractious younger sister. There was something about Nick that reminded Diana of her sister Sarah. Something dutiful. Overly apologetic. Way too responsible. And always worrying about something. Diana was sure that Nick, like Sarah, had been the valedictorian of his high school class. When he'd first joined the group, he had been married to his college girlfriend, who had subsequently left him. Now he was seeing a woman who seemed perfect for him, except that she lived in Boston. If this new woman, Lauren, hadn't appeared on the scene, Diana might have introduced Nick to Lucy. They would have gotten along. But that was a non-starter now. And given past history, Diana probably should stay out of Lucy's personal life anyway.

The thought of her sisters reminded her of her Aunt Adele. Her dad was picking Aunt Adele up at the airport at that very moment. Diana figured this was all pretty stressful for him. Being abandoned as a little kid by your only sister, and then having her turn up as an old lady all these years later.

She'd mentioned it to Blattner during their most recent Skyping session. "Crazy shit," he had replied, and had told her a story about an estrangement between his own father and grandfather, which was sort of upsetting to hear but quite useful for the book.

"Guess what, guys?" she said. She might as well tell the group about Aunt Adele. She'd mentioned her before, so they undoubtedly would be interested.

Poppy scowled at her. "My story?" she said. "What the hell?"

"We'll get back to it," Diana said. "This is material for all of you to think about. My dad's picking up my Aunt Adele at the airport tonight. They're going to see each other for the first time since 1954."

"Fuck," Poppy breathed, her expression rapt. "Circus Adele?" She had apparently forgiven Diana for the digression. "She must be, like, a hundred years old at this point."

"Oh, Diana!" Marcia said, her eyes widening. "Maybe she'll be here when the baby arrives! How magnificent!"

"Family," Gideon said, shaking his head. "They'll surprise you in the end."

Nick, putting his phone away, seemed completely speechless.

"So yeah," Diana said, gratified by their response. "Circus Adele. Although she hasn't said anything about what she was actually doing for all those years."

"I think the circus thing was just a throwaway line," Gideon said. "Something you say to a kid when you're not sure what to say."

All the Pinskys thought that was a possibility. Diana nodded. "But the thing is, she could have joined the circus. She's the type you could imagine doing such a thing. There's circus people, and not circus people." In her family, it was clear that she, Diana, was circus. The rest of them were not circus. They all knew that.

She gestured around at the other four. "So you take our group. Poppy and I are circus. The rest of you are not circus."

Poppy, Gideon, and Marcia all nodded.

"Go, Team Circus!" Poppy said, offering Diana a fist bump.

Diana could feel the baby offering a fist—or foot?—bump in solidarity. Would the baby be circus? Philippe was the opposite of circus. Maybe it would be like him.

"I'd say my older son is sort of circus," Gideon mused. "The rest of us, definitely not."

"Yeah," Marcia said. "My middle child, circus all the way. She's off in Tibet right now."

Nick was silent, which often was the case. He was looking thoughtfully at Diana. "So you're seen as the circus one in your family, Diana, but seriously," he finally said. "I mean, I get that you were kind of irresponsible as a kid and when you were, like, a younger adult, but where did you actually go, anyway? You live right here, with everyone else in your family. You never moved away. You're completely enmeshed with them. I'm more circus than you when you think about it. My parents live four hundred and fifty miles away." He paused. "Except that they're moving here soon. But still. Maybe you're not so circus after all."

Diana, in turn, was speechless. She had never thought about it that way. Nor, she was sure, had anyone in her family. Being circus was a major part of her identity. It had represented her role in the family structure. What if she had been not circus all along? What then?

Four

Howard

Howard paced around the baggage claim area at National Airport. The plane had arrived twenty minutes ago, so where was she? They had arranged to meet near the baggage carousel disgorging the luggage from her flight. Honolulu to Los Angeles, L.A. to D.C. Would he even recognize her? Would she recognize him? They hadn't exchanged photos. And he looked somewhat different at seventy-five than he had at eleven.

Was she mobile? Would she need a wheelchair? The idea of Adele, his vibrant teenage sister, as an elderly woman in a wheelchair was stunning, and he felt the need to sit down and catch his breath. Dropping into one of the black vinyl chairs lining the windows, he felt his pulse. He was supposed to see Dr. Goldstein in two days. So that was good. Get everything checked out, see if his heart was okay.

Sarah had said maybe he should also go to her therapist. Just to talk, she'd said. It's a lot to deal with when your sister reemerges after sixty-four years. But Howard wasn't sure. He'd never gone to a therapist, although Marilyn had urged him to over the years. What the hell would he say? His sister ran away at sixteen, when he was eleven, and he'd never seen her again? But people dealt with far worse circumstances. His life had turned out okay without Adele, hadn't it? A fantastic wife, three wonderful daughters, two delight-ful grandsons, and another grandchild on the way. A successful career. What did he have to complain about, really?

His thoughts returned to that day when he learned of Adele's disappearance. Off to join the circus. He'd obsessively researched circuses. Demanded to attend whenever the circus came to town. Over the years, as he progressed deeper into adolescence and went off to college, he'd doubted that Adele had anything to do with the circus at all. Maybe she had found work in an office somewhere. Gone to college somehow. Gotten married. His dad had just tossed out the line about the circus because he didn't know what else to say. Still, the idea of the circus had been so deeply lodged in Howard's brain that it had become immovable. Permanently attached.

He remembered his first date with Marilyn. He was a senior at Columbia and she was a junior at Barnard, fixed up by a friend of hers who was dating a friend of his. The four of them had gone to a movie, *Lawrence of Arabia*, and then the other two had departed, leaving Howard and Marilyn alone. They had ended up in a late-night diner, eating omelettes, for some reason, and talking for hours. And she'd mentioned she was an only child and did he have any siblings? And although he rarely talked about Adele with any-one, he found that he was unburdening himself to Marilyn, and revealing his questions about whether Adele actually had joined a circus—a decade of exhaustive circus-going on his part had turned up nothing—and his parents' reluctance to say anything further about the entire thing, and the fact that Adele had called one time, three years ago, but he'd been away at school already and had missed it.

And Marilyn had been fascinated, and had peppered him with questions, and several hours later proclaimed herself ready to help him track his runaway sister down. Which was a relief to

Howard, because he'd been convinced he'd messed things up with this incredibly attractive girl by blabbing on about Adele. And so it had begun.

"Howard?"

Howard jumped up, but it wasn't Adele. It couldn't be Adele. This woman was about fifty, maybe, with blonde hair pulled back in a knot. Could Adele be ageless? Maybe she had had multiple facelifts?

"Betsy O'Neill," the woman said, an apologetic smile on her face. "From the office. Sorry, you looked very preoccupied."

"Oh, sorry, Betsy, of course," Howard mumbled. Of course this wasn't Adele. This was one of the partners at his former law firm. Not someone he'd been especially close with, but a good colleague nonetheless. "I just had my mind on something else." She probably thought he was senile. Retired a few years back and then gone completely to seed.

"Back from a trip?" Betsy inquired. "I'm just back from Chicago." She gestured at her wheeled suitcase. "Work, work, work. You know how it can be."

Howard nodded. "I'm picking up my sister." It sounded so strange. And yet, to Betsy, probably so normal.

"Nice," Betsy said. "She's coming to visit you?"

Should he tell her the whole thing? No, probably not. She undoubtedly had somewhere to go. "Yes, that's right."

"Well, great seeing you, Howard," Betsy said, smiling again and turning toward the doorway. "Have fun with your sister."

"Thanks," he managed. "Send my regards to everyone at the office."

She waved and departed.

Howard looked at his watch. It was now more than half an hour since the plane had landed. Where was she? Could this be an elaborate hoax? Get his hopes up and then not show after all?

Maybe he should check his phone. Max and Will had taught him how to use it when he'd finally submitted to the need for a smartphone a couple of years ago.

"We can text you," Will had proclaimed gleefully.

"You probably have no idea how to text, so we'll show you," Max had added helpfully.

Sure enough, there were multiple texts.

"Is she there yet? Is she there yet?" This, from Will.

"Don't want to bother u, but any news?" From Sarah.

"How u doing, Gramps?" From Max.

"Hope ur holding up ok." From Lucy.

Nothing from Diana, but that wasn't surprising. And Marilyn didn't tend to text often, at least not to him.

He had nothing to reply, so he didn't answer any of them. Instead, he put his phone back into his pocket and started pacing around again. Was she playing him for a fool? Getting him all worked up, and then bailing? He walked toward the baggage carousel for the L.A. flight, where there were still several pieces of luggage circling forlornly. Was one of them hers? Maybe something had happened to her. Maybe she'd had a stroke. Been taken ill. Should he go up to the security line and explain the situation? Try to get through somehow? But they'd agreed to meet here, so what if she got here and couldn't find him?

His heart was pounding, so he took a couple of deep breaths. He'd called his cousin, Morty, the other day, after the phone call from Adele. Cousin Morty, a couple of years younger than Howard, had also grown up in West Orange, a few streets away, and after Adele's departure, was the closest thing to a sibling Howard had. He was also a lawyer, but a far more flamboyant type of lawyer, with a flourishing practice in Manhattan that focused on celebrity divorces. Cousin Morty himself was on his third wife, a thirty-something former model named Lucretia.

"What the fuck, Howie?" Cousin Morty had bellowed over the phone. "Adele? After all this time? Is she dying or something? Wants to make amends?"

Dying? Howard hadn't contemplated such a thing. Oddly enough, although Adele certainly was up there in years, Howard had always assumed she was alive and well, somewhere. He hadn't assumed Hawaii, although that was about as far as you could get from New Jersey and still be in the United States.

"I don't know," Howard had replied. "I'll keep you posted."

Now, staring at the baggage carousel, the thought came back to him. What if Adele were indeed dying, and he would find her only to lose her soon again?

"Howie!"

He turned around to find his sister, very much recognizably Adele. Her hair was an attractive silvery gray, and she was wearing incredibly high heels that made her almost as tall as he was, and he was about five-ten. Although he'd shrunk an inch or so in the past few years. High heels? Marilyn had given up on them a few years back. Not that she'd worn them all that often anyway.

Howard's heart was pounding even faster and a feeling of light-headedness swept over him.

"Adele," he said. And he found himself caught up in a fierce embrace. The same kind of embrace that made him feel better after Bobby Slotnick picked on him, or after he was chosen toward the end for baseball in the vacant lot down the street and then proceeded to strike out repeatedly, or after his fourth-grade teacher sent him to the principal's office for talking back. He let himself sink into it.

And, as if he were that kid again, the first thing he asked her was, "Did you really run off to join the circus?"

Five

Max

His mom was on the phone with Vilma, even though it was like three in the morning in Finland, and Will was involved with Fortnite on the computer, so Max decided he might as well take Phoebe, their elderly, somewhat obese basset hound, for her evening walk.

"Come on, Phoebs," he said, attaching the leash to Phoebe's collar. Phoebe, always amenable, wagged her tail and barked happily. Max waved at his mom, who smiled at him and waved back. Will, who was playing the game remotely with some of his friends, didn't seem to notice Max's presence or absence. So he and Phoebe left.

It would be nice to have friends to play Fortnite with. But at the moment, that wasn't something Max had. Ernesto had moved back to Argentina in December and was often hard to reach, and Lucas was all absorbed with this girl, and Seb seemed like he thought he was just too cool to hang out with Max any more and was spending all his time with the popular kids.

"You got any friends, Phoebs?" he asked Phoebe, who barked and pulled at the leash, tugging Max toward the park. Clearly, Phoebe did have friends, and she thought she'd find them at the park. Maybe she would. Maybe at night when everyone was asleep,

Phoebe and all the other neighborhood pets slipped out windows and doors and made their way to the park and had a giant party.

Maybe right now his grandparents and Aunt Adele were having a giant party at the house. Gramps should be back from the airport by now with Aunt Adele, and Grandma would be stressing out over the whole thing, and actually there was no way they'd be having any kind of party. His grandparents seemed like they couldn't even begin to deal with the reappearance of Aunt Adele.

He thought about it. What if Will left and he didn't see him for sixty-four years, until—he thought for a second—the year 2082? Holy crap. That seemed like a totally unreal kind of year, like something from *Star Trek*. He and Gramps and Will had watched the new *Star Trek* series and found it pretty cool, although he had to admit he liked the old original series with Captain Kirk and Mr. Spock better. Not that he would admit having anything to do with *Star Trek* to Seb, at least not these days.

Phoebe started barking frantically, and Max noticed none other than Seb's mom, walking their poodle, Baxter, heading toward him. Baxter started barking too, and Seb's mom pulled on his leash.

"Hey, Max, good to see you," Mrs. Wong said over the sound of the two dogs. She smiled pleasantly at Max. "You'll have to come over and see the new basketball hoop we just put up. Test it out with Seb, okay?"

Max nodded and smiled back, feeling sort of numb inside. Up till a few months ago, he would have been over there nonstop. He would have been discussing and playing basketball with Seb, the way the two of them always did. Until things shifted. He wasn't sure what had happened, exactly. Just that all of a sudden, Seb was avoiding him. Talking to the kids who had scorned Max and Seb and Lucas and Ernesto. Joking around with those other kids at the bus stop.

"I'm heading this way," Mrs. Wong said, pulling a reluctant Baxter away from Phoebe. "See you later!"

"Yeah," Max said. He wished he could tell Seb all this weird shit going down with Aunt Adele. I mean, who would do that? Who would leave and not contact their only sibling for sixty-four years, anyway? What kind of person was she? Circus, his family would say. She's circus. Max had always thought it was really cool to have an aunt who might have joined the circus, but lately he'd been thinking this circus stuff was total crap. Probably Gramps had bought into it because he was just a kid at the time, and Aunt Adele really had run off to do drugs or something. Join a commune. Although maybe that was later. Like, the sixties, not the fifties. Will still seemed to believe in the circus story, though, and Max didn't feel like sharing his doubts and bursting Will's bubble. It would be like telling a kid the tooth fairy didn't exist. Not that Will still believed in the tooth fairy any more. Or like telling someone about Santa or the Easter Bunny. Of course, that was irrelevant since his family was Jewish. But still.

They had reached the walking trail around the park, and no one else was around, so Max let Phoebe off her leash. He knew he wasn't supposed to do that, but the park was empty and it was almost nine at night. And Phoebe never seemed eager to go anywhere, anyway. She stayed near Max's feet and they ambled slowly around the path together.

The other night Will had been practicing his bar mitzvah portion, and Max had asked if he was nervous. Max remembered how nervous he had been for months before his bar mitzvah. How his stomach always seemed upset and he was always running to the bathroom. Gramps had said he went through the same thing, and his mom remembered totally freaking out before her bat mitzvah.

The worry gene seemed to have come straight down the line. He wondered if the donor had been a worrier too. He and Will often speculated about the donor. Lately he'd been thinking he might want to try to track him down at some point. One thing was clear: the donor probably looked like their mom. She must have picked someone who resembled her. Because he and Will both looked like her. Dark curly hair, largish features, slender. Not short. Well, Will wasn't so tall yet. But Max had grown five inches in the past year. Sometimes he felt as if this body wasn't really his. This lower voice wasn't really his. All these zits weren't really his. He envied Will, who still hadn't hit puberty. And didn't seem nervous at all about his bar mitzvah, which was weird. Why hadn't Will gotten the worry gene?

His mom seemed worried all the time lately. And Max was stressing out about it. Maybe it had to do with the bar mitzvah, and maybe she had too much work. And maybe she was thinking Aunt Adele's visit was too much for Grandma and Gramps. But Max couldn't help thinking maybe his mom and Vilma were having problems. Why else would Vilma be away so much? Well, his mom had always worried, even before Vilma went away, so maybe it was nothing. Just the worry gene at work.

Diana certainly didn't have the worry gene. Diana was circus, that was for sure. He could easily imagine her taming a lion, or flying through the air on a trapeze. Not the way she looked right now, of course, about to have a baby. He wondered if the baby would be a boy or a girl. He could babysit for it. That would be fun. A little cousin. He could teach it to read, or teach it to ride a bike, or teach it to play the guitar.

Max loved playing the guitar. He'd been spending hours and hours up in his room with the door shut. Lately, when he wasn't doing homework, he'd been playing this Bob Dylan stuff his grandma had gotten him into. All those hours spent at his grand-parents' house, maybe he was turning into an old person. Maybe that's why he didn't have any friends. Maybe he was just super-weird and that's all there was to it. At the bus stop, no one talked to him. Seb and the other kids all clustered around one another, leaving Max on the periphery with a couple of other kids who didn't seem to care. This new girl, who always had earbuds in her ears and was really into theater, and this totally weird kid who had never talked to anyone, ever since kindergarten.

Maybe Max really was circus, underneath it all? Maybe he was the one who would run away. Escape from Bethesda. He'd thought Will was more likely to be circus, because Will never seemed worried about anything. But Will seemed too content to be circus. Circus meant rebellious. Discontented. Alienated. Not that Max had ever rebelled against anything. But maybe he could. Maybe he could join a band. Guitar was a cool instrument, right?

"Max?" A voice sounded behind him. He jumped, and turned around. It was that girl from the bus stop, the one with the earbuds. Except she didn't have earbuds tonight. She had a dog. A huge dog. A Great Dane? He wasn't sure. The dog started barking, as did Phoebe. Max slipped her leash back on.

"Shirley!" the girl said. "Stop it! Calm down!"

Shirley? This dog didn't look like a Shirley. And what was the girl's name, anyway? This was embarrassing. She knew his name, and he couldn't remember hers. Shit. He knew she had played Hermia in the school play of *A Midsummer Night's Dream* last November. But that wasn't her name in real life. What was it? Something unusual, he thought.

"It's okay, Phoebs," Max said, patting Phoebe, who subsided and suddenly looked very happy. Sometimes he could swear Phoebe was smiling at him. It made him feel better.

"Phoebs?" the girl said. "That's kind of cute."

"Phoebe," Max said. "And I like the name Shirley for your dog. Kind of unexpected." He was proud of himself. He actually had managed a coherent sentence or two while talking to a girl. This was unusual.

"She belonged to my grandma, who loves Shirley Temple movies," the girl said, smiling at him. "Gram had to move to assisted living, so Shirley came to live with us."

"Cool," Max said. "I mean, not about the assisted living, but about Shirley Temple." She was some kind of old movie star, right? "I mean, there's nothing good about having to move to assisted living, is there. Like, that must be totally difficult. And having to leave your pet on top of it. Like, yeah, difficult." He was glad his grandparents hadn't reached that point yet. Seb's grandma had gone into assisted living last year. He'd visited her with Seb a couple of times at the home. God, he was sounding awkward. And he still had no idea what this girl's name was.

"Yeah, it sucks," the girl said. "Thanks."

"So you take Shirley for walks at night a lot? I haven't seen you out here before." Oh, crap. Maybe he was sounding stalkerish or something. Like some weird #MeToo type of situation. Why did he always say the wrong thing? Why couldn't he be more like Seb? Or Lucas? Or even Will, who seemed to have no trouble talking to anyone?

The girl nodded. "Most nights, yeah. Sometimes my brother does it. But usually I don't come down this street."

And she probably never would again, now, Max thought gloomily.

"Well, gotta go," the girl said, pulling Shirley along. "See you at the bus stop tomorrow!" And she disappeared down the street in the other direction.

Max checked his phone. There was a text from his grandfather. "The eagle has landed," it said. "Heading home now."

Six

Marilyn

"You'd think she could at least offer to help," Marilyn muttered to herself as she set the dining room table for eight. Everyone was about to show up and the house was a mess. Adele's possessions were strewn all over the first floor, which Marilyn felt was the sign of a bad guest. A good guest would keep their things in the guest room. Who left scarves and shoes and sweaters all over someone else's house? And the shoes? What kind of eighty-year-old wore such high heels? And seemed so secure in them? Marilyn had one pair of shoes with slightly high heels and every time she wore them she sensed vertigo descending upon her.

She banged down the plates and frowned. She still hadn't had the chance to give Adele a piece of her mind. Adele had been closeted with Howie most of the time. They'd arrived home from the airport last night, and then the two of them had vanished into Howie's office. Marilyn had been asleep when Howie came to bed, sometime in the middle of the night. Probably normal bedtime in Hawaii. But of course Howie wasn't on Hawaii time, which Adele didn't seem to realize. And then this morning Howie had taken Adele out for brunch, and out to the National Gallery—apparently Adele fancied herself an artist—and then they'd squirreled themselves away in Howie's office again.

Well, she could understand. The idea of seeing a long-lost relative after so much time was probably quite exhilarating. But from what Marilyn had seen of Adele, she found her very inconsiderate. To begin with, she hadn't even greeted Marilyn. Marilyn had smiled her warmest smile at Adele and even approached her as if to hug her, but Adele had sort of looked through Marilyn, as if she wasn't there, and then had asked for some water. Really. And then once she finally deigned to notice Marilyn, she had given her a scrutinizing kind of once-over and said Marilyn didn't look how Adele had expected her to look. Well, what did that mean? Did she look worse? Better? Older? Grayer? But Adele hadn't explained. Instead, she'd taken Howie's arm and said the two of them had a lot to catch up on.

The doorbell rang. Marilyn hurried to the door to pay for the Chinese food, and brought it all back into the dining room, where she arranged it on the table. She'd put out the best tablecloth, and the nicest plates. But she had drawn the line at preparing a homemade feast. Adele had proclaimed she was vegan, and although all three girls had gone through vegan phases at various points and Marilyn was quite sympathetic to the vegan point of view, she didn't have it in her right now to cook a gourmet vegan meal. Especially not for Adele.

She counted the places at the table again. Herself, Howie, Adele, Sarah, Max, Will, Diana, Lucy. Philippe was at the restaurant, and Vilma, well, would she ever come back again from Finland? The bar mitzvah was coming up in a matter of weeks—Marilyn and Cat had talked about placing bets on whether the bar mitzvah or the baby would happen first--and you'd think Vilma, who was the boys' stepmother, after all, could do something to lessen Sarah's burden. But no.

She heard the door open. All the girls and the grandsons had keys, so it was only natural that they'd be in and out. Sarah's house was only a short drive from Marilyn's, and the other two lived in apartments that also were not far away.

"Mom?" It was Lucy. She came into the dining room and gave Marilyn a hug, which Marilyn returned.

She looked closely at her youngest daughter. Lucy looked too thin. Fine lines were appearing around her eyes. Even Marilyn's baby was showing signs of age. It was startling.

"So I'm teaching *The Comedy of Errors* starting this week," Lucy began. Lucy tended to talk shop with Marilyn rather than discuss anything personal. "Did you ever teach that one?"

Marilyn had, and Lucy helped her bring some serving utensils and bowls to the table as the two of them discussed Shakespeare and the best way to approach him with middle-schoolers.

"I guess she's still in with Dad?" Lucy whispered after a while.

Marilyn nodded. She'd been in touch with Lucy and with Sarah—Diana was often impossible to reach—and told them the situation.

"And I haven't had a single moment with Dad to get a debrief," Marilyn said. "I don't even know if they discussed the circus at all."

Lucy sighed. She pulled her curly brown hair up on her head, reached into her jeans pocket for a clip, and fastened it in place. "Hang in there," she said, patting Marilyn on the shoulder. "At least this gets your mind off Diana and the baby."

Perhaps this was true. Marilyn had been in a frenzy over Diana for weeks now. Why didn't she have a crib? A changing table? Any baby clothes? Diana hadn't wanted a shower, which was fine; Marilyn thought showers were overdone anyway. But the baby was due in less than four weeks—the same day as the bar mitzvah, actually--which meant he or she could be arriving at any point, and Diana and Philippe had done absolutely nothing to prepare.

Marilyn wondered, not for the first time, what Lucy thought of all of this. She knew Lucy and Jeff hadn't wanted children. But Lucy hadn't said much about the whole thing, and she hadn't told Marilyn and Howie why the marriage had broken up, and she certainly hadn't said anything about how it made her feel that Diana was having a baby. She hoped Lucy was opening up to someone about her feelings. It didn't have to be herself or Howie. But keeping everything inside all the time was never a good thing.

She heard the door again.

"Grandma!" Will rushed into the dining room, followed by Sarah and Max. "I just got this huge check from Cousin Morty! Like, a bar mitzvah check! My first one!" Will waved a piece of paper in her face excitedly.

Everyone hugged one another, and Marilyn examined the check before handing it back to Will. Eight hundred dollars? What? Since when did people give checks for eight hundred dollars for a bar mitzvah? Well, Cousin Morty was one for the big gesture. Marilyn couldn't stand Cousin Morty. Or his ever-younger stable of wives. Cousin Morty's values were terrible. All about money and status. What about being a decent human being? She stomped into the kitchen and filled a pitcher with cold water from the refrigerator dispenser.

Sarah had trailed her into the kitchen and took the pitcher from her. "Are you okay, Mom?" she asked, a worried expression on her face. Sarah had always worried too much, ever since she was a little girl.

"Yes," Marilyn said. "And you?" She wanted to ask Sarah if Vilma would be back in time for the bar mitzvah. She assumed so, but she just wasn't sure. Still, she didn't feel comfortable asking. There had to be some boundaries, didn't there?

"Fine, just a lot going on at work," Sarah said, heading back into the dining room with the pitcher.

"I think we can go ahead," Marilyn said, returning to the dining room herself. "Diana must be on her way. Max, can you go get Gramps and Aunt Adele? They're in the office."

Max nodded and disappeared down the hallway, at which point the door opened again and Diana swept in. She looked even more gigantic than ever. Had she, Marilyn, ever looked that huge when she was pregnant? She didn't think so. She had carried all the weight in front. From the back, she hadn't even looked pregnant at all. Diana was wearing that crazy Blattner outfit, and she was greeting everyone in the Blattner voice.

"How the hell are you, Will?" Diana growled, ruffling Will's hair.

Will waved the check at her. "From Cousin Morty," he said triumphantly.

"Morty? One of my pals," Diana said, still in character. "So he's your cousin? Holy shit."

Marilyn didn't think Diana should be talking that way around Will, but Lucy had assured her that Will heard worse than that every day at school.

"How's the bar mitzvah prep going, kid?" Diana continued, giving Will a look that eerily duplicated the expression Gary M. Blattner often had on his face while appearing on the financial news shows. Marilyn had to admit--although she didn't like to boast about her kids, even to herself--that Diana was an incredible actor.

"Okay, Gary," Will said. "Hey, Grandma, can I sit down and eat now?"

"Go see what your brother's doing," Marilyn said, shooing Will down the hallway. Where were they, anyway?

"I really need to sit down, Mom," Diana said in her own voice, plopping herself down in a chair. "The baby's really active right now. You want to feel?"

Marilyn leaned over and felt a series of kicks. Her future grandchild. It was truly a miracle. She felt as if she might cry. "Oh, Diana," she said, overcome.

"Let me," Sarah said, and sat down next to Diana, resting her hand on Diana's stomach. "Hi, baby, it's your Aunt Sarah. I can't wait to meet you!"

Lucy, Marilyn noticed, was busy on her phone.

"Do you actually want to be called Aunt Sarah?" Diana asked. "I mean, the boys don't call me Aunt Diana, and they don't call Luce Aunt Lucy."

"Actually, they did call her Aunt Lucy when she was reading those Paddington books to them," Sarah said, removing her hand from Diana's stomach. "Remember? Paddington's Aunt Lucy?"

Lucy looked up from her phone and smiled weakly. "If this baby wants to call me Aunt Lucy, that's fine," she said.

And then there was a flurry of footsteps and in came Max and Howie.

"Will wants to introduce Adele," Max said, as he and his grandfather sat down. "You know how the bar mitzvah kid gets introduced to everyone at the party, this big-deal buildup before he walks into the room? I think he's practicing for what he wants someone to say about him."

Sure enough, Marilyn turned to see Will approaching.

"Ladies and gentlemen," Will pronounced. "Straight from Hawaii, the mysterious long-lost possible circus performer we've waited our whole lives to meet! It's the one, the only, the amazing Aunt Adele!" And with a flourish, he gestured behind him at Adele, who was beaming in what Marilyn thought was a thoroughly Diana-like way. God, the two of them really looked alike.

She hadn't realized it before.

"My family!" Adele said, and went around the table embracing them all. Except Marilyn.

Seven

Will

Will had managed to sneak his phone out of his pocket onto his lap, under the table, and was texting with Carson and Arjun about the upcoming Nats game and about Fortnite and about how annoying Sra. Machado's Spanish class was and then he heard his name.

"...bar mitzvah, right, Will?"

It was Grandma. She seemed to be in a terrible mood. Will wasn't sure why. He looked up from his phone.

"Coming up soon, yeah, I think I'm ready." It was his all-purpose bar mitzvah-related answer. He had no idea what Grandma had been asking him, but figured his response would do the trick.

Grandma smiled at him. "I'm so proud of you," she said.

Well, that was good. Will glanced back down at his phone.

"Put the phone away, Will," his mom said from the other end of the table. He'd deliberately sat in a seat where she couldn't see him too well, but as usual she seemed to be able to sense what he was up to.

"Yeah, okay," he grumbled. He probably should pay attention to the conversation, after all. It wasn't every day that he got to meet a long-lost relative. He had tons of things he wanted to ask her. But when he'd tried, in Gramps's office, she really hadn't answered many of them. Including the question about the circus. She'd, like, avoided saying too much. Maybe she was a spy. Maybe he should ask her some espionage-related questions. When he was younger, he and his friend Jayson used to be really into spy stuff. Jayson had all this spy gear and they'd listen through walls and once they'd heard Jayson's sisters talking about how annoying Jayson was and then his sisters got in trouble. That was probably the high point of their spying careers.

"Yes, I was named after Adele Astaire," Aunt Adele was saying. "My mother loved Adele Astaire. And after Great-Uncle Abe. He had just died the year before I was born."

Will had no idea who Adele Astaire was. Or Great-Uncle Abe for that matter.

"...Adelaide Montgomery?" he heard Diana asking.

And who the heck was Adelaide Montgomery, anyway?

"No, I kept Diana Pinsky," Diana said. "Back when I first started acting, a couple of people told me I should change it, but I didn't."

"Different times," Aunt Adele said. "Adele Pinsky, back then, wouldn't get you where Adelaide Montgomery would. And I wasn't exactly eager to be tracked down."

Why not? Why had she felt like running away? When she was only a few years older than Will was now? A year older than Max was now? Will couldn't imagine Max running away. Lately Max spent all his time up in his room playing the guitar. All these songs Grandma had them listen to. Bob Dylan. Joni Mitchell. Joan Baez. Will knew more than any other kid his age about 1960s folk singers, he was sure of that. Not that he talked about it with anyone at school. He wasn't that into old music anyway.

"...Phoebs?" Max was saying now. "We probably should get home so I can walk her."

Since when did Max want to walk Phoebe all the time?

"Phoebe will be fine for a while more," their mom said, a look of slight puzzlement crossing her face. "There's no hurry. We're still enjoying our dinner."

Although his mom didn't look like she was especially enjoying her dinner. Will glanced around the table and then helped himself to some more chicken with broccoli. Grandma was frowning. Diana and Aunt Adele seemed to be discussing acting, which Aunt Adele apparently had done at some point. Gramps was staring into space, looking kind of tired. Max was sighing and resting his chin on one hand. Lucy was focused on Diana and Aunt Adele, listening to their conversation. Everyone but him seemed to be taking a break from eating.

Lucy seemed really stressed out lately, Will thought. He spent a lot of time with Lucy, given that he often hung out in her classroom after school when he didn't have another activity, and he had become sort of fascinated by this glimpse into the inner workings of teachers' lives. Lucy was a sixth-grade English teacher, and some of the other English teachers—including Will's current seventh-grade English teacher, Ms. Collins, and his last-year's English teacher, Mr. Shapiro—were constantly coming in and out to talk with her.

Ms. Collins always seemed amused to see Will there. "Getting your homework done, Will?" she tended to ask in that jokey way a lot of teachers had around kids when they interacted outside their particular classroom. Will would smile and joke back with Ms. Collins, who was a pretty good teacher even if she was kind of strict and gave a lot of quizzes.

Mr. Shapiro was another thing entirely. He was probably the coolest teacher in the whole school. He was sort of young, for a teacher, and he coached the boys' soccer team, which Will was on, and the girls would whisper about him and get all embarrassed when he called on them in class. And Will was convinced that Mr. Shapiro really liked Lucy. He was always coming into her classroom and acting all dorky and saying the wrong thing and behaving nothing like the way he behaved in his own classroom. It was sort of how Will acted around this girl Katelin C. who was in a few of his classes. He never was quite sure what to say to her.

But Lucy acted like she couldn't care less about Mr. Shapiro. Sort of like he annoyed her and she didn't like him very much. It was puzzling. He'd discussed it with Max the other day when they were shooting hoops at the park.

"That would be good," Max had said, after dribbling around Will and sinking a layup. "If Lucy ended up with some new person. I mean, after what happened with Jeff."

No one seemed exactly sure what had happened with Jeff. One day he was their uncle, and the next day he wasn't. It was weird.

"Yeah," Will had said. And then he'd asked Max about something else he'd been thinking about. Vilma.

"Where is she all the time?" he'd inquired. He held onto the ball, forcing his brother to pay attention.

Max had frowned. "I'm kind of wondering about her and Mom," he'd said. "Like, are they okay?"

"Okay how?"

"Like, okay, okay," Max said. He shook his head and smiled at Will. "But I'm sure it's all going to be fine, so don't worry about it. Now pass me the ball, all right?"

Will wasn't so sure. And he didn't think Max was so sure either. Would Vilma even be back for the bar mitzvah? She talked to him and Max on the phone sometimes, and texted with them too, but why was she always away?

He couldn't remember life pre-Vilma, but Max could. Max remembered the first time they'd met Vilma, and she'd given them these dinosaur puzzles and they'd all gone to the zoo. And their mom had seemed really happy.

Which she didn't seem to be right now.

"...could stay on longer, for the baby and the bar mitzvah!" Aunt Adele was proclaiming.

"Cool," Diana said.

"Yes, of course," Gramps said.

Grandma looked as if she were about to explode and shoot laser beams out of her eyes like the guardians in Will's Zelda: Breath of the Wild game. But why? Will's mom also looked super-unhappy. Will thought maybe it had to do with Vilma being away. And also with all the planning for his bar mitzvah. He felt a little guilty.

"...dessert?" Grandma was asking. "I have some ice cream, and I made some brownies, and there's some fruit."

Grandma's brownies were the best.

"Yeah," Will said. "Brownies and ice cream."

"Oh, I never eat dessert," Aunt Adele said, waving one hand in the direction of Grandma.

"But Grandma makes the best desserts," Will blurted out. "You should try the brownies."

"Max, Will, why don't you help me get everything out of the kitchen and bring it in," Grandma said, smiling at Will and getting slowly up from her chair. Maybe her knee was bothering her again. Maybe that's why she was in a bad mood.

"Hawaii just seems so far away right now," Aunt Adele said. "Howie?"

Gramps nodded. "Yes?" He turned toward Aunt Adele.

"Go help Grandma," Will's mom hissed at him and Max. "Come on!"

"Maybe we could go look at some apartments," Aunt Adele said. "I might be interested."

Eight

Sarah

"It's too bad we couldn't have kept the crib Max and Will used," Sarah's mom said, gazing around the store at the dozens of cribs on display, an overwhelmed expression on her face. "This is all just too much."

"Do you really need a crib, anyway?" Aunt Adele asked, turning to Diana. "Perhaps you could just put the baby in the bed with you. Co-sleeping, I believe it's called?"

Diana snorted. She was dressed in her Blattner garb and had added a fedora to the mix. "I'm not co-sleeping. I want to be able to get some sleep, if at all possible, and I'd be stressing out the whole time if she or he was in the bed with us."

"Consumerism run amok," Aunt Adele said, gesturing imperiously at the rows of cribs. "One reason why I chose never to have children. None of my husbands were all that eager, either. They wanted to save me for themselves. I hear the sex gets a lot worse after there's a child in the house."

Sarah sighed and looked around to see if anyone was listening. How had she been roped into this expedition, anyway? Lucy had pleaded an overload of work, but somehow that kind of excuse never worked for Sarah. Three weeks until the bar mitzvah, and she had so much going on at the office, and here she was spending her Saturday morning shopping for cribs with her narcissistic sister, her even-more-narcissistic aunt, and her beleaguered mother. The way things tended to happen in her family, Diana, seizer of spotlights, would go into labor right in the middle of Will's bar mitzvah. Sarah just knew it.

Her mom had not wanted Aunt Adele to come along on the crib-buying trip. But, as they were all learning, whatever Aunt Adele wanted, Aunt Adele got. Like Lola in *Damn Yankees*. Sarah's parents had watched that movie with her and Vilma and the boys a few years back, and it was quite a hit with Max and especially Will, given that it took place in D.C. and was about baseball.

"What about this one?" her mom said now, gesturing at a white crib with simple wooden slats. "This looks nice. Very classic. Sort of like what I had for you two. Of course, when Lucy came along, we had given everything away, so we had to get a whole new set."

Diana frowned and tilted her head to one side. "No, too plain," she said. "I was thinking of something a little more edgy."

"Babies don't need edgy," their mom said. "They need a comfortable place to sleep."

"Ah, I see just the thing," Aunt Adele said, pointing at a gray and black crib with interesting curved lines. "Diana, behold."

Diana lumbered over and started to examine it, Aunt Adele striding behind her on her high heels.

"Ridiculous," Sarah's mom said to her. "That's probably the most expensive crib in the place, too."

Sarah nodded. It probably was. She remembered going shopping with her mom all those years ago for Max's crib. They had picked something more like the classic one Diana had rejected.

Sarah's phone buzzed. She glanced down. A text from one of her college roommates, inquiring about the hotel room block

Sarah had booked for the out-of-towners who'd be descending for the bar mitzvah. She couldn't deal with it right now. She'd been fending off a nonstop series of texts and emails all morning. From the caterer. From the DJ. From Monique at the office, who was working on the weekend, making Sarah feel horribly guilty. From Will, at the batting cages with his team, who said he'd forgotten his special bat and Gramps had to go back to the house for it.

"Oh, shit," her mother said, elbowing Sarah in the side. "I think Adele's actually convinced her to buy the edgy crib."

Sarah could tell her mother was at the end of her rope with Aunt Adele. For some reason, Aunt Adele treated Sarah's mom like a servant of sorts, ordering her around and failing to acknowledge anything Sarah's mom did for her. It was awful. And this had been going on for almost a week now.

Sarah had talked to her dad.

"Can't you make Aunt Adele be a little more considerate?" she'd asked, during one of the rare moments Aunt Adele wasn't glued to her father's side. "Mom's doing so much for her, and Aunt Adele's acting like a total jerk."

Her father had sighed. "I've tried," he said, shrugging his shoulders. "It's very hard to get Adele to do anything she doesn't want to do."

The understatement of the year.

Diana and her stomach were making their way toward Sarah and their mom, Aunt Adele in her wake. "I've decided. That gray and black one. And I bet there's a changing table to match." And she headed toward another part of the cavernous store where changing tables were lined up.

Sarah and her mom exchanged glances.

"So much more interesting than the white crib," Aunt Adele sniffed. And she followed Diana over toward the changing tables.

Sarah noticed that her mother looked mutinous. Her lips were clamped shut and her face, normally quite pale, was turning bright red.

"Sit down, Mom, okay?" Sarah said, leading her mother over toward a bench, where a group of men—expectant fathers?—were seated, eyes glued to their respective phones.

"That woman," her mom sputtered, as the two of them sat down. "I just can't take it any more. And she's planning to look at apartments tomorrow with Dad. The thought of her moving here for good..." And her voice trailed off.

Sarah noticed her phone was buzzing again, and she took a look. Vilma.

"Mom, it's Vilma," she said. "I need to get it."

Her mother nodded, pulled a copy of The New Yorker from her capacious bag, and started fanning herself with it.

Sarah retreated into a corner, near an enormous display of diapers. "Hey," she said. "I miss you." Sometimes lately she wondered if she really did miss Vilma, or if Vilma's absence was becoming the new normal.

"I miss you too," Vilma said, her lightly accented voice causing Sarah to sink into an even deeper state of worry. Why on earth was she not sure she was missing the true love of her life? Vilma's parents were in Finland, so clearly she had responsibilities there beyond those of her job, and the two of them had discussed it all before Vilma took this new job, and Sarah had been completely understanding at the time that Vilma would need to spend much of the next year in Finland. But six months in, Sarah wondered what they'd gotten themselves into.

"...bar mitzvah?" Vilma was saying. Vilma, who had considered converting to Judaism but hadn't done so yet, had thrown herself wholeheartedly into the preparations for Max's bar mitzvah a couple of years back, perhaps taking on even more of the work than Sarah herself. This time, Sarah felt completely alone.

"The caterer called, and I need to get back to him, and I'm not sure about the room block at the hotel, and..." Sarah wasn't even sure what Vilma had been asking about the bar mitzvah anyway, but she felt the need to unburden herself. "And Max is spending so much time in his room lately."

"It's all going to be fine," Vilma said soothingly. It was one of the many things Sarah loved about Vilma. Vilma was not one to worry unduly about anything. Sarah had told Vilma all about the dreadful Aunt Adele, with new and more hellish updates every day, and Vilma had listened sympathetically and said that maybe Aunt Adele's visit would do them all some good. Shake them out of their family overdependence. It was a theme Vilma had stressed for years now. But was Sarah's family really too intertwined? She needed to help her parents, and they needed to help her with the boys. She needed to help Diana, who was completely incapable of taking care of herself, and Philippe was no better. And Lucy, well, that was another story.

"We're in Buy Buy Baby right now," Sarah said. "Getting Diana the crib and changing table. And probably some baby clothes too."

"You and Marilyn are doing that for Diana?" Vilma said, somewhat disapprovingly.

"No, no, Diana's here too, and Aunt Adele. They're conspiring to buy an edgy crib."

And she and Vilma both started laughing, and it felt so good to have someone who understood, and she wished beyond anything that Vilma would come back sooner than planned. The plan was for her to arrive a week from tomorrow, which would be almost two weeks before the bar mitzvah.

"Sarah?" Sarah heard her sister's voice, and then saw Diana

approaching. "Can you help with the baby clothes? I have absolutely no idea what to get."

Sarah nodded at Diana and held up one finger. "Vilma? Diana and I are going to check out the baby clothes now, okay?"

"Hang in there," Vilma said. "Talk later. I love you." And she hung up.

As she followed Diana toward the baby clothes—she noticed her mom and Aunt Adele sitting on the bench, not talking to each other—her phone buzzed again. Her dad.

"Your mom's not picking up her phone," he said. "I just heard from Cousin Morty. He and Lucretia want to come down for a few days to see Adele. They asked if they could stay at the house."

Sarah looked over at her mother. It probably was just as well she wasn't picking up her phone. This news would not improve her mood.

Nine

Howard

Less than two weeks later, and Howard was back at the baggage claim at National Airport. This time, he was waiting for Cousin Morty and Lucretia. And this time, Adele was waiting with him. He'd asked Marilyn if she wanted to come along, but she, predictably, had declined. He was getting a little worried about Marilyn. She'd been giving him the cold shoulder for the past few days.

"I'm getting the house ready for Cousin Morty and Lucretia," she'd practically spat at him that morning, as she gathered up bundles of Adele's belongings that were tossed about the living room. "Here," she said, thrusting the pile of scarves and sweaters at Howard. "Take this and figure out what to do with it."

Howard had tried to reason with both Marilyn and Adele. It wasn't his fault that they seemed to hate each other. But he wasn't getting anywhere with either of them. Since Adele's arrival, Howard had felt torn between his wife and his sister. Why couldn't they just get along? Why couldn't they just let Howard sink peacefully into the sepia-toned nostalgia that had overwhelmed him since his sister's reappearance?

Having Adele back meant that Howard had someone with whom to relive some of his childhood memories. Memories that he'd started to question over the years, not having anyone else to verify them with. Had his father really worn a toupee for a couple of years? Had his mother really almost burned the kitchen down one night making a difficult chicken recipe? Had his grandparents' home in Elizabeth really had a nubby gray sofa in the living room that he wasn't supposed to sit on? Cousin Morty remembered some things, but, despite his ubiquitous presence throughout Howard's childhood, he had lived in a different house, with different parents.

"Remember when you and Chuck would put me in the back seat of his dad's convertible and take me with you to Gruning's for ice cream?" Howard asked now. "I'd get the strawberry?"

"Oh, yes!" Adele said, her eyes, still as dark and mischievous as they'd been when she was a girl, lighting up. "And I'd get the chocolate with the sprinkles. Delicious. I wonder what ever became of Chuck."

Howard had heard over the past ten days about the four husbands, countless boyfriends—or "lovers," as Adele tended to call them--and other men in his sister's past. He remembered himself and his parents going over to Chuck's house after Adele left, asking him if he knew anything. But he'd seemed as shell-shocked by her disappearance as they were. Chuck had matriculated a few months later at Princeton, and Howard and his family had lost track of him after a while. Howard shrugged.

"You know, Howie, I had a lover named Chuck. After Herman died." Herman was her third husband. "Not the same person, of course. The second Chuck wasn't as handsome. I couldn't really cope with him after a while." And Adele made a shooing gesture with her hands, as if to recall the dismissal of this particular Chuck.

Howard nodded. Sometimes he wondered about how he, Mr. Monogamy, had ended up in the same family with Adele and Cousin Morty.

As if reading his mind, Adele tilted her head and frowned at him. "Howie, what's it like sleeping with only one person for your entire adult life?"

He could tell he was turning red. He looked around the waiting area. A college-aged kid with earphones was a few seats away, and a mother with two screaming babies—twins?--was beyond him. No one seemed to be paying attention, fortunately.

How could his eighty-year-old sister still have the ability to embarrass him, a seventy-five-year-old man? He remembered being in sixth grade and having a crush on a girl in his Hebrew school class, and Adele, when she saw him attempting to talk to this girl—Betty? Beth?—had made some comment about how cute the two of them looked together. He'd been so mortified he hadn't talked to Betty/Beth again for years.

And what business was it of Adele's, anyway?

"No comment," he said. That had become his all-purpose response to some of Adele's overly inquisitive questions.

"Come on, Howie," Adele said. "I'm assuming you don't indulge in any hanky-panky on the side. You don't seem like the type. So you're in bed with the same woman, from age, what, twenty-one to age seventy-five? How can that even be possible?"

Howard glanced around again. The woman and the twins had left. The kid with the earphones still seemed absorbed in whatever he was listening to. He was tapping one foot up and down and drumming on his knee with his hand. He reminded Howard of what Max might look like in a few years.

"Well?" Adele persisted.

Hanky-panky on the side? Lately he and Marilyn hadn't had much hanky-panky at all. One of them always seemed to be too tired. And he needed the medication for anything to happen anyway. But that, too, was none of Adele's business. He remained silent.

"Now, I'm assuming Cousin Morty is more similar to me than not," Adele continued. "Third wife, much younger woman. I had a lover who was half my age. I was seventy, he was thirty-five. He couldn't get enough of me. But then he moved back to Novosibirsk."

Howard sighed. Clearly Adele's life had been far more colorful than his own. But would he trade Marilyn, the girls, the grandsons, the stable legal career, for anything else in the world? Even if it were offered up to him on a silver platter? Of course not.

"You see this ring, Howie?" Adele gestured at a large green stone on her right ring finger. An emerald? He wasn't too knowledgeable about such things. Diana would know. "Given to me by this particular gentleman. Evgeny. As a token of his esteem."

Howard wasn't sure what to say. He needed to change the subject. Fast. Her apartment search would have to do. She had turned her nose up at all the places they'd seen the previous Sunday.

"So," he said. "Are you seriously thinking of moving here?" Or was this just a whim? He had mixed emotions about the whole thing. Having her back in his life was wonderful. Having her right in the neighborhood? Well, maybe if Adele and Marilyn could patch things up. And he had to admit that Sarah didn't seem too keen on Adele either.

"Can't you do something about the way she treats Mom?" Sarah had pleaded with him on the phone the other night. "I mean, she's so rude to her. Mom's not her servant, you know."

"...new luxury apartments in downtown Bethesda," Adele was saying. "I saw something on the computer about them."

"So what we saw wasn't fancy enough?" Howard said. He hadn't been entirely clear about why Adele didn't like the apartments. They'd been really nice. Maybe Howard could move into one of them himself. With Marilyn, of course. He was fine with the idea of selling the house. But Marilyn said she couldn't imagine such a thing. She'd die in the house, she'd say. She'd never leave it.

"I've told you, Rudy left me vast quantities of money," Adele said. Rudy was her fourth, most recent, husband. He had passed away a few years ago, from what Howard gathered. Honestly, he couldn't keep all these husbands and lovers straight. "I can afford the fanciest."

"Fucking hell, if you don't look exactly the same!" A booming voice sounded, and Howard turned to see Cousin Morty and Lucretia heading in their direction. Cousin Morty, who was pushing a luggage cart piled high with bags—how long were they staying, anyway?--was wearing a weathered leather jacket and jeans. His abundant hair was more salt than pepper, but was impressive for a seventy-three-year-old. Lucretia was wearing high heels—similar to Adele's—and a short flowered dress that didn't leave much to the imagination. Wasn't she going to be cold? It wasn't that warm out. It was only April, after all.

"It's little Cousin Morty, all grown up!" Adele jumped up and threw her arms around Cousin Morty. He embraced her too, and Howard noticed tears flowing down Cousin Morty's face. Cousin Morty had always been quite emotional.

Lucretia was staring at Adele with fascination. Maybe she was wondering if she could be like Adele in, what, forty-five years? Howard wondered what it would be like to be married to someone the age of his youngest daughter. And why would someone Lucy's age want to be with someone in his seventies, anyway?

"Cousin Adele, you look beautiful," Cousin Morty said, wiping his eyes with a tissue. "Lucretia, my beloved, here's my ageless cousin Adele."

Howard wondered if Adele would take against Lucretia, the way she had with Marilyn, but no. Adele hugged Lucretia and

Lucretia hugged her back.

"I have heard so much about you!" Lucretia breathed. She spoke in a Jackie Kennedyesque way, Howard thought. But with a Central European accent. "You are like a family legend."

Adele released Lucretia and preened. "Yes, I suppose I am," she said.

"And you joined the circus?" Lucretia continued, twisting one lock of long blonde hair around her finger. "I had wanted to run off when I was a girl, but I ended up coming to New York and modeling rather than joining the circus."

"Oh, I've done some modeling in my time," Adele said, nodding. "In fact, there's a catalog for older women that recently asked me to model some summer fashions."

"And you said yes?" Lucretia whispered, transfixed.

"I said no, actually," Adele said, bestowing a smile upon Lucretia. "My modeling days are over."

Howard noticed how skillfully Adele had turned the conversation away from the circus. She'd been here for ten days now, and he wasn't any closer to figuring out about the circus than he had been before she'd reappeared in his life.

"Cousin Howie," Cousin Morty said, noticing him. He slapped Howard on the back and offered him a fist bump.

"Cousin Morty," Howard said, slapping him on the back in return. He fist-bumped Max and Will on occasion, but he didn't think he needed to fist-bump Cousin Morty. "Lucretia." He hugged Lucretia, who kissed him on the cheek.

"Thank you so much for having us at your house," Lucretia said. "We just wanted to be spending as much time with Cousin Adele as possible. Right, Morty?"

Cousin Morty nodded. "Let's get this shit into the car and head home," he said. As they all left the terminal and headed toward the parking garage, Cousin Morty put his arm around Adele and drew her into conversation, leaving Howard and Lucretia to push the cart.

"So how long exactly are you staying?" Howard asked. He counted the bags on the cart. Two large wheeled bags, two smaller wheeled bags, and a couple of carry-ons.

"Oh, we thought a visit of three, four days?" Lucretia breathed. "Dear Cousin Marilyn should not be inconvenienced."

Well, at least someone was thinking of Marilyn. That was a plus. But he wondered, given Marilyn's current frame of mind, if she'd survive three or four days with not just Adele residing in the house, but also Cousin Morty and Lucretia. He wasn't sure.

Ten

Lucy

Her last class of sixth-graders had just departed, and Lucy collapsed into her chair. She had been explaining *The Comedy of Errors* to the kids, and it was her fifth time that day teaching the same lesson, and she had mixed up Adriana and Luciana, which the kids thought was hilarious, given that her name was Lucy—most of them were aware of that fact—and one girl in the class was named Adriana. So they all were in hysterics by the end of the period. Including Lucy.

She pulled together a huge stack of papers that needed to be graded by Monday. At least it was Friday. The weekend. But what did she ever really have to do on weekends any more, anyway, except grade papers?

The scene from last night popped into her head again. She'd been at this Italian restaurant in Bethesda with her college roommate Stacy, and the two of them had been discussing Stacy's three-year-old twins, and Stacy's job at a PR firm, and Stacy's husband Adam's job at a lobbying firm, and how Stacy's sister-in-law Amanda seemed to be head over heels in love with a professor who lived in New York. Lucy had happily settled into this voyage through Stacy's life, not wanting to say much about her own.

And then Stacy had stopped, her mouth open in mid-sentence. "Oh my god, Luce, there's Jeff." She had paused. "With that woman from his office."

Lucy had turned around in her chair, to find her ex-husband entering the restaurant, hand-in-hand with none other than Matea Barker, the other partner in Jeff's political consulting firm. Parker-Barker, it was called. Which Lucy had always found completely absurd, but no one else seemed to. Plus, why should it be Parker-Barker rather than Barker-Parker? Why not go in alphabetical order? Why not let the woman's name come first?

Lucy stared at them, her fork, which held a piece of cheese ravioli dripping with tomato sauce, frozen in place near her mouth. This was not possible. Matea Barker was absolutely gorgeous, of course, and incredibly brilliant. But she had kids. Three of them, to be precise. Her divorce had come through last year, and she had custody of the kids most of the time. Lucy knew that for a fact. So what on earth was Jeff doing with her?

The ravioli fell off Lucy's fork and onto her white sweater, creating a splotch that ricocheted onto her tan pants. Shit. She picked up the ravioli and replaced it on her plate, wiping her fingers on her napkin. And of course, Jeff chose that moment to notice Lucy's presence, and escort Matea over to Lucy's table.

"Luce," he said. "Great to see you." His white teeth gleamed as he smiled at her. "And Stace. You too."

Stacy glared at him, while Lucy tried to hide her splotchy clothing under the napkin. "Hi, Jeff," she managed. "Hi, Matea." Try to be civil, her therapist had suggested, after the time Lucy had bumped into Jeff on the Metro and had immediately run in the opposite direction. Literally.

Matea waved at Lucy and wrapped one arm around Jeff, who looked uncomfortable.

"Come on, let's go sit down," he said, and escorted Matea off to a table in the corner. A romantic-looking table. The kind of place she and Jeff would have sat. Up until last year. When the whole thing happened.

"Hey, Lucy." Will's cheerful voice broke into Lucy's musings. Her nephew had entered the classroom, lugging a heavy-looking backpack. "Are you going to drive me to baseball practice this afternoon, or is Grandma going to?"

Will was on a baseball team and a soccer team, and Lucy was glad to help out, but she was completely overwhelmed with work today. As she usually was. "I'll see if Grandma can do it," she said, and texted her mother. She probably would need a break from her visitors, with Aunt Adele, Cousin Morty, and Lucretia all staying at the house. Her mother had sounded like a woman on the verge of a nervous breakdown last night on the phone.

"Yes, of course," her mom promptly replied. "I'll pick him up at school in half an hour. Good to get out of house."

Lucy often wondered why Sarah wouldn't just let Will stay at home by himself, whether or not Max was there. Sarah argued that she did, quite frequently, but that Will just spent all his time playing video games if no adult was around. Sarah's caution, though, meant that Lucy got to spend more time with Will, and that was all to the good.

"Get some of your homework done, okay?" Lucy said in her no-nonsense teacher voice that brooked no backtalk. Even from a beloved nephew. She'd done the same thing with Max when he was in middle school.

Will complied, pulling his binder out, unzipping it, and plopping it down on a nearby desk. "I have math, English, and World Studies," he said. "No Spanish or science today. But we have a quiz in math tomorrow, so I need to study. I bet Benjamin that I'd do better than him this time." He sat down. "He's kind of my rival, you know?"

Lucy nodded. She'd had Benjamin in class the previous year. He was alarmingly intelligent and quite competitive. As Will turned his attention to his math, Lucy started grading some of the papers. Then her mind started wandering again. Back to the night about a year ago when she'd heard about Diana and Philippe trying IVF. Up till that point, Lucy hadn't known Diana and Philippe even wanted to have kids. She'd assumed they were like her and Jeff. People who didn't want kids. But then her mom had called, a combination of worry and excitement in her voice.

Jeff had groaned when Lucy told him it was her mom and she should pick up. He thought Marilyn called too often. That Lucy's family was too intrusive. That she needed to get away from them more of the time. She agreed, for the most part. But it was difficult. And she loved hanging out with Max and Will.

"This is a joke, right?" Lucy had asked her mom. "Diana's not really trying to have a baby, is she?" She couldn't imagine such a thing. Her irresponsible older sister and her absent-minded brother-in-law trying to become parents? Being organized enough to set up appointments with fertility doctors and schedule an IVF cycle? When she and her mother concluded their conversation, Lucy's head was spinning.

"That's absurd," Jeff had snorted. "I mean, I love them both, but Diana and Philippe with a baby? No way." He leaned back on the sofa and patted the seat next to him. "Hey, come over here, Luce, watch the game with me." He had the hockey playoffs on, and the Capitals seemed to be in the midst of their usual swoon into oblivion.

Lucy had sat down next to him, but her mind wasn't on the game. She had agreed with Jeff, when they'd been married more than a decade earlier, that kids were not something they wanted. She was teaching. Her students and her nephews were more than enough. But ever since the arrival of Stacy's twins, something had started to shift. Not enough to really change her mind. Not enough to talk to Jeff about. But still.

"Hey, Ms. Collins," Will was saying.

Lucy returned to the present. She was in her classroom, not on the sofa in her old apartment with Jeff. And there was her best teacher friend, Kathleen Collins, who happened to be Will's English teacher this year, standing in the doorway.

"Make sure you do a good job on that essay, Will, okay?" Kathleen said jokingly.

"Hey, I'm Lucy Pinsky's nephew, I'm sure I will," Will replied. They smiled at each other.

"So I'm leaving now, Lucy," Kathleen said. "I'll see you in the morning, okay?"

Lucy nodded. Kathleen had two kids, and spent a lot of time shuttling them to various activities. Like Lucy did with Will and Max. Except she was their aunt, not their mother. Kathleen departed, and Lucy mentally returned to the previous year. Diana's IVF news had marked the beginning of the end for Lucy and Jeff, although Lucy hadn't known it at the time. Jeff was adamant about not having kids, and Lucy was edging toward wanting to try to have one, and they couldn't agree, and divorce seemed the only option. So that's what happened. Shortly thereafter, they were over. Twelve years down the drain. And now here was Jeff, dating a woman with three small children? A spark of fury shot through Lucy. She got up from her desk and started pacing around the room.

Will looked up. "Getting your steps in?" he inquired. "You know, Will Z. got an Apple Watch the other day. For his bar mitzvah. It has a fitness tracker on it. I really want to get an Apple Watch too." And he launched into a list of things he'd like to get with his bar mitzvah money. Lucy doubted Sarah would let him get half the things on the list, but it was good to dream.

"And Will R. has this really cool gaming computer. I was over at his house the other day and I got to use it."

Lucy reflected on the fact that almost every other boy in Will's grade was also named Will. If they weren't named Alex. The fortunate thing was that Will hadn't been dubbed "Will P." The connotations of that appellation, in the mind of a kid, were not good. He somehow had avoided that fate and was just called "Will." It was a testament to the fact that he seemed to get along with everybody. Max was far more like the rest of the Pinskys. Well, except Diana, of course.

Lucy was heading around the corner of the room, still trying to walk off her stress—she figured she'd go for a run later--and toward the classroom door, when the door, which had been slightly ajar, opened further and whacked into her arm.

"Oh, sorry, Lucy." Of all the people she didn't want to see, it was Jonah Shapiro. "Are you okay?" A concerned expression spread across his mobile, way-too-good-looking face. "Hey, Will, what's up?"

"Hey, Mr. Shapiro." Will gazed at the two of them with curiosity. Had he somehow figured out, in that middle-school kid way, that something had transpired a few months earlier between his aunt and his former English teacher? Of course, it would never happen again. Never. It was entirely the wrong thing to have happened. Lucy had been vulnerable, that's all there was to it.

"I'm fine," she snapped. "What do you want?"

"Um, just wanted to go over some stuff with you about lesson plans, but this probably isn't a good time." He gestured at Will.

"No, not a good time," she replied. "I have this huge stack of papers to grade." And she pointed at the papers on her desk.

"Okay, well, I guess you both are okay here, Will, Ms. Pinsky, I mean, Lucy, I mean, Aunt Lucy, I mean, yeah." And Jonah backed out the door and closed it behind him. Good. He was too young. He was her colleague. He was Will's former teacher and current soccer coach. It was all wrong.

Will was cracking up. "He really likes you, Lucy," he said. "I mean, jeez, he called you Aunt Lucy?"

And Lucy couldn't help it. She started laughing too. The whole thing was ridiculous. Her whole life was ridiculous. Maybe that's why she reached into her bag for her phone and invited Aunt Adele for coffee.

Eleven

Marilyn

"Are you sure I cannot help you with the dishes, Cousin Marilyn?"

Lucretia was nothing if not helpful, Marilyn reflected as she stood with Lucretia amidst a pile of dishes in the kitchen. But Lucretia had no idea where Marilyn kept everything, and how certain things needed to be dried a certain way and other things could be left in the drying rack, and how to load the dishwasher, so her help would actually not be helpful at all.

"Thanks so much, Lucretia, but I'm okay here," Marilyn said. She had pulled together what her own mother would have called the perfect Friday night dinner: roast chicken, potatoes, some healthy green vegetables, a salad. Plus a challah Marilyn had found in the freezer that afternoon.

"Then I will stay here and talk to you while you clean," Lucretia said, leaning one skinny hip against the kitchen island. Howie and Cousin Morty had gone out for a walk with Adele, so they had the house to themselves. Lucretia paused. "What do you think of Cousin Adele?" she asked tentatively.

Marilyn wasn't sure what to say. "Well, it's certainly interesting having her reappear after hearing so much about her for all these years," she ventured.

"Oh, yes!" Lucretia said, and started discussing how amazing

Adele was and how she hoped she could be like her when she was eighty.

Marilyn found her mind drifting elsewhere. To Adele's look of triumph that afternoon, when Marilyn was about to head out the door to pick up Will. Adele had hung up her phone and proclaimed that Lucy had just invited her to coffee on Sunday. And she'd shot Marilyn a glance, indicating Adele's full awareness that Marilyn would not be pleased.

Why would Lucy do that? Marilyn felt somewhat betrayed. Sarah, she knew, would never do that. She shared Marilyn's opinion of Adele. Diana, absorbed in herself and the baby, was not inclined to take that kind of initiative either. But Lucy? Lucy had always been the most enigmatic of her daughters.

Marilyn's phone buzzed, and she picked it up from the kitchen counter. Diana. Her heart leaped. Was it the baby?

"Sorry, Lucretia," Marilyn said. "It's Diana. I need to get this."

Lucretia nodded understandingly and stopped talking.

"Mom?" Diana asked. In her own voice, not the Blattner voice. "Did you ever have a craving for this particular type of cookies when you were pregnant? Those really soft chocolate chip cookies with big chocolate chunks? They have some at the Giant, in the bakery, I think."

Marilyn hadn't. But she could pick up some cookies for Diana and drop them off. It would get her away from her house of horrors for a while. "Are you at home, sweetheart?" she asked. "I can bring some over to you."

"Oh, thanks, Mom," Diana said.

Marilyn heard the door open, and the voices of Howie, Cousin Morty and Adele. She was more or less done with the dishes. She'd leave now. It would be good for her to spend some time at Diana's. Philippe was at the restaurant at night, and Diana could probably use some company.

And a half-hour later, she was at Diana's apartment, cookies in hand. Diana opened the door, dressed in all black, and Marilyn handed the plastic container of cookies over.

"Yum," Diana said, opening up the container and popping a cookie into her mouth. "You're the best, Mom!"

"Oh, I needed to get out of the house anyway," Marilyn said, collapsing onto an armchair. All Diana's furniture had originally been in either Marilyn's parents' house in Queens or Howie's parents' house in West Orange, and Marilyn felt a jumble of emotions when she saw it in its new setting. This particular chair had been in Howie's parents' basement, and had gone into storage once they'd moved his parents to the Hebrew Home down here, and then Diana had claimed it once she and Philippe had moved in together.

Diana sat down in another chair, which had been in Marilyn's parents' guest room. "I couldn't fit into the Blattner clothes today," she said, looking mournful. "I tried. But I just couldn't. Which meant that my writing was far less productive than usual." She reached into the container for another cookie and offered the container to Marilyn, who took one.

They sat there chewing in unison. "It's okay," Marilyn said after a few minutes. "You'll be able to get back into them soon enough. But shouldn't we talk about what happens once the baby arrives? With your work and everything?" She'd tried, on multiple occasions, to get Diana to focus on hiring some help. Especially if she was planning to go right back to this Blattner project. But Diana didn't seem to want to think about any of that. Marilyn had tried enlisting Philippe in the effort, and he'd smiled his beautiful smile and said of course, of course, and then—of course—he'd done nothing.

"It's going to work out," Diana said. "Philippe's going to take off the first week. He has a friend from culinary school who's between jobs and is going to fill in at the restaurant."

Philippe's restaurant, which had opened a couple of years earlier, just before Diana and Philippe's wedding, featured Belgian cuisine. Mussels, stew, fries, waffles. Located along the U Street Corridor, the restaurant, called Diana's, was becoming quite trendy.

"That's good," Marilyn said, taking a deep breath. The depth of Diana and Philippe's impracticality knew no bounds. How could they have reached their forties and not learned some basic things? "But what about after that first week? Babies don't sleep through the night for months. And with Philippe at the restaurant, you'll be the one who's doing most of the caretaking. Especially if you're planning to breastfeed." Which she thought Diana had said she was planning to do.

"Oh, I know," Diana said blithely, reaching for another cookie. "It's not as if I didn't see Sarah with Max and Will, or tons of my friends who have kids. I mean, I'm forty-four years old, Mom. So we're not exactly likely to have another one after this, so I'll be able to handle it. I've heard it's only with the second baby that your life gets out of control."

Marilyn thought about this. "One baby can make your life go out of control," she finally said. "In a wonderful way, of course. But I couldn't get much work done at all when Sarah was born. She took over my whole existence." Marilyn had been working on her dissertation at the time. It had been put aside for years, until both Sarah and Diana were in elementary school.

"Oh, well, things are different now," Diana said, putting her feet up on the coffee table. Which had been in Howie's parents' living room. Marilyn remembered the first time she'd set foot in that living room. She'd been twenty years old and completely terrified to meet her boyfriend's parents. She'd clutched onto Howie's arm as he'd made the introductions. "Those were the old days," Diana continued. She smiled at Marilyn. "No offense, Mom."

Marilyn felt a wave of weariness sweep over her. Maybe she could just stay at Diana's tonight. Not go home at all. Let Howie deal with his crazy relatives. "None taken," she said. She closed her eyes. She heard Diana talking about some episode in Blattner's life where his father wasn't speaking to his grandfather, and then all of a sudden they were all at the hospital and Diana and Philippe were displaying the baby, who was dressed in a mini-Blattner outfit, and Adele was there too, reaching for the baby, and then Marilyn distantly heard her phone buzzing. She opened her eyes and sat up straight in the chair, disoriented. Had she fallen asleep?

"Your phone, Mom," Diana said, looking up from *What to Expect When You're Expecting*. "It's ringing. You've been asleep for an hour and a half."

Marilyn fumbled around in her bag. She could never find her phone in here. Especially not when she was half-asleep. Damn. By the time she found it, the ringing had stopped. Then it started up on Diana's phone.

Diana looked at her phone. "It's Dad," she said. "Hey, Dad. Yes, she's here." A pause. "No, she fell asleep. She seems kind of tired." Another pause. "Should he come over here and pick you up?" Diana asked Marilyn.

Marilyn shook her head. "I'm fine," she said. Except that she didn't want to go home.

"No, that's okay," Diana said into the phone. "She says she's fine." A longer pause. "I'm fine too, yeah. No, not yet. No. Yeah, I know. Okay, bye." She sighed as she hung up. "Dad was asking if we'd set up the crib and the changing table yet, and I said not yet. Philippe's friend André, the pastry chef? He's supposed to come over and set everything up tomorrow morning. He's very handy."

Marilyn pictured a pastry chef setting up a crib and a changing table, depositing little pink and blue pastel cookies and cakes around the edges of the furniture. Not that the baby would be able to eat anything like that for a while. "Good," she said. And she reached for another cookie. She didn't need to rush off anywhere, did she?

Twelve

Will

The rabbi was saying something about Aidan's Torah portion, and Will was sort of listening but sort of not. A couple of boys he knew were goofing off in the row in front of him, and Will could see the rabbi look down and glare at them. They should know better, Will thought. He hoped they wouldn't do that at his bar mitzvah. Which was in just two weeks at this point.

He peered up at Aidan on the bimah. Aidan had breezed through his Torah portion and was about to start on his Haftarah. Aidan's parents, looking proud, were sitting up there next to the cantor. Will wondered what would happen in two weeks. He pictured his mom and Vilma up there, looking proud the way Aidan's parents were. Vilma was supposed to come home soon, so that was something to look forward to.

Will shifted around in his seat. His blazer was getting uncomfortable. It was a hand-me-down from Max, as were most of Will's clothes, and it was getting too small. Maybe he, Will, was finally growing a little? It seemed that most of his friends were shooting up in height. Some of their voices were changing. He still sounded like he always had.

"I was kind of a late bloomer too," Max had said the previous evening, when they were sitting around in Max's room tossing an old Nerf football back and forth. A rare occurrence, because lately Max didn't let Will in very often, so Will had been pleased. He needed some big-brotherly advice.

So he'd asked Max whether Max thought he, Will, would ever get taller, and Max had been all reassuring, saying it had taken time for him, too, and how he'd been the shortest kid in his grade for a while—Will wondered if Max was just saying that to make him feel better—and then, lo and behold, he'd grown five inches this year, and maybe that would happen to Will soon.

And then Will started querying Max about why he'd been so eager to walk Phoebe lately. Will hadn't walked Phoebe for more than a week. He kind of missed it. Not that Phoebe went very fast, so it wasn't like you could get any exercise walking her, but there was something soothing about, like, ambling along with Phoebe.

"Good exercise," Max mumbled, turning away from Will. And Will knew that couldn't possibly be true. But Max didn't seem like he was going to say anything else, so Will figured he'd change the subject, and he told Max about the whole Aunt Lucy episode in the classroom.

"Something's up with them," Will said.

"Well, let me know if you figure it out," Max said. "I have to get some stuff done now, okay?"

And Will had left. And now he heard the rabbi telling everyone to rise for the Aleinu, and he and all the other blue-blazered, khaki-pants-wearing boys stood up, and soon thereafter the service was over.

"You're next, dude," Aidan said, as Will offered congratulations at the Kiddush lunch after the service. "Good luck."

Will nodded. He thought about the party he'd have after the service. Bowling, pizza, all his friends. It would be cool, right? He'd even invited girls, Katelin C. and a bunch of others. Max had asked him the other day if he was nervous. And maybe he was, just a little, even though he hadn't admitted as much to Max. It was the thought of messing up his portion in front of Katelin C. that stressed him out a little. Otherwise, he felt okay. His speech was written, his tutor kept telling him he was doing well, and the rabbi had been all complimentary at their most recent meeting.

He wondered if Aunt Adele would still be here for the bar mitzvah. She seemed to be saying she would, but it was hard to figure her out sometimes. Will hadn't had much time alone with Aunt Adele, but the other day he'd been over there and she'd beckoned him into the guest room.

"William," she'd said. She sat down on the bed, which was unmade and covered with rumpled clothing, and gestured for Will to sit on the chair. He shifted aside some scarves and perched on the edge. "You realize you were named after my father. Howie's father too, of course."

Will nodded. He knew that. Max was named for another great-grandfather on Grandma's side of the family.

"He was quite something," Aunt Adele said, a reflective look on her face. "He came to this country as a child, with nothing, and eventually managed to open his own store, which was highly successful. Shoes. We always had the most beautiful shoes." Aunt Adele looked down at her feet and smiled.

"How come you wear those high heels?" Will inquired. He'd been wondering that since Aunt Adele's arrival. Some of the girls in his grade wore high heels to bar and bat mitzvahs, but they looked like they'd fall over. And then they took them off for the dancing. His mom pretty much never wore high heels. Vilma only did when she was going to fancy-type parties or something. And Grandma was afraid of tripping. "Is it because of your dad's business?"

"Comfort, my dear William," Aunt Adele said. "Many women,

your grandmother for example, find them uncomfortable, but it's just the opposite for me. And it adds to my height."

Will thought about that. He nodded. Adding to your height was definitely a good idea.

"Do you remember how tall Gramps was as a kid?" Will asked. "Like, was he super-tall, or super-short, or kind of in the middle?"

"Kind of in the middle, I'd say," Aunt Adele said. "But he always seemed short to me. He was my kid brother. It was quite a shock meeting him at the airport and finding him taller than I."

Will nodded again. He imagined that was probably true.

Will Z. jabbed Will in the side, returning him to the temple and the Kiddush lunch. "Did you try the desserts?" Will Z. asked. "They're awesome. Better than at my bar mitzvah." Will let Will Z. lead him over to the table with the desserts, and he took a plate and started loading it up. His mom wasn't at this particular bar mitzvah, so there was no one to tell him that he'd had enough sweets and he should try something from the fruit platter.

"So you know Katelin C.'s here," Will Z. said, stuffing a cookie into his mouth. "She asked if you were here. There were so many people in there it was hard to see everyone."

She had asked if Will was here? Really?

"Okay," Will said. "That's cool." He started looking around the room to see if he could see her anywhere. He saw a couple of her friends, Emma P. and Ayesha, but there was no sign of Katelin C.

Will Z. drifted off and Will sat down with his plate of desserts next to a few other kids he knew, who were busy eating and texting.

"Sup?" his friend Marco asked Will. "Here, check out this video." And Marco handed Will his phone, which showed a video of a really bad, out-of-tune marching band. The two of them played the trumpet in the seventh-grade band, so they often sent each other funny band videos.

"Dude, Mr. Cromwell would never let us get away with that." Will said, starting to laugh.

And then he felt a tap on his shoulder, and he looked up from the phone to find Katelin C., trailed by Emma P. and Ayesha. He noticed they were all wearing high heels. They probably would tower over him. It was good he was sitting down. "So are you nervous, Will?" Katelin C. asked. "For your bar mitzvah?"

"Like, um," Will said. "Uh, nervous? Well, um." He couldn't think of anything else to say. This wasn't going well. He sort of sounded like Mr. Shapiro the other day in Lucy's classroom.

"Will's never nervous," Marco said. "Right, dude?"

"Right," Will managed. "Never."

"Cool," Katelin C. said, and she and her friends disappeared to the other side of the room.

"I think she likes you," Marco said, elbowing Will in the ribs.

"No, I doubt it," Will said. And he turned back to the marching band video. It was far less stressful.

Thirteen

Lucy

"So you slept with your coworker?" Aunt Adele asked loudly. "And now you feel bad about it? But why? I slept with coworkers all the time over the course of my life. Where else does one meet people, anyway? Well, nowadays there's all this swiping left and right, but I'm not sure I want to start with that at this point."

Lucy tried to imagine Aunt Adele on Tinder. Weirdly, she could imagine Aunt Adele trying it out better than she could imagine trying it herself. And why didn't Aunt Adele seem to know to keep her voice down? The Starbucks was really busy and noisy, but you never know who might be listening. Maybe someone from school. Maybe a parent. Or worse, a student. She looked around nervously but didn't see anyone she recognized. She heaved a sigh of relief.

"So how was it?" Aunt Adele inquired, her eyes fixated on Lucy. She took a sip of her cappuccino.

"What?" Lucy said. Had she known the direction this conversation would take, she might not have asked Aunt Adele for coffee. The whole morning had been a little weird. She'd come by the house around ten to pick Aunt Adele up, and her mother had glared at her. Why? Lucy wasn't sure. She had the sense that her mother and Sarah really disliked Aunt Adele. And she knew her mom was stressed out beyond belief with Cousin Morty and Lucretia added to the guest list. She probably should do something to help. The house looked like a shambles.

"You know perfectly well what I'm talking about. How was it?"

The thing is, it had been amazing. Totally different from anything with Jeff. Everything had been fine with Jeff, but not amazing. Still, it was all wrong. Sleeping with a colleague was not something she, Lucy Pinsky, should do. Especially not a colleague who was so much younger. Lucy shook her head. She wasn't going to discuss that kind of detail with Aunt Adele. She hadn't even told Stacy any details. And she certainly hadn't mentioned anything to Kathleen.

"He's my colleague. He was Will's English teacher last year. We work in a middle school where everyone notices everything. He's twenty-six." She picked up her iced coffee and took a few sips.

"So?" Aunt Adele said. She thrust her hand into Lucy's face. "See this emerald ring? This was given to me by a lover who was half my age."

Interesting. Lucy studied the ring, which was beautiful. "So what happened?" she asked. "Between the two of you?"

Aunt Adele removed her hand from Lucy's face and waved both hands in the air dismissively. "Different paths in life," she said. "He returned to Siberia."

Siberia? Was this during the Cold War or something? Was Aunt Adele a spy? "How old were you?"

"Seventy."

So the giver of the ring was thirty-five? Her age? This was sort of like Cousin Morty and Lucretia, but in reverse.

"Like Cousin Morty and Lucretia," Aunt Adele said, as if reading Lucy's mind. "But when the woman's older, all of a sudden everyone gasps in shock. A cougar, they say." She shook her head and sipped angrily at her coffee. "Ridiculous."

"Jeff's ten years older than I am," Lucy said.

"And look how that turned out," Aunt Adele retorted.

Terribly. But when she'd met Jeff and they had first fallen in love, she never would have imagined such an ending. It had all seemed so perfect. He was even Jewish, which she could tell pleased her parents, although they said it didn't matter. And what did the terrible ending have to do with Jeff's age, anyway? It could have ended the same way whatever age Jeff was.

"You're too tied up in knots," Aunt Adele said, waving one end of her gauzy scarf at Lucy. "You need to chill."

Chill? This coming from the woman who ran away and tectonically shifted the whole landscape of her family, with impacts reverberating into the third generation now? Who deserted her little brother and her parents? Without whom, Lucy might not even be here? How could she expect Lucy and her family to chill when she reappeared after sixty-four years? Didn't she get that it was stressful for them? Lucy was starting to understand why her mom and Sarah were upset.

"Jeez, Aunt Adele," Lucy burst out. "Do you understand the impact your absence had on my dad? On all of us? And now you're back and you expect us to chill?"

Aunt Adele tilted her head to one side and nodded. "I suppose it's difficult, yes."

"And look," Lucy continued, on a roll now. "I probably wouldn't even have been born if you hadn't run off. So I suppose I should be grateful to you, in a weird way."

"What?" Aunt Adele looked baffled. As well she might. But Lucy and her sisters thought that their parents decided to have a third child, who turned out to be Lucy, because they were worried

Diana would run off to join the circus and leave Sarah alone. Of course, they'd never asked their parents about this. But it made sense. Lucy recounted the theory to Aunt Adele, who seemed fascinated.

"I'd like to give myself credit for your conception," she said. "You're a delightful young woman. But perhaps you were a simple accident. Perhaps it had nothing whatsoever to do with me."

Oh my god! A simple accident? Lucy was speechless.

"It happens all the time," Aunt Adele said. "Fortunately never to me. But I suppose you'd have to ask your parents."

"And of course I'd never do that," Lucy said. She couldn't imagine discussing anything like that with her parents.

"So getting back to your colleague, who cares if you work with him and he's almost a decade younger than you are? And the fact that he was William's English teacher last year is not germane."

"And he's also Will's soccer coach," Lucy said.

"If I had stopped myself from jumping into situations because I came up with one ridiculous excuse after another, I would have missed out on some of the better experiences of my life," Aunt Adele said. "Evgeny, for example."

"The one who went back to Siberia?"

"Exactly."

"I'll consider what you said," Lucy said. She didn't feel like talking about Jonah Shapiro any more. Or thinking about him. Which was difficult most days, given that he taught in the classroom next to hers. "So what made you live in Hawaii, anyway?" She'd been wondering about that. Plus, she needed to change the subject.

"Art, beauty, distance from New Jersey," Aunt Adele said. "Of course, I didn't go directly from New Jersey to Hawaii. I took a rather circuitous route."

"Jeff and I went to Hawaii a few years ago," Lucy said. "He was working on a political campaign out there. If I had known you lived there, I could have looked you up." Of course, Matea and her then-husband had been on the trip too, along with their kids. They'd all spent several days hanging out together once the election was over, and each night Jeff and Lucy would go back to their hotel room and Jeff would laugh and say that the kids were fun for a few hours but he was so glad he didn't have to deal with them all the time, and Lucy would say she agreed. Even though she wasn't sure she did. And now here Jeff was with Matea and, presumably, the three kids. Ironic.

But she needed to get her mind off Jeff. Thinking about him wasn't doing her any good either.

"Tell me some stories about my dad when he was a kid," Lucy said. That was a safe topic, she assumed.

"Oh, he was really a fan of those building sets, not Legos, what are they called? He'd sit there on the floor building all kinds of things. And he had these two friends from the neighborhood. One was a great little kid, like your dad, and one was a holy terror. And then there was Cousin Morty, a few blocks away. He was always over at our house." Aunt Adele had a nostalgic look in her eye. "And Howie did well in school. We both skipped a grade, you know. I skipped first grade and so did he, five years later. I graduated high school at sixteen. That's when I left."

"But why?" Lucy asked. That was really the key, wasn't it? To how their family ended up the way it had? All tangled up in one another's business?

"Wouldn't you want to escape from West Orange?" Aunt Adele said. And that was all Lucy could get out of her.

Fourteen

Max

Max had taken Phoebe out for a walk every single night for the past two weeks. And it had paid off. He had managed to have several conversations with the girl. Conversations that actually were becoming slightly easier as the days progressed. The only problem was that he still wasn't sure what her name was. And that was getting a little awkward.

"Hi, Max!" she'd greet him in the park, as he pulled Phoebe along and she restrained the exuberant Shirley.

"Hi!" he'd reply, hoping she wouldn't notice how he never used her name.

And she'd start talking about the drama class she was taking, and about the parts she really wanted to play, and about the music she liked, and all kinds of other things, and he'd listen, enraptured. And he'd even managed to say a few things. About how he played the guitar. About how he'd like to join a band one day. About how maybe he'd try out for the school jazz band. Auditions for next year were coming up.

And then he'd see her at the bus stop, and she'd stopped wearing the earbuds all the time, so now he actually had someone to talk to instead of watching Seb and the others ignore him. Since no one talked to her, either, it wasn't possible to figure out her name that way. He'd tried searching for a program from the fall play, to see the list of actors. But he hadn't been able to find one. He'd even texted Ernesto, in Argentina, to see if he had any idea of the mystery girl's name.

"You know that new girl who played Hermia in the school play in November?" he'd texted.

"Dude! Is she hot?" Ernesto had texted back.

Well, yeah, she kind of was, but that wasn't the point. "What's her name?" Max texted desperately.

"Didn't see play, don't know," Ernesto replied. "Why?"

"Oh, nothing," Max had written back. "She's at my bus stop." And that was that. He couldn't just come out and ask her what her name was. Not at this point. Not after they'd, or mostly she'd, spent all this time talking at the bus stop and on the bus and in the park. It would just seem too weird.

He couldn't ask Seb. They really weren't speaking any more. The only other possibility was Lucas. He didn't live in Max's part of the neighborhood and he didn't ride the same bus, but maybe somehow he would know. Max felt weird texting Lucas, because he wasn't really in touch with Lucas too much either lately.

So that day, right before Spanish, the only class he had with Lucas—fortunately Lucas's inseparable other half, Clara, was not in their class—Max pulled him aside.

"You know the girl who played Hermia in the school play in November?" he whispered.

"No," Lucas had said. "I didn't see the play."

And then Sra. Bautista had asked everyone to sit down and announced that they were having a pop quiz. Great.

So there he was in the park again, with Phoebe, hoping that this would be one of the nights Ms. Nameless would be walking Shirley. He made a couple of circuits round the path, and the park was still empty, and he wondered where she could be, and maybe this was one of the nights her brother would be walking Shirley instead. Maybe he could ask the brother what her name was. But then the brother would probably tell her, and that would be totally embarrassing.

The thought of Aunt Adele popped into his head. Aunt Adele never seemed embarrassed by anything. That night, they'd all been over at his grandparents' house for dinner. Cousin Morty and Lucretia were leaving the next day, and Grandma wanted everyone over there for a family dinner, so everyone turned up except Philippe, who, to Max's disappointment, couldn't get away from the restaurant. Philippe was, like, really great to talk to. But in any case, Grandma seemed super-stressed out lately. Max figured having all those houseguests probably wasn't easy. And Grandma was the one doing all the work.

So after dinner, Max had been about to ask Grandma if he could help with the dishes, but then Aunt Adele had taken Max's hand and dragged him off to sit with her on the living room sofa.

"I know when I was your age everyone would ask, How's school going?" Aunt Adele said, still holding Max's hand. "How are your classes? Where are you thinking of going to college? So I won't ask you that."

"Thank you," Max had replied. He wondered where this conversation was leading.

Cousin Morty wandered in. "I'll ask you, then, Max. How is school going?"

Max sighed. Except for the fact that he didn't have any friends, fine. Well, maybe one friend, if the nameless girl counted as his friend.

"Morty, let the boy talk about something besides school. What are your passions?" Aunt Adele asked. "What do you think you'd like to become?"

"An attorney," Cousin Morty butted in. "Like his grandfather and his mother. And of course, like me." Cousin Morty didn't have any kids, so he took a great interest in what Max and Will planned to do with their lives. Max assumed he'd been the same way with Max's mom and aunts when they were younger.

"No," Max said. He didn't think he wanted to be an attorney. He wanted to do something with music. But he didn't really want to tell anyone that. It would sound too unrealistic, right?

"Well, what, then?" Cousin Morty persisted, sitting down on Max's other side. "You're halfway through high school, almost. You must have some thoughts on the subject."

"Any girlfriends?" Aunt Adele said. "A handsome boy like you, there must be girls falling all over you."

Not exactly. Max could tell he was turning red. He'd need to switch the conversation to another topic. Fast.

"Or boyfriends," Aunt Adele said. "If that's what you prefer."

Max shook his head. It wasn't. Even though he'd joined the Gay-Straight Alliance in middle school and then in high school, in honor of his mom and Vilma. Vilma was supposed to come home tomorrow, which he hoped would put his mom into a better mood. She rivaled Grandma for the bad mood award. But he wasn't sure. Was everything okay with his mom and Vilma? It just seemed weird that Vilma would be away for so long. He knew it had to do with her job, but wasn't it true that sometimes people took jobs away from their spouses because they didn't really like them any more? Why did people leave, anyway?

"Why did you leave?" Max asked Aunt Adele. Maybe he'd leave too. Maybe he'd take off for Alaska, since she'd already claimed Hawaii. Maybe then no one would expect him to be a lawyer. Maybe he'd be some kind of fisherman. Or work in a national park. But maybe the way things were going there wouldn't be any national parks by the time he finished high school.

"New Jersey was too small for me," she answered. "I sought adventure elsewhere."

"Come on, Cousin Adele, New Jersey was a fine place to grow up," Cousin Morty said, shaking his head. "West Orange was good enough for me and Howie. Why not you?"

Aunt Adele smiled. "To each her own," she answered.

And then Max's mom showed up and said they should be leaving because he and Will had homework, and Max had been fine with that, because then he could go walk Phoebe, and so they'd left.

And now it didn't seem like the nameless girl would be showing up tonight, and he figured he'd do one more loop around with Phoebe, just in case, and then at the end of the loop he heard barking, and Phoebe started barking too, and then he saw Shirley and the girl heading toward them.

"Max!" she said, sounding a little breathless. "I'm glad you're still here. I was planning to get here a little earlier, but I was studying for a French test, and then before I knew it, it was past nine, so I rushed over."

She rushed over? Because he was there? Could that be possible? He nodded, but it was dark, so he couldn't tell if she could see him. He probably should actually say something. Like, that he was glad she had rushed over. But he felt sort of tongue-tied.

"You know jazz band auditions are on Friday," she said, as they walked slowly around the path, the two dogs stopping every few feet to check out their surroundings. "Are you trying out?"

"Yeah," he said, his voice coming out unevenly. "I mean, there are tons of kids who play guitar, and there's no reason they'd pick me, but, yeah."

"Hey, I have an idea," she said. "Why don't you bring your guitar with you when you walk Phoebe, and I can listen? I told you my dad's a guitarist, right?"

What? No, she hadn't.

"He played with Dylan, Joni Mitchell, all these people a long time ago," she said. "You know, he's a lot older than my mom. He's almost seventy. It's his mom who just went into assisted living. She's ninety-two."

Max was speechless. Her dad had played with Bob Dylan?

"Do you want to meet him? He's away on tour right now, but he'll be back tomorrow. Maybe you could come over after school?"

He nodded again. "Yes," he managed to say. This was incredible.

"You can Google him," she said. "Logan MacLeish."

Logan MacLeish. That was a clue! Max could look her up in the school directory now, assuming she had the same last name as her dad. If he Googled her dad, maybe it would mention his family.

"I don't like to talk about him a lot, because at my old school there were these kids who thought I was boasting. But I didn't mean to do that. I mean, I'm just proud of him. It's sort of cool, don't you think?"

"Of course," Max said. He realized they had circled around the park a couple more times. And that they were walking kind of closer to each other than they had been before. When the dogs weren't pulling them apart, that was. Did she realize that? Did she want him to do something? Like, hold her hand? He didn't know. So he didn't do anything.

And then his phone started buzzing. His mom. He reluctantly answered it.

"You have homework, and poor Phoebe must be exhausted. I think you should come home now."

"Yeah, okay." And he hung up.

"Your mom?" the girl asked. "I probably should be going too. But I'll see you at the bus stop tomorrow. And then you'll come over after school, right?"

"Right," he said. "I'm looking forward to it."

And in the darkness, he could see her smiling at him.

Fifteen

Sarah

Vilma's plane should be taking off from Helsinki right now, Sarah thought, as she gazed at her office computer. Tons of emails she needed to deal with. A meeting with a couple of Hill staffers over lunch. A performance evaluation for Asif, her intern. And then she needed to catch up on some reading about arts programs in California that she'd meant to get to a few weeks ago. And answer a bunch of messages about the bar mitzvah. She had to ask Will what music he wanted for the slide show, and she needed to fill out a form for the temple with everyone's Hebrew names. She sighed. And then there was Aunt Adele. At least Cousin Morty and Lucretia were leaving that morning. Her dad and Aunt Adele were taking them to the airport.

Her mom had escaped to a yoga class with Cat, which Sarah thought was a great idea. She wished she could go with them.

Will was the only one who didn't seem stressed out, which was astonishing considering he was the one who would be standing up there in front of a hundred and fifty people in less than two weeks. But Will had never seemed all that stressed out about anything. She wondered how that could be possible, that a child of hers, a grandchild of her parents, seemed to lack the capacity for anxiety. It was good, of course, but weird. The donor? Some throwback?

The same genetic place Diana and Aunt Adele had come from?

"Yeah, Mom, I've got this," he had said to her when she asked him that morning if he was feeling okay about everything. And he'd headed out the door to the bus stop. She'd driven by a few minutes later, on the way to the office, and she'd seen the kids, heads bent over their phones, in a line, like penitents, or pilgrims, waiting to board the bus.

That phone, those screens, would drive her insane one day. Screens were why she had him spend time with Lucy and her parents after school. If he went home, whether or not Max was there, all Will would do was play video games. He needed supervision. And unfortunately her schedule didn't allow her to do much of that until she left work.

Max, on the other hand, spent most of his time in his room playing the guitar. He had gone through a video game phase, too, but now he seemed intent on playing the guitar every free minute of his day. And he was getting his homework done, too, which was good. Sarah wasn't sure why he was spending so much time walking Phoebe lately, though. She'd have to ask Vilma what she thought about that.

Sarah enjoyed walking Phoebe. It gave her time to clear her head. She walked her in the morning, and then Max walked her after school, and they all used to take turns walking her at night, but lately Max seemed obsessed with the nighttime walks. And these walks seemed to be lengthening. Phoebe was elderly. She probably didn't need such long walks. Although she was looking a little slimmer.

"Sarah?" It was Monique Johnson, Sarah's number-two, her right-hand woman, peering in at her. Monique had worked at Arts Alliance for eight years now, half as long as Sarah. They'd both been hired by Sarah's predecessor as executive director, her role model in life, Caroline Martino.

Sarah had heard amazing things about Caroline Martino, the founder of Arts Alliance, for years before she'd ever met her. And when Sarah was starting to feel burned out from working on the Hill as a staffer focusing on education issues, she ventured over to Arts Alliance for an informational interview with Caroline. And it turned out there was an opening, and although it represented a bit of a pay cut, Sarah leaped at the opportunity.

And, she reflected now, she'd never regretted it. She loved her job. Except that she had relied on Caroline's sage advice, and now Caroline, who at seventy-nine had recently been widowed, was moving to New Zealand where her son lived with his New Zealand-born wife and their kids. Which was sending Sarah into a total panic.

"Hi, Monique," Sarah said. Lately she wondered if Monique and everyone else in the office had picked up on Sarah's own unease. Could she really handle this job without the backstop of Caroline's counsel?

"Oh, jeez," Monique said, and she plopped herself down in one of the spare chairs and launched into a familiar litany of dread, about the problems facing Arts Alliance, and similar groups, given the current political situation. The idea behind Arts Alliance, which Caroline had founded back in the 1970s, was to get arts programs into schools, particularly in underserved neighborhoods. In Sarah's own neighborhood, parents chipped in to provide extra funds for artists to visit the schools. Clearly this was not an option in most places.

Sarah tried to reassure Monique, while feeling increasingly worried herself. What if Arts Alliance fell apart on her watch? What if the kids they served didn't end up getting exposed to the arts any more? What if Monique and everyone else on the staff ended up losing their jobs? And what about her own job?

And then there was the fact that Monique was six months pregnant—Sarah felt surrounded by pregnancy lately, given Diana—and was planning to take time off once the baby, a girl, arrived, which was fine. Sarah had done the same thing when Max and Will were born. Caroline had always been incredibly generous with maternity benefits. But, based on some things Monique had said, Sarah had a feeling Monique might not come back. And then what would Sarah do? No one else in the office had the institutional memory that she and Monique possessed.

Vilma, she reflected, was far better than she was at sounding confident in the face of long odds. Maybe Vilma should stop by the office tomorrow if she wasn't too jet-lagged and give everyone a pep talk. Including Sarah. Monique was Lucy's age, and everyone else in the office was younger than that, and Sarah knew they all looked up to her. They all saw her the same way she saw Caroline. But now Caroline wouldn't be available for biweekly lunches and impromptu phone calls. She, Sarah, would have to manage somehow.

"Sorry to be such a downer," Monique muttered, getting up from her seat. "Gotta make a couple of calls now, see you later." And she left.

Whereupon Sarah's phone rang. It couldn't be her mother. She was at yoga. Her dad was taking everyone to the airport. The boys? Had something awful happened at one of their schools? It was a constant worry. She reached for the phone. Diana. The baby?

"Diana? Is everything okay?"

"So if I'm having this kind of pain on the right side, like, my lower stomach area, what does that mean?"

At least she wasn't having the baby right now. Sarah thought about Diana's question. She vaguely remembered something like that.

"Ligaments, I think."

"So nothing's imminent?"

Sarah sighed. She wasn't a doctor, a fact that didn't seem to stop Diana from asking her this type of question every couple of days. "I'm not a..."

"Doctor, I know," Diana interrupted. "But you've been through all of this, twice, and Mom says she can't remember because it was so long ago, and I could ask some of my friends but they're all really busy."

And I'm not? Sarah thought.

"And, you know, I can't fit into the Blattner clothes any more, and it's making it harder to get into character, so the first draft might not be done before the baby gets here, and I can't seem to get Blattner's voice right in my head."

This was the most doubt Sarah had heard Diana express in years. If not forever.

"This is all normal," Sarah said. "If you get the first draft done before or after, it's all going to be okay." She thought back to her own pregnancies. She'd had had a few months off each time and after that the boys had been at a wonderful day care and...

"...and Mom's been on my case about getting someone to help. But I don't think I need anyone," Diana was saying. "I can handle it. And Philippe's taking the first week off."

"One week isn't enough," Sarah said. "Is there any way he can take more time?"

"Not really," Diana said. "Not with the restaurant and everything. Anyway, I need to get back to work. See you." And she hung up.

Sarah's parents had insisted that she hire someone to help her for the first month. Especially given that she was a single mom. She remembered the nervousness she'd felt, the day she went over to tell her parents that she'd decided to try to have a baby through donor insemination. But you're on your own, she was afraid they'd say. How can you do that? Why don't you wait until you meet the right person?

But Sarah hadn't met the right person, and she was thirty years old, and she felt the time had come. She had a great job, and she knew Caroline would be supportive. She just wasn't sure about her parents. She'd be asking a lot of them, and they were both still working, and would they be willing to pitch in?

"Of course," her parents had chorused in unison. Her dad was incredibly busy all week but he could help out on weekends, and her mom's schedule was fairly light in comparison and she would be delighted, and how exciting, and a grandchild, and how exactly does a sperm bank work anyway?

And Sarah had explained the whole thing, and over the next few months her mom delved into research on single parenting by lesbian moms, and her dad read up on the paternal role played by grandfathers in the lives of fatherless children. They'd thrown themselves completely on board, and once Max arrived, they doted on him endlessly.

And by the time Will was born, her mom was having such a great time with Max that she decided to retire and be there even more for Sarah and the boys, and a few years later Sarah met Vilma and then the boys had yet another parental figure in their lives.

Sometimes Sarah worried that she'd loaded the boys with too much baggage. That having a sperm donor for a dad and a two-mom situation at home would lead to teasing. Mocking. Bullying. She worried that living in Bethesda, where there were only a couple of other single-sex-couple families at the boys' elementary school, was the wrong idea. Takoma Park might have been a better choice. But it was logistically easier to be right near her parents, and they'd been so generous in helping her pay for the house, and so far the boys seemed to be thriving.

Will was so easygoing and had a real gift for making friends, and as far as she knew, no one had ever bullied him or made fun of him. Max was more complicated. She remembered one incident where a new boy had joined Max's fifth grade class and had started throwing homophobic slurs Max's way, and Max had gotten into a fistfight with him, and both boys had been sent to the principal's office.

And Max had told the principal—and Sarah, when she was called into school from work—that this boy had shouted all these things at him and said that Max and Will and their mom were probably going to hell for being gay, so Max had to beat him up. And the principal had been appalled, and the other boy had been disciplined, and Max had eventually gone back to class, after being told by the principal that fighting wasn't the answer to anything.

But that night she'd heard him crying in his room, and she'd gone in, and through his tears he'd explained that he hoped she understood that he hadn't fought the boy because he thought being called gay was bad. He'd fought him because the boy was a bigot and a jerk. And she'd been incredibly proud of him and told him of course she understood, but she'd added that she agreed with the principal, fighting wasn't the answer. It was one of those times she was glad her boys had her dad in their lives. He could answer a lot of those boy-type questions. Like about the role of fighting.

Still, that whole incident had been an aberration, as far as she knew. Neither boy had been targeted specifically since. Which was a huge relief. Because she could take it if it was directed at her, but at her kids? Who had nothing whatsoever to do with her sexual orientation? Both boys had told her about anti-gay slurs and anti-Semitic slurs and other bigoted comments being casually tossed around at school, especially since the most recent presidential election. So were her worries justified? Probably. But sometimes she felt as if she just didn't know the right way to handle any of these issues.

Would she ever know? She'd always assumed that by the time she hit her forties, she would be mature. Wise. Knowledgeable about the ways of the world. And here she was, forty-six years old, and she had no clue about anything.

Something Aunt Adele had said at dinner the previous night stood out in Sarah's mind. "No regrets," Aunt Adele had said. "I have no regrets about any of the decisions I made in my life."

Now how could that be? How could anyone have lived eighty years without regretting anything? Especially someone who'd estranged themselves from their family the way Aunt Adele had? She must have had some regrets to contact Sarah's dad, right?

Sarah's mom had snorted audibly upon hearing Aunt Adele's pronouncement, and the two had glared at each other. "No one has no regrets," her mom had said. "If you have no regrets, you're just running away from your problems."

An awkward silence had ensued before Sarah's dad had jumped into the void. "I suppose everyone handles regrets in their own way," he said. And he had deftly turned the conversation onto the topic of Robert Mueller, and the skirmish had ended.

But it was something to think about. Did people who were circus—Aunt Adele, Diana--really have no regrets about anything? Or was it all just a sham, a way to avoid those feelings of existential dread? It was yet another thing about which Sarah had no idea.

Sixteen

Marilyn

It was a gentle yoga class, but Marilyn still found it challenging. Maintaining her position in down dog. Balancing in tree pose. Cat, on the other hand, was executing all her moves perfectly. The point, Marilyn knew, wasn't to compare herself to Cat. That was completely not the point. But she just couldn't help it sometimes. And the whole ridiculous dinner last night kept running through her head. No regrets? Who had no regrets? No one, that's who. What was Adele running away from? There must be something.

"And hold the warrior pose for four breaths," Margo, the yoga teacher, was saying.

Marilyn felt herself wobbling slightly and adjusted the position of her back foot, which helped. Breathe in, breathe out. She pictured Adele floating upward in a bubble. Floating away. Out of their lives again.

At least Cousin Morty and Lucretia were on their way back to New York. Lucretia, she had to admit, wasn't too bad. She had tried to help out, and she seemed genuinely interested in Pinsky family history, which was nice. But Cousin Morty had always driven Marilyn crazy. He was too loud. Too convinced that his way was the right way. Too willing to push his views on her kids and grandkids. She'd overheard him last night telling Max to be a lawyer. Well, maybe that isn't what Max wanted to be. Why couldn't Cousin Morty see that not everyone wanted to do what he wanted them to do?

Margo was telling everyone to lie down for shavasana, and Marilyn complied. She breathed in and out and imagined she was in a peaceful meadow. She was sitting on a bench watching happy little cartoonlike animals frolicking around. One of them, a chipmunk, was wearing a yarmulke and a tallis, and it started reciting the prayer before the Torah reading, and she realized the chipmunk was Will. The chipmunk was reading the Hebrew prayer in an Israeli accent, though, which surprised her, as she had never heard Will do anything like that. And then she heard Cat's voice.

"I guess she fell asleep," Cat was saying. "Well, let's let her sleep a little more, then," Margo's soothing voice replied. "I don't have another class for twenty minutes."

"She's been under a lot of stress," Cat offered in a confiding tone. "Her sister-in-law reappeared after sixty-four years and has been staying with her and Howard and apparently is wreaking havoc."

"Oh, dear," Margo said. "How difficult."

How long had she been asleep? This really had to stop. Until the past couple of years, Marilyn had not been the type of person who took naps. In fact, she had found it almost impossible to do so.

"At least you can nap when the baby's napping," she remembered her mother saying when Sarah was a newborn and hadn't learned to sleep through the night yet. "Catch up a little."

But of course Marilyn couldn't nap. So she didn't sleep at all. Day or night. Now she seemed to be unable to stop sleeping.

"...forty-four," Cat was saying. Now she must be talking about Diana.

"Well, that's wonderful," Margo said. "My best friend had her son at forty-two. And I was thirty-seven and thirty-nine when my kids were born, so I wasn't that far off." Margo was in her fifties, but looked as if she were in her thirties.

"It's wonderful, yes," Cat said. And then Marilyn heard her start to tell Margo the whole story about Skip and the boat, and Marilyn tuned out. What could Adele be running away from? She needed to figure that out.

Howie was no help. She felt as if she had no opportunity to talk to him about anything since Adele's arrival. Adele monopolized him completely.

And she hadn't had much time to talk one-on-one with Adele, either. Maybe she should do that. Do what Lucy did. Invite Adele to coffee. Marilyn hadn't been too happy when Lucy had done that, but maybe Lucy had the right idea.

Not that Marilyn knew what Lucy and Adele had discussed. Was Lucy actually confiding in Adele? Telling her what was on her mind? Because clearly something was. Relating to the divorce, Marilyn assumed. But maybe it was something else. Could it be a problem at work? Was there someone new in Lucy's life?

She thought back to Lucy's birth, when Marilyn herself was thirty-nine. It had been an easy pregnancy, easier than the first two, which was surprising given that Marilyn was a whole decade older. And Lucy had been such an easy baby. Sarah, at eleven, had been a huge help, while Diana, nine, had sulked around the house complaining dramatically about not being the youngest in the family any more.

And unlike Sarah, who tended to share her troubles with Marilyn, at least most of the time, and Diana, who shared everything with the entire world, Lucy kept her feelings to herself. She was a self-contained child, and later a self-contained teenager and young adult. And when she walked into the living room with a young man and announced she was going to marry him, Marilyn and Howie had been shocked. Not by Jeff, though he was a bit older than they might have expected, and not really by the idea of Lucy getting married at twenty-three. Although none of her friends were anywhere near getting married, and her sisters, so much older, had yet to find anyone to settle down with. The shock came from the fact that Marilyn and Howie had no idea Lucy was even dating anyone. And they'd seen her at family dinners every couple of weeks.

"...think we should wake her now," Cat was saying. "Marilyn?"

Marilyn was sort of awake anyway, but sort of not. She liked this half-awake state, in which she had no responsibilities. And they'd all descend on her again once she opened her eyes.

"The next class is coming in," Cat said, a bit louder. "Marilyn? Are you okay?"

She'd have to open her eyes. So she did. "Sorry about that," she said. "I think my houseguests are getting to me."

"Roll over on your right side, in fetal position," Margo said. "Then work your way slowly up to a sitting position before standing up."

Marilyn wondered how the process of standing up had become so difficult. She used to be able to do it with ease. She thought the yoga would help, and maybe it was, but everything seemed to take a while.

Margo reached one hand out and effortlessly helped Marilyn up.

"Thanks," Marilyn said, feeling somewhat absurd. She rolled up her yoga mat and put it in its case, and followed Cat out the door. The yoga studio was within walking distance of their houses, so they started heading homeward.

"So what's with the sleeping?" Cat asked. "Falling asleep at

Diana's. Falling asleep now. That's not like you. Are you okay?"

"Yes, I'm fine," Marilyn said. She just wanted to escape. Maybe she should take a leaf from Adele's book and escape to Hawaii. They could switch places for a while. She imagined herself with a lei around her neck, sipping a tropical drink on a hotel veranda. Lucy had traveled to Hawaii a few years back, with Jeff, and seemed to have a good time. She'd sent back some pictures of the two of them, arms around each other, smiling into the camera. Who would have known their marriage would end so soon after?

Marilyn and Howie had discussed a trip to Hawaii for years now, but had never ended up following through. Too much else going on. It had been a couple of years since they'd gone anywhere except up to New York for family-related celebrations involving various second cousins.

They probably should embark on any big travel plans now, before they got too old to enjoy it. Cat had taken her whole family—both sons and their wives and kids--on one of those Alaska cruises. Maybe she and Howie could do that with the girls, Vilma, Philippe, and the grandkids. Although at this point, Howie would probably insist on inviting Adele to join them, and Marilyn didn't think she could handle that. Well, it probably wouldn't work in the end. Vilma would be in Finland, and Philippe wouldn't be able to leave the restaurant, and how old would a baby need to be to go on a cruise, anyway?

"...Adele?" Cat was asking.

Marilyn wasn't entirely sure what Cat had said. But it probably had to do with how annoying Adele was. "Why would someone say they have no regrets over anything they'd done in their entire life?" she asked. She glanced over at a beautiful pink dogwood tree in full bloom. It made her feel momentarily better about things.

"That's impossible," Cat said, shaking her head. "Everyone

must have some regrets. Although I wonder if the current inhabitant of the White House is self-aware enough to have any."

"Probably not," Marilyn replied. "But I think Adele's running away from something again. That's why she's here."

"Her health," Cat said. "I've always thought it must be something health-related."

But Adele seemed fine. Not that that meant anything, Marilyn knew. Could it be her health? Or was it something else entirely?

Seventeen

Diana

Philippe had taken to calling her every hour or so to check in. It was sweet, really. But she had nothing to report. She was the first one at Starbucks again, and she was waiting for the other four to arrive.

"I will leave the restaurant for more than a week if you would like me to, Diana," he said in his delightful accent. "I can leave it in the capable hands of Lillian."

Diana wasn't so sure. Lillian was Philippe's able sous chef, but Diana feared the entire restaurant would collapse without Philippe there. His absent-mindedness about pretty much everything else in life turned into a fierce focus when it came to his work. It was astounding.

She remembered early on in their courtship, when he was working as the chef at a French restaurant downtown, and she had disguised herself as a man, just for the hell of it, and had been hired by Henri, the supercilious restaurant manager, as a waiter, and had seen a completely different side to her mild-mannered, somewhat bumbling suitor as he barked orders and whipped up fabulous cuisine. Of course, he'd figured out immediately that the new waiter was none other than Diana, but it had been fun. She loved disguises. Not that she could disguise herself as much of anything right now.

The baby whacked one of its ever-growing body parts into Diana's ribs and she gasped. She was definitely ready for her or him to come out. Enough already. Will had been a week early. She wondered if that would be the case with her own baby. A week early would be five days from now. Was she ready? As much as she'd ever be, she figured.

"Diana, hello!" Marcia waved and sat down next to her. "So no baby yet. Every week I think, maybe this will be it! And then here you are again." The previous week, the group had discussed Marcia's new chapter, which featured a clash between Marcia's plucky heroine and a goblin. Diana had enjoyed it, much to her surprise. She imagined Marcia's book actually being published one day, and her, Diana, reading it to the baby.

"Hi, Marcia." Diana had given up on the Blattner voice for now, since she couldn't get into the outfit. "I really did enjoy your chapter last week. Good work."

Marcia beamed. "Thanks. So how's Philippe holding up? I remember Dexter was a nervous wreck each time I was about to give birth. I felt like he was another child I had to look out for."

Diana considered that. Was Philippe a nervous wreck? He was so easy-going, except when it came to the restaurant, that it was hard to tell. "He's been calling me every hour," she reported.

"Ah, yes," Marcia said, nodding. "That's typical nervous-wreck behavior."

"I did that," Gideon said. He had appeared behind Marcia and sat down on Diana's other side. "I called Serena every few minutes toward the end. The idea that this baby would actually be appearing into the world, it was overwhelming. It was a little easier the second time around."

"I doubt there'll be a second time around for us," Diana said.

"Keep in mind how old I am." Part of her felt sort of sad about that. That this baby would be an only child. But she knew Max and Will would be there for him or her. First cousins. Diana hadn't had any of those. Her mom was an only child, and her dad might as well have been. Until now. And Aunt Adele didn't have any kids anyway.

"You're eternally youthful," Marcia said. "Don't you agree, Gideon?"

"Of course," Gideon said. And they both smiled at Diana.

"What's all the smiling for?" It was Poppy, who was scowling. "I just broke up with Pietro, so I'm not in the mood for happy stuff tonight." And she sank down into a chair. "It turns out he hooked up with my so-called friend Giselle. More than once."

"How dreadful," Marcia said, her smile turning to a frown. "You poor thing." She put her arm around Poppy and patted her shoulder.

"Sorry, Poppy. That sucks," Diana said. "But you can put this into one of your stories. Once the hurt wears off, which it will." That was the good thing about fiction writing. If someone got on her bad side, that person could eventually find their way into one of her stories. She'd put this woman who'd been overly flirtatious with Philippe into one of her stories. One of the ones that actually had been published. But she wasn't sure the woman read *Glimmer Train*, so perhaps it was all for naught.

"Writing well is the best revenge," Gideon said, nodding. "You'll find someone better."

Poppy sniffled into a tissue. "But I really liked Pietro," she said. "I mean, before this happened."

Diana recalled a time when something similar had happened to her, with this guy Carlos she'd been completely infatuated with back in college. Another drama student. And they'd had the most incredible sex ever, but a few days later she learned he'd also been sleeping with her then-best friend, and she banished both of them from her life. She recounted the story to Poppy, who wiped her eyes and blew her nose.

What she didn't tell Poppy and the others was that often she, Diana, had been the one with whom guys cheated on their girlfriends. The homewrecker, you might say. It had given her a thrill at the time, like she could take any girl's boyfriend away if she wanted to. Needless to say, these days it wasn't something she was proud of.

"Hey, guys." It was Nick, as usual the last one to arrive. He pulled up a chair between Diana and Gideon and sat down.

By now, Poppy was wailing into Marcia's comforting arms. Marcia must be used to this kind of thing after years of soothing her own kids and her young students, Diana realized. Would she, Diana, be able to comfort the baby if it cried? She assumed somehow she'd figure it out.

"What's going on? Poppy, what's wrong?" Nick's brow wrinkled.

"My fucking boyfriend was fucking someone else, that's what's wrong," Poppy said, lifting her head momentarily. Her eye makeup was running down her face in globs. "So I dumped him." Poppy put her head back onto Marcia's shoulder and sobbed.

Nick reached for Poppy's hand and squeezed it. "Jeez, Poppy, I'm sorry. The guy didn't deserve you."

Diana could feel the baby joining in, as if he or she also wanted to squeeze Poppy's hand. But instead, it kicked Diana in the ribs again.

"Ow," she exclaimed.

"Are you okay?" everyone asked in unison, including Poppy.

"Yeah, the baby just hit me in the ribs again," Diana said. "I'm all right." She pulled her water bottle out of her bag and took a few sips.

"My sister's having a baby in August," Nick said. "Did I tell you guys that?"

Everyone shook their heads and offered congratulations.

"Maybe you and Hannah could get together once you both have your babies," Nick said. "Have a playgroup or whatever."

Diana nodded. Finding other people with babies would probably be a good idea. Most of her friends' kids were older. "Yeah, I'd like that," she said. "So listen, guys, I thought I'd show you a story I'm working on. Since I might not be here for a few weeks." For some reason, she'd been having trouble sleeping lately, which had never been a problem before, and she'd get up in the middle of the night, lumber into the living room, pull out her laptop, and write. It was a story unlike the others she'd written. It was told from the perspective of a teenage girl whose family didn't understand her.

Everyone expressed interest, so Diana passed out copies of the work in progress, and watched as they read it. Generally this was an enjoyable moment for Diana. She liked watching everyone's faces as they reacted to what she'd written. But this time, she felt slightly tense. She wasn't sure why. Maybe her hormones were out of whack, given the baby and everything.

Her phone started ringing, and she picked it up. Philippe again. "Everything is well, chérie?" he asked.

"Yes, mi amor," she said. She liked to mix up her languages a little. "So are you a nervous wreck?"

She could hear Philippe laughing. She loved his laugh. "Probably, yes," he said. "I love you so much."

"I love you too," Diana said. All of a sudden she felt like crying. What was going on with her, anyway?

"I will call again soon," Philippe said. And he hung up.

"Wow, Diana, this is great," Nick said, his eyes wide. "Your story, I mean, not your phone call. I mean, not that I was listening or anything." And he smiled sheepishly.

Diana was well aware that Nick probably had been listening. But that was okay.

"Wait, Nick, I'm still reading," Poppy said. She had pulled a pen out of her pocket and was marking up the story. "Don't get ahead of the rest of us, dude, all right?" She seemed more like herself now, Diana thought with relief.

Marcia, whose pink sweater was stained with Poppy's black makeup, also was making some notes, as was Gideon.

Nick leaned over and whispered to Diana, "So this is kind of autobiographical, right? Like, how your main character's family underestimates her and thinks she's an airhead, so she acts out and becomes who they think she is?"

Diana hadn't exactly thought of the story that way. But now that Nick had mentioned it, yeah. Her character, Artemis, did resemble herself as a teenager.

"Artemis, Diana, that's the first clue," Nick said. "Very clever."

But she hadn't meant to do that. It had just happened. The story had emerged from some deeper part of herself that she had somehow tapped into. The baby kicked her again, and Diana started rubbing her stomach to see if it would calm the baby down. What kind of legacy would this baby inherit? How had her parents done this three times? How had Sarah done it twice? Could she really do this? Could she be responsible for another human being? She put her head in her hands and sighed.

Eighteen

Howard

Howard was in the car on the way to pick Will up from a soccer game. It was at a field further out River Road. The traffic was slow, it being afternoon rush hour, and his mind was restless. He'd taken Adele to see more apartments that morning, but again she'd seemed dissatisfied. He wasn't sure why, as the apartments had been top of the line.

"Just not quite right," she'd said as they headed back to his house. "I'm used to a certain je ne sais quoi, and I'm just not finding it here."

Howard refrained from saying that someone who was used to living in Honolulu might find Bethesda a bit different. If she was so used to Honolulu, maybe she shouldn't be moving here at all. But he didn't want to say that. He didn't want to say anything that might make her leave again.

Which had put him into increasing peril with Marilyn. The other night, in bed, he'd tried to give her a hug, nothing more, and she'd wriggled away with surprising agility to the edge of the bed, where he'd sensed the fury emanating from every fiber of her being.

"No regrets, my foot," she'd grumbled, before falling asleep.

He figured she was referring to something Adele had said at dinner that night, about how she had no regrets about anything she'd ever done in her life. Which was absurd, of course. He agreed with Marilyn on that.

But he was willing to cut his sister some slack. Getting to spend all this time with her after so long, when he'd been convinced he'd never see her again, was absolutely priceless. And here she was, planning to attend Will's bar mitzvah, which in a strange way seemed to make up for the fact that she hadn't come to Howard's.

He remembered arguing with his parents when he was Will's age. "But there must be some way to send her an invitation," he'd pleaded. "We can just write to the circus and they'll give it to her. We just need to figure out exactly which circus to write to."

His parents had acted vague and unhappy and had never engaged fully with Howard on the matter, so he'd taken it into his own hands. He had squirreled away several invitations, and had addressed them to Miss Adele Pinsky, care of Ringling Brothers, or whichever other circuses he had found. And then on the day of his bar mitzvah, he'd kept one eye out for her as he stood on the bimah chanting from the Torah. But she hadn't turned up.

And now here she was, just in time for her great-nephew's bar mitzvah. After missing not only Howard's but Max's, plus the bat mitzvahs of Sarah, Diana, and Lucy. And Marilyn's adult bat mitzvah a few years ago. But Adele also would be here for the arrival of the baby, another milestone. So he should count his blessings.

Which reminded him. If the baby turned out to be a boy, was Diana planning to have a bris? Philippe wasn't Jewish, but he didn't seem to care one way or the other about religion. Diana didn't seem to care about it either, but maybe at a time like this she would. He didn't know. He'd discussed it with Marilyn that morning.

"I can't even get her to focus on getting some help in the apartment after the baby comes," Marilyn had said. "Philippe's taking off one week, and then she's planning to start right back with that

Blattner project, and I'm at my wit's end." She'd stopped, in the midst of folding some of their laundry. "Maybe you could take that on," she said. "The bris situation. You should call Diana and talk to her about it."

And now he realized he'd forgotten to make that call. He was nearing the field, and he pulled the car into a lot and got out, listening for the sounds of a soccer game.

And there it was, right in front of him. He caught a glimpse of Will, running down the field with a group of other boys, one of whom was kicking the ball.

"Will! Go to your left! Over to your left!" a young man was shouting. The coach? He looked Jewish, Howard thought, which for some reason surprised him. "Mohammed! Pass the ball! Juan and Alex! Back him up!" The boys galloped up and down the field, and suddenly the ball was rocketed past the opposing goalie and Howard saw his grandson raising his arms in triumph. "Great goal, Will!" the coach shouted, clapping his hands together. "Way to go!"

Howard pondered the fact that Will was actually good at soccer. He'd been at enough of his games to know that. Will played on his school team in the fall, and then on this other team in the spring, with the same coach and a lot of the same kids. The donor must have been athletic, because it certainly didn't come from the Pinsky side of the family. Not that he, Howard, hadn't been okay at basketball as a kid, and the girls had all participated in various sports when they were younger—Lucy was still an avid runner--and Max liked to play basketball too, but this was different. It made life easier to be athletic. Max was musical, which was good, but Howard feared that was a harder path to tread as a teenage boy.

Howard saw Will waving at him and gesturing toward the goal, and he gave Will a thumbs-up. It was nice that Will wasn't embarrassed by him yet. He was getting the sense lately that Max was a little embarrassed by everyone in the family. Even though he was still an incredibly sweet kid. He'd shown Max how to shave a while back. It was the first time he'd taught anyone to do that, being the father of girls, and he found himself tearing up a little.

"Thanks, Gramps," Max had said, examining his face in the mirror. "This is kind of weird, you know?"

Howard had nodded. He remembered his father teaching him how to shave. Back in the bathroom in the West Orange house, with the black and white tiles. He was the last kid among his friends to go through puberty. One of the drawbacks to skipping first grade was that he was always the youngest in his class. Bobby Slotnick, who was older to begin with and had gone through puberty early, had tormented Howard for years about how his voice still hadn't changed. He hoped Max and Will weren't picked on by a present-day Bobby Slotnick. Of course, Bobby had turned out all right. They still kept in touch. He probably should call him and tell him Adele had reappeared. Bobby was living in Boca. Stuart Bernstein, meanwhile, was still in the New York area.

The coach was energetically running up and down the sidelines, calling out encouragement to the players. Ah, youth. Howard remembered when he didn't feel so tired all the time. When he could work an eighteen-hour day and come home and wake up the next morning ready to start all over again.

The game seemed nowhere near finished, so Howard fished his phone out of his pocket and dialed Diana.

"Hey, Dad," she said.

"How's it going, sweetheart? How are you feeling?"

"Oh, fine. I mean, as fine as I can when this baby's punching and kicking me and I feel like an elephant."

She sounded a little out of breath.

"Are you taking a walk?" he inquired.

"Yeah," she said. "I couldn't really focus on Blattner right now, so I decided to walk up to Friendship Heights and go shopping. Maybe see if there's anything I need for the baby."

Well, that was good. Very enterprising of Diana. "Wonderful," he said. "So that reminds me, sweetheart, let's say the baby's a boy, okay?"

"Okay," Diana said. "I dreamed the other night that it was a boy."

"And you remember when Max and Will were born that we had a bris for each of them."

"Uh-huh," Diana said. "I remember that. I think I drank too much of the Manischewitz." And she started laughing. "Remember that boyfriend I had at the time? Zeke? I brought him to Max's bris? The one who ended up being arrested for drug dealing?"

This was not something Howard particularly wanted to remember, but yes, he did remember it.

"I mean, he was a great actor, but he did have a lot of issues," Diana said in a reminiscent tone.

"Well, putting Zeke aside, I wondered if you and Philippe were considering a bris for the baby. If it's a boy, of course."

"Oh," Diana said, sounding completely surprised. "We hadn't discussed that at all. You know, Philippe's not Jewish."

"Yes, I know that," Howard said. Of course he knew that! Sometimes he thought his daughters considered him half-witted at best. "But maybe you should discuss it. You're Jewish, after all, and the baby is Jewish, or at least half-Jewish, and it's something worth discussing."

"Yeah, good idea, Dad," Diana said. "Hey, I'm at this store that has some cute baby stuff in the window, so I'm going to go in and take a look." And she hung up.

Howard peered back at the soccer field to find it empty. Will was approaching, along with his teammates and coach. They all looked sweaty, and were gulping from their water bottles as they lugged various bags filled with soccer gear. Howard recognized a couple of the other boys, who he thought were also named Will.

"Hey, Gramps, you saw the goal? That was our game-winner!" Will said proudly. "Two to one."

The other boys all scattered.

"This is my coach, Mr. Shapiro," Will said, gesturing at the young man. Shapiro. Yes, undoubtedly Jewish. A nice-looking young man, Howard thought. "He was my English teacher last year. He teaches in the room next to Lucy."

"Howard Pinsky, good to meet you," Howard said, sticking out his hand, and the young man, who had turned bright red for some reason, stuck out his hand, and they shook.

"Will's a great kid," Mr. Shapiro said. "Definitely, I mean, yeah."

"Well, thank you," Howard said. "We think so too."

And they headed back to the parking lot, Will chattering away about the game and Mr. Shapiro and Howard occasionally chiming in. Mr. Shapiro's car, an old Toyota Corolla, was parked next to Howard's Toyota Avalon, and they all said goodbye and got into their respective cars.

"He has this major crush on Lucy," Will said, pointing at Mr. Shapiro's car, which was ahead of theirs leaving the parking lot. "But she doesn't seem to, like, reciprocate."

Howard mulled this over. Well, he seemed kind of young for Lucy. But then Lucy hadn't fared too well with someone older. The story Adele told about her young suitor who gave her the green ring popped into his mind. And of course Cousin Morty and Lucretia. They seemed to get along famously, despite their age difference. What was age, anyway? It didn't really matter, did it? He'd need to discuss this with Marilyn once he got home. He was sure she'd have some thoughts on the matter.

Nineteen

Sarah

It was so wonderful to have Vilma back, Sarah thought, as she wrapped herself around Vilma in their bed and sighed contentedly. Of course, Vilma had already drifted off to sleep. She'd only been home since the previous night so she was still jet-lagged. But she'd been eager to meet Aunt Adele, so Sarah had brought her over to her parents' house for a quick visit.

"Vilma, dear, welcome home!" Sarah's mom had exclaimed, embracing Vilma. Sarah knew her parents were very fond of Vilma. And her dad had joined in, also giving Vilma a hug. Sarah had a sense her parents were worried that things were dicey between her and Vilma. Which wasn't true, of course. But they weren't used to the kind of marriage where one person went away for most of an entire year. Her parents had been in the same place all the time, ever since their college days.

And then Aunt Adele had emerged, in her usual high heels, her scarves trailing around her neck.

"And this must be Vilma," she said. "The famous Finn."

Vilma shot Sarah a glance before smiling at Aunt Adele. Sarah could tell Vilma was about to start laughing. "That's me," she said. "Finnish, but probably not so famous."

And Aunt Adele had enfolded Vilma in her arms. "My fourth

niece," she said. "I'm so delighted."

Sarah could see her father gazing fondly at his sister and his daughter-in-law, while her mother looked annoyed. Things didn't seem to have improved between her mom and Aunt Adele.

Vilma had brought some Finnish chocolate for Sarah's parents and for Aunt Adele, and everyone tried some and said how delicious it was, and then Sarah's mom pulled her into the kitchen.

"Can you please talk to Diana?" she asked.

Sarah sighed. Now what?

"Your dad tried talking to her about the bris, but she didn't seem very motivated," her mom said. "And I just have my hands full, and I can't seem to take that issue on, on top of keeping the house clean with all those damned scarves and high-heeled shoes all over the place. I almost tripped over one of those shoes this afternoon."

"So what do you want me to do, exactly?" Sarah said.

"Explain to her that if the baby is a boy and she's thinking of a bris, that she needs to figure out the plans. Let the relatives know she's considering it. Maybe Cousin Morty and Lucretia would want to come down again, unless they're already here for the bar mitzvah. It all depends on the timing. I mean, there's the mohel and the caterer and everything to arrange. I'm sure Cat will want to come, and of course Diana and Philippe's friends." Her mom took a breath, and continued. "And if it's a girl, she'll want to consider a baby naming party of some kind, and probably the same people would want to come. Maybe the rabbi would want to come. He could say a blessing for the baby. So either way, she's going to have to think about it."

"Okay," Sarah said, resigned to the fact that once again she'd have to organize Diana. It was something she'd been doing as far back as she could remember, so it wasn't as if she didn't know the drill.

"Thanks, Sarah, dear, I don't know what I'd do without you. My reliable one." And her mom hugged her.

The reliable one. Sarah had always been the reliable one, Diana was the circus one, and Lucy was the baby. It was hard to break out of those roles, not that Sarah had ever tried. She was destined to be reliable, no matter what.

In the car on the way home, Sarah filled Vilma in on the conversation with her mother.

"Why can't Diana and Philippe just do what they want to do?" Vilma asked. "Why do you and your parents need to be involved in this at all?"

Sarah thought about this. Vilma had a point. But she'd already promised her mom.

And now here she was, trying to fall asleep. She wrapped her arms more tightly around Vilma. She could feel Vilma's breath going in and out. It was soothing. But various worries kept swirling around in Sarah's mind. There were still a bunch of last-minute details she needed to figure out for the bar mitzvah. She had to make sure Will's suit, which she'd bought him a couple of months ago, still fit. Max needed a new suit, too, she suddenly realized. Nothing fit him any more. He was taller than she was now. She'd need to get him something. Unless he could wear one of her dad's suits. She should see about that. They were about the same height. Or maybe Max had surpassed her dad by now.

She'd discussed the whole Max situation with Vilma. Why was Max walking Phoebe every night, for what seemed like endless amounts of time? And last night, Sarah had noticed Max sneaking out of the house with not only Phoebe but also his guitar. Was he planning to serenade Phoebe in the park? What was he up to? She almost felt like sneaking out after him, but she figured he'd see her and then accuse her of not trusting him. Did she trust him? He'd been acting very strangely lately. But she needed to give him some leeway. Walking the dog and playing the guitar weren't bad things in and of themselves. In fact, they were good things. In moderation.

Earlier that night, she and Vilma had returned from a meeting at the temple about the tablecloths for the Kiddush lunch, and only Will was home. He was hunched over the computer in the family room, apparently talking to himself.

"Excuse me?" Sarah said, confused by what he was saying.

"I'm not talking to you," Will said, his eyes on the screen and his hands flying over the mouse and the keyboard. "I'm on Discord with Benjamin and Marco playing Fortnite."

"Where's Max?" Sarah asked.

"I don't know," Will replied.

"What's he doing?" Vilma inquired, following Sarah upstairs. "He's on some chat site playing Fortnite?"

"Will, or Max?"

"Will. From what you say about Max, he's probably out walking Phoebe again." Vilma loosened her knot of blonde hair, and it fell over her shoulders. Sarah felt undone. She remembered Vilma doing just that the first time they'd spent the night together. The boys had been at a sleepover with Sarah's parents.

"God, I missed you so much," Sarah said, resting her head on Vilma's shoulder. Vilma was almost five-ten, a few inches taller than Sarah.

"I missed you too," Vilma said, pulling Sarah in for an embrace. "It's only for another couple of months." Then she'd be opening her company's D.C. office, which would be a lot of work but at least they'd be in the same place.

"I think my parents are worried about us," Sarah said. "Like, they think we're having problems." She looked at Vilma.

"What about the boys?" Vilma said, a concerned expression

crossing her face. "Do you think..."

Sarah's heart sunk. She hadn't thought of that. What a terrible mother she was. They might very well be worrying about the situation between her and Vilma. She should have talked to them about it. Reassured them that despite the distance, all was well between their parents. Maybe it explained Max's peculiar behavior. "Should we..."

"Tomorrow," Vilma said. "It's getting late, and I'm exhausted. Maybe a family meeting at dinner?"

So Sarah had agreed. Max had returned shortly thereafter, with Phoebe but without the guitar, and, as she finally was about to fall asleep, she realized she had completely forgotten to call Diana about the bris.

Twenty

Lucy

Lucy was in the teachers' lounge getting some coffee during her free period when it hit her. She'd been so preoccupied thinking about Jonah Shapiro and thinking about how strange it was that Jeff would be with Matea given her three kids that she hadn't thought about how long Jeff had been involved with Matea. As in, had this been going on when Jeff was still married to Lucy? When he and Matea had been in the office together at Parker-Barker every single day? Going on trips all over the country, the two of them? How could she have been so stupid? Matea's marriage had ended a year before theirs, when her youngest was not even four years old. At the time, Jeff had said something about Matea and her husband growing apart, that they'd been together for years and were just too different to remain together.

But was there more to the story? Had he been unfaithful to her, Lucy, while she was happily oblivious to the whole thing? Was the child issue just a ruse to get rid of her so he could be with Matea? She pictured Matea, her sea-blue eyes and straight flaxen hair, in her large office at Parker-Barker. Sirenlike, she called to Jeff, who was in the equally large office next to hers. And he heard her call and was drawn to her side. Or maybe it had happened the other way around. Jeff was whatever a male siren was—was there such a thing?--calling to Matea.

This was horrible.

She grabbed her phone and her bag, ran out of the teachers' lounge and into the parking lot, and before she could think about it, she had dialed Jeff's number.

"Luce," he said, sounding surprised. "I'm about to go into a meeting, but what is it?"

"Matea," she said. She seemed unable to put a coherent sentence together. "You and Matea. When did it start?"

"Oh, god," Jeff said. "Look, this really isn't a good time."

"When is a good time?" She couldn't breathe. What an idiot she had been. A trusting, foolish idiot.

"Look, Lucy, our lives are separate now. We wanted different things. Isn't that what we decided?"

"I thought this had to do with kids," Lucy said. She could tell her voice was rising. And she was out in the parking lot of the school. Some kids were hanging around on the paved area outside the cafeteria. She needed to be quiet. They might be able to hear her. "Was I wrong? Was there more to it? Were you telling me the truth?" She walked further down the line of parked cars, away from the kids, her head spinning.

"This isn't a good time, Lucy. And does it really make any difference now?"

"Yes," she screamed into the phone. At this point, she really didn't care who heard her. She was too far gone. "It does make a difference."

"Okay, I'll call you later," he said. She could hear him sighing. "Once you're out of school and I'm done with the meeting."

She hung up, feeling as if she couldn't breathe. She was shaking. Everything she'd thought about her marriage had been wrong. Kathleen was teaching this period, so she couldn't talk to her. She knew Stacy was in New York for the day for a meeting. And she didn't want to call anyone in her family. It would just upset them.

"But what happened? You seemed so happy," her mother had said when Lucy had broken the news of her impending divorce.

"Did he do anything?" her father had asked suspiciously. "Anything to..."

"No, no," Lucy had reassured them. "Just a parting of the ways. We wanted different things. It's very amicable."

She glanced at her watch. It was almost time for her next class. She had to pull herself together. Pretend she was Diana, playing a role. Lucy had never been much of an actress, but right now she needed to try.

And somehow she managed to go through the motions with her last three classes, and she knew Will was taking the afternoon bus because Vilma was home and was going to drive him to baseball practice, and she paced around the room, after closing the door for privacy, and then her phone rang. It was Jeff.

"Yes?" she said coldly.

"Oh, jeez, Lucy," Jeff said. His once-familiar voice sounded broken. Cracked with emotion. "I didn't want it to come to this. I thought it would be better if..."

"Better if what? Better if you lied to me? Better if you slept with Matea and then came home and slept with me and told me we wanted different things and led me to believe something that wasn't true?" By now she was on the verge of screaming again. She had to get some control over herself. She didn't want anyone to hear her. "You betrayed me, Jeff. And you're a fucking hypocrite. What's it like to be spending time with three little kids, Jeff? When you told me you didn't want any kids? When I wasted all those years with you and..."

"But you didn't want kids either," he broke in. "Until that

whole thing with Diana."

"I'm going to be thirty-six on my next birthday," she yelled. "I might not ever be able to have kids now at all."

"We can't have this conversation if you're going to yell at me," he said. "Can you pull yourself together, please?"

"No, I can't fucking pull myself together. You lied to me. You cheated on me. You told me it was all about having kids, when it wasn't. I can't stand this any more." And she hung up.

She sat down and put her head on her desk. She was shaking again. She could hear her phone buzzing, and she figured it was Jeff calling back, but she didn't answer. It cut off and started buzzing again, but she ignored it, and then it stopped for good.

A knock sounded on her classroom door. She didn't want to see anyone. She probably looked horrible. But what if it was a student? What if it was someone who needed her help? She pulled her hair back from her face, walked hesitantly over to the door, and opened it.

And there was Jonah Shapiro. "Are you okay, Lucy?" he asked. "I thought I heard..."

"I'm fine," she snapped. "I'm fine. I don't need any help from anyone. I'm absolutely fine." What had he heard, anyway? This was just so awful. And so embarrassing.

"You don't seem fine," he said. He had that concerned expression on his face. It made him look even more attractive than usual. He needed to leave. "Can I..."

"There's nothing you can do," she said, practically pushing him out her classroom door. "Nothing anyone can do."

"You know how to reach me," he said. "If you change your mind and you need someone to talk to, just let me know."

And she shut the door on him. She didn't need to talk to anyone. She especially didn't need to talk to Jonah. She started pacing around the room again. When had it started between Jeff and Matea? How had she not noticed anything? How could she have been so gullible?

A pile of papers, waiting to be graded, lay on her desk, and she angrily pushed them all onto the floor. They fluttered in various directions, some ending up under the desk. She couldn't deal with them now. She'd have to pick them all up and take them home with her, but right now they could stay on the floor for all she cared.

She walked around for a while, trying to take deep breaths. She knew Kathleen had left already because her son had a doctor's appointment. There was no reason for her, Lucy, to stay here. She should go home. Curl up in bed. Call her therapist and make an emergency appointment. Normally she'd go for a run, but she felt sapped of all energy.

She started gathering the papers up and stuffing them into her bag. Jeff had kept their huge apartment near Logan Circle. It had been in his name all along. She had been fine with that. If she were starting over, she'd rather start over in her own new place. It was in Bethesda, a small studio, which was all she could afford right now, even with help from her parents.

She slunk past Jonah's classroom. She really didn't want to talk to him. What would she say? He was probably too young to understand, anyway. Her mind went back to that night. She'd been out at a happy hour with some of the other teachers to celebrate the thirtieth birthday of her friend Natalia Reyes, who taught in the Spanish immersion program. Kathleen had been there, and Jonah, and a half dozen others. And eventually everyone else besides Lucy and Jonah had left, and it was the day after she had signed her official divorce papers, and she had had two glasses of wine and a glass of Sangria, which was far more than usual, and she and Jonah kept sitting there and talking about the school, and teaching, and what had first gotten them into the profession, and how his girlfriend had recently dumped him for a lawyer who made tons of money, and then he said Lucy seemed kind of sad and she explained about signing the divorce papers, and he got this really sympathetic look on his face and he said something about how Jeff must have been an idiot to end things with her.

And before she knew it, she had invited him back to her apartment, which was only a few blocks away, and one thing led to another, and it was the first time she'd slept with anyone except Jeff since college, and she thought Jonah would think she was all wrinkled and old and ugly, but he kept marveling over how beautiful she was, and she was completely swept away.

And the next morning he'd looked at her with this awe-struck expression and said how incredible she was and he'd never felt anything like that before with anyone else, and she said she was feeling the same way. And he'd gone back to his apartment to change, and they'd seen each other at school and she'd felt sort of shy and embarrassed but pleased.

But by the time he texted her that evening to see if she wanted to go out for dinner, she was feeling overwhelmed, so she declined. It was all too much, she told him. She was still recovering from her divorce. She needed to take some time and think about what she wanted. And he couldn't have been more understanding. Nothing more had happened since then.

And now it was three months later, and by the time she got home, she was feeling even worse, and the papers fell out of her bag in the elevator and she had to collect them again, and she collapsed into her bed with her clothes on and pulled the covers around her, and all of a sudden it was dark outside and she looked at the clock to find it was already eight at night.

And loneliness was sweeping over her like a wave, and even

though she knew it was entirely the wrong thing to do, she texted Jonah and asked if he could come over. Now. And he texted right back and said yes.

Twenty-One

Max

Family meetings always stressed Max out. And this one especially. He was convinced his mom and Vilma were going to tell him and Will that their marriage was over. Ever since Lucy got divorced, Max had been thinking a lot about divorces. Lots of kids at school had divorced parents. And unlike Will, Max had vague memories of their family's depressing pre-Vilma existence. Vilma was, like, this calming presence. He had been so relieved when she finally got back a couple of nights ago.

It had been a few hours after he met Logan MacLeish for the first time. The night he'd learned of Logan MacLeish's existence, back on Sunday, he'd spent huge amounts of time Googling him. Guitarist, born 1948 in Cleveland, played with Bob Dylan, Joni Mitchell, Crosby, Stills, and Nash, Bruce Springsteen, and on and on. Now on tour with his new album, *All Torn Up*. Of course, Max had downloaded all the songs, which were amazing, and attempted to play them on his guitar.

It had been harder to find anything about Logan MacLeish's personal life, but he managed to find an article from about ten years ago in an obscure music publication. It indicated that after a couple of unhappy marriages with no kids, Logan MacLeish had settled down with his third wife, Lourdes Rivera, an economics professor, and their two kids, Ricardo, six, and Isla, five.

Isla! That must be her! He had rushed downstairs to search for the high school student directory, and had unearthed it under a pile of magazines near the computer in the family room. He checked under MacLeish, but didn't see anything, so he checked under Rivera.

Rivera-MacLeish, Ricardo (11th).

Rivera-MacLeish, Isla (10th).

Score!

And the next day in school, he hadn't been able to focus on much of anything. All he could think about was how he was about to meet a legendary guitarist who just happened to live in his neighborhood. And just happened to be connected to someone who he also couldn't stop thinking about. Because Isla had been on his mind a lot, he had to admit.

And after school, Isla had brought him over to her house, one of the big new houses that had popped up here and there in the neighborhood, and there he was. Logan MacLeish. He was probably the coolest-looking person Max had ever seen. He was kind of skinny, and had this whitish-blondish hair and green eyes, and was wearing jeans and a white t-shirt and an old leather jacket, and it flashed through Max's head that that's what he, Max, should start wearing. It was totally lit. And Logan MacLeish had smiled at him and said Isla had told him all about Max, and how would he like to try one of Logan MacLeish's guitars, and maybe they could play something together? And Max felt as if he'd just levitated up to heaven, or whatever was up there, because Max wasn't sure he believed in God, or in heaven, and were Jewish people supposed to believe in heaven anyway? He wasn't sure. He'd have to ask the rabbi at the next meeting of the Hebrew school confirmation class.

And Logan MacLeish had escorted Max into a room that was

filled with guitars and electronic equipment, and Isla had followed them in, and Logan MacLeish had handed Max an electric guitar, a really cool Fender Stratocaster, and he asked if it really was okay for him, Max, to play this guitar, and Logan MacLeish had smiled and said of course. And Isla had nodded encouragingly.

So Max had started to play this Dylan song he'd been working on, "Changing of the Guards," and at first he was messing everything up, but then he got more comfortable with it, and he settled into it, and he didn't even feel all that self-conscious with the singing part, which he usually did, and it was as if no one else was in the room, just him and the guitar and the music, and when he stopped, both Isla and Logan MacLeish were applauding.

"You remind me of myself when I was your age," Logan MacLeish said. "Try it again." And he took out another guitar and joined in, and it sounded really incredible, and when they finished playing, Isla had this huge smile on her face. She didn't really look much like her dad, Max thought. She had dark curly hair and dark brown eyes. She probably looked more like her mom. But she and her dad had the same smile. "Do you take lessons?" Logan MacLeish asked Max.

"I used to," Max said. His guitar teacher had graduated from Maryland the previous May and moved to New York for a job. And Max had decided it was fine if he took some time off from lessons and just played what he wanted to. His mom had agreed, given that Max wasn't exactly ignoring the guitar.

"Maybe we could set something up," Logan MacLeish said. "No charge. I'd really like to work on some things with you."

Max was speechless. "Okay," he said. "I mean, like, yes."

Logan MacLeish had smiled. "Great," he said. "Why don't we say next Monday, then. And every Monday afternoon I'm in town."

And Max had nodded, and he'd said goodbye to Isla and her

dad and almost floated home. This was unbelievable. It was so unbelievable that by the time he got home, he was convinced it hadn't really happened. So he didn't say anything to his mom, or to Will, or—when she returned—to Vilma.

And that same night he'd brought his guitar to the park and he and Isla had tied Phoebe's and Shirley's leashes to the poles of the swing set so the dogs couldn't run away—not that Phoebe would be inclined to run anywhere anyway--and he and Isla had sat down on the swings and he'd played a couple more songs for her while she swung back and forth.

And again he'd wondered if maybe she wanted him to do something more than just play the guitar, but he wasn't sure. So again, he didn't do anything more. And when his mom texted that he still had homework to do, he untied Phoebe's leash, preparing to head home, and Isla untied Shirley's leash. And then she leaned over and gave him a quick one-armed hug, with the arm that wasn't connected to Shirley's leash, and he was taken by surprise but managed to hug her back without tangling himself up in Phoebe's leash, and they parted from each other and he went home.

"...this family meeting," his mom was saying. He was jolted back to the present. He was sitting at the kitchen table with his mom, Vilma, and Will. Oh no. His mom was about to tell him something awful, he knew it. "So I know it's been a tough time for you guys, with Vilma's job in Finland, and also an exciting time, with Will's bar mitzvah coming up, and then of course there's Aunt Adele, and I thought it would be good for everyone to have an opportunity to say something. Whatever's on your mind."

Max could see that Will had his phone in his lap and was texting with someone.

"Will, hand me the phone," their mom said. "Now."

"I'm in the middle of..." Will began.

"Come on, Will," Vilma chimed in.

And Will handed it over, looking annoyed. "I'm fine with my bar mitzvah," he said. "I'm done with the speech, and I know my portion, like, inside out."

"Well, great," their mom said. "Max, I wanted to know what's going on with you, okay?"

Should he tell them? Maybe he'd tell them next Monday, after his first lesson. If it really happened.

"What's going on with these long walks with Phoebe?" his mom asked, her eyes boring into his.

"Yeah," Will jumped in. "I haven't gotten to walk her in a long time now. I want to walk her sometimes too."

"If you came home in the afternoons, you could walk her then," Max muttered. He knew his mom didn't want Will unsupervised in the afternoon because he'd just play video games and not get his homework and his trumpet practicing done, plus Will had all these sports things, but sometimes it just pissed him off.

"You're responsible for walking Phoebe in the afternoons," their mom said. "But Will can certainly walk her sometimes in the evenings. And why did you have a guitar with you the other night?"

"Were you playing songs for Phoebs in the park?" Will said, snickering. "Oh, Phoeeee-beeee, I love you soooooo," he warbled, completely off-key. And he started laughing.

Max could see his mom and Vilma exchanging glances, clearly trying not to laugh too.

"Just practicing outside," Max said. He could tell he was turning red. "You know, different acoustics." Jeez, what was this, some kind of interrogation?

"Okay," his mom said. "Fine. But give Will a chance to walk Phoebe sometimes, Max, all right?"

Max nodded. He'd figure something else out. He could go for a walk without Phoebe, after all, couldn't he?

"So guys," Vilma said. She and Max's mom exchanged glances again. Oh, no, Max thought again. Here it comes. "I know it's been tough with my job, but I wanted to let you know it's only for a couple more months. They want me to open the D.C. office sooner than expected. So I'll be moving back for good around the time school's out for the summer."

"Hooray!" Will cheered. "On both things, you coming back and school being over. I'm so tired of school. It's so annoying."

Max waited. Surely there was more?

Vilma looked at Max's mom again. "I hope you boys weren't thinking my absence meant something more than just a temporary job thing," she continued. "Because it doesn't. Your mom and I are fine."

Max felt a huge weight lift off him. He expelled a deep breath he wasn't aware he'd been holding in.

"You were worried, sweetheart, weren't you," his mom said, leaning over and giving Max a hug. "I'm sorry, I should have made that clear all along. I've been stressed out, yes, but not because Vilma and I are having problems. It's mostly because of work. Okay?"

Max hugged his mom back. He didn't hug her all that much lately. It seemed kind of infantile. But right now it felt great. "Yeah," he mumbled into her shoulder.

"Cool," Will said. "That's like the best news ever. Family hug? All four of us? We haven't done that for a long time."

"Oh, Will, sweetie," their mom said, looking as if she might cry.

And they all joined in, and Max sort of felt like he might cry too. But it was the kind of crying that you did when you were happy. Relieved. Overwhelmed. And he sunk into the family hug, and he thought maybe he'd tell them about Logan MacLeish after all. But not about Isla.

Twenty-Two

Marilyn

Marilyn was sitting with Adele on the family room sofa watching Rachel Maddow. Howie had gone off to his study with a book, presumably to do what he often did, read with the Nationals game on the radio in the background, and, to Marilyn's surprise, Adele hadn't followed him.

"I'm a big Rachel fan," Adele said, waving her scarf at the screen. "She really sticks it to the administration."

Marilyn nodded. "I agree."

Although short, that was the most pleasant interaction she and Adele had had so far, in more than two weeks, and it filled Marilyn with a sudden optimism. She'd had an enjoyable day. She and Cat had gone down to the National Gallery and spent the entire afternoon there, losing themselves in the art. And tomorrow would mark the start of a new adult-ed class she and Cat were taking, focusing on the literature of exile.

"Rachel's not going to let them get away with anything," Adele said. "You know, I had a stint on local television. Back in the seventies. I covered all kinds of stories." She leaned back on the sofa, pulling her high-heeled shoes off, placing her feet daintily on the coffee table, and tossing the shoes onto the floor, from whence Marilyn would probably need to pick them up to avoid a tripping hazard.

"Like what?" Marilyn asked. "And where was this?"

"Hawaii," Adele said. "Of course."

"So you were already in Hawaii in the seventies?" Marilyn still didn't have a handle on Adele's peregrinations across the country.

"For a while. Then I spent time in California, Nevada, Arizona, and then back to Hawaii. It was during my time in Arizona that I met Herman."

Her third husband, Marilyn knew. The one, it seemed, she'd been with the longest.

"So he went back to Hawaii with you?"

"He went to Hawaii for the first time. He'd never been there before."

"Right." Marilyn didn't feel like letting Adele get to her. Was this a good time to have it out with Adele? Ask her why she was so rude all the time? But it was a pity to turn what was a somewhat neutral conversation into a confrontation, so Marilyn opted against it.

"So I understand you and your friend are going to a class tomorrow?" Adele inquired. "Howie told me."

Adele had met Cat briefly, earlier in the day, when Cat had come by to pick Marilyn up. Howie had plans to take Adele apartment-hunting again.

"Yes," Marilyn said.

"Why aren't you teaching that kind of class, rather than taking it?" Adele asked, fixing Marilyn with a stare. "You must have something to offer, no?"

It was a good question, one Marilyn had asked herself over and over. Actually, she had taught a bunch of adult-ed classes, in the years following her retirement. But then she'd spent the year taking care of Cat, and after that she just hadn't gotten back into it.

"You're right," she said. "I used to, but not for a while now."

"Get back into it," Adele said, nodding. "It would do you good. Here you are, getting all caught up in this family stuff, and you're not using your brain enough."

"All caught up in this family stuff?" A pulse of annoyance shot through Marilyn. Maybe it would have done Adele good to be a little more caught up in family stuff over the past six and a half decades. But she held her tongue. She wanted to continue the pleasant atmosphere of her day.

"You don't have to micromanage everything," Adele continued.

Did she micromanage everything? Marilyn didn't think that's what she did. She just wanted to help everyone, that's all. Right?

"You know, I had a wonderful time with Lucy the other day," Adele said. And she focused her attention back on Rachel Maddow, adjusting the volume way up so Rachel's voice blasted through the room.

Marilyn's mind turned to the conversation she'd had with Howie the previous day, when he'd come back from dropping Will at home after his soccer game. Apparently, at least according to Will, Lucy had a younger admirer, another teacher at the middle school, and Howie wanted to know Marilyn's opinion about age. Did it matter? Well, Marilyn replied, it depended on the people involved, didn't it? There were some people for whom it didn't matter at all. And then there were some people for whom it did. Where Lucy fell on that spectrum, Marilyn wasn't entirely sure.

"His name's Mr. Shapiro," Howie had said. "Jewish, I assume."

Mr. Shapiro? Yes, probably. It was interesting, if Lucy actually had some connection to this Mr. Shapiro and it wasn't just a figment of Will's imagination, that Lucy seemed to gravitate toward Jewish men. Or vice versa.

Sarah had occasionally dated Jewish women, but nothing

had ever worked out, and then she met Vilma, and that was that. Assuming everything was okay between Sarah and Vilma. Marilyn had her doubts.

And Diana's vast array of dubious male companions over the years were almost never Jewish. Not that Philippe was dubious. He was lovely. But he was the exception. That Zeke, for example, the drug dealer. And then there had been the one who'd been arrested for some kind of weird bank fraud. What was his name? Corbin? Corwin? Something like that. Marilyn had never entirely understood what he had done to get arrested, but it hadn't been good.

She decided to find out what she could about Mr. Shapiro, so she clicked onto the middle school website and ran down the listing of teachers.

"Aha!" she announced to Howie. "Here he is. Jonah Shapiro, sixth-grade English, boys' soccer coach." She wished there were a picture.

"That's the one," Howie said from his chair across the room. "Good-looking kid."

Marilyn tried to uncover more about Mr. Shapiro on Google, but there were dozens of Jonah Shapiros, so she gave up. "I'll go to Will's game next week," she said. That way she could check out Mr. Shapiro and see what she thought. She hadn't gone to one of Will's soccer games in a long time.

"Okay," Howie said, and then Adele came into the room and started talking about her apartment in Hawaii and how it was so much nicer than anything she'd seen here, so the subject of Mr. Shapiro was dropped for the time being.

The thought struck Marilyn now that perhaps Lucy had confided something in Adele about Mr. Shapiro. If there were something to confide.

"So, Adele," she ventured, speaking loudly over Rachel

Maddow. "Speaking of Lucy, did she mention anything to you about someone named Mr. Shapiro?"

"Mr. Shapiro?" Adele repeated, a shifty look appearing on her face. "I'm not exactly sure. Why?"

"Oh, nothing," Marilyn said. Adele probably knew something, but Marilyn wasn't about to beg her. So she listened to Rachel Maddow, and when the show ended, she turned to Adele and asked if she wanted to watch anything else.

"I think I'll go to my room now," Adele said, maneuvering herself around the shoes and managing to drop her scarf on the floor in the process.

Marilyn sighed and shut off the TV.

"I was wondering," Adele said. "Can one still sign up for the class on the literature of exile? I was thinking I might like to join you."

Twenty-three

Will

The family meeting turned out to be really good, Will thought. Everyone seemed to be in a lot better mood now. And dinner had been delicious because Vilma had cooked it. She was a much better cook than Will's mom. Vilma had made this really amazing chicken with rice, and then she'd made this chocolate cake for dessert, and Will had probably eaten too much but that was okay.

He was done with his homework, and he'd practiced the trumpet, and he didn't feel like playing Fortnite, for once, and he was kind of hoping Max would let him walk Phoebe. Maybe the two of them could walk Phoebe. But then, from his vantage point in the living room, he noticed Max attaching Phoebs's leash to her collar, and he realized Max wasn't going to ask him to come along. In fact, Max was slipping out the front door with Phoebe, closing it quietly behind him. He could hear Phoebs barking a little as they left.

Well, this was just too annoying. He was tired of being left out. So he took his key and followed Max out the door. He didn't feel like telling his mom and Vilma. They'd just start getting all involved and asking questions. He had his phone, so if they needed to reach him, they could.

Max was halfway up the block with Phoebs, who was going a little faster than usual. Maybe all this walking had gotten her into better shape. Will loitered around a little, kicking a stone down the road so as not to catch up. He'd have to employ those spying skills he and Jayson had perfected back in elementary school.

He was kind of using them to figure out what was going on with Lucy and Mr. Shapiro. So far he'd figured out that Mr. Shapiro really liked Lucy, and even though it seemed as if Lucy didn't like Mr. Shapiro at all, he had a sense she actually did. There was no reason for her to be so rude to him otherwise, right?

It reminded him of something that happened to Will Z., when he kind of liked this girl Chelsea and she was always being all rude to him but it turned out she liked him too and they'd gone to the movies once but then things had ended because she decided she liked someone else instead. Will Z. had been salty for a while, but he'd gotten over it pretty fast.

He wondered what would happen if Lucy ended up marrying Mr. Shapiro. That would be so incredibly cool, to have Mr. Shapiro as his uncle. Even cooler than Philippe, who was a pretty fun uncle. Jeff hadn't been all that fun, so Will didn't miss him a whole lot. If Mr. Shapiro were his uncle, everyone at school would be totally jealous. But maybe he was getting ahead of himself. Lucy had just finished getting divorced, so she probably wasn't about to get married anytime soon.

He'd slowed down so much that he'd lost sight of Max and Phoebe. He assumed they were going to the park, so he turned the corner, and there they were, heading in that direction. He followed along behind them, and saw Max and Phoebe turn into the park and head up the pathway.

And before he could follow them any further, he was intercepted by Max's friend Seb's mom. She was walking Baxter, their poodle.

"Hey, Mrs. Wong, hey, Baxter," Will said, crouching down to

scratch Baxter behind his ears. He knew Baxter liked that.

"Hi, Will." Mrs. Wong said. "How's seventh grade going?"

"Fine," Will said, standing up again.

"And the bar mitzvah's right around the corner, isn't it," Mrs. Wong said. "We're really looking forward to it."

Will hadn't even realized the Wongs were invited, but it made sense. Max had been, like, best friends with Seb as far back as Will could remember, and the two families had become close over the years. Although now that he thought about it, Seb hadn't been around lately. He wondered why.

"Yeah, I think I'm all ready," Will said. His all-purpose answer, which just happened to be true. He did feel ready. He couldn't wait to get the whole thing over with.

"I saw Max up ahead," Mrs. Wong said. "I guess you're catching up to him?"

"That's right," Will said. Sort of right, anyway.

"Okay, see you next week, if not before!" Mrs. Wong said cheerily, and she and Baxter disappeared down the street.

Will walked toward the park, and took up a position behind a tree. He didn't want Max to see him, at least not right away. The park was pretty well-lit, so he wasn't sure how long he could keep Max from seeing him. Max and Phoebe were circling around the path, and then they passed by and headed around again, so he figured he'd follow along the path a little ways behind.

They were ambling along, and Phoebs was snuffling around in the grass, and then Will heard some really loud barking coming from down the street, and Phoebe looked up and started barking too, and then Will saw a huge dog approaching. He couldn't tell who was walking the dog at first, but as they came closer he could tell it was a girl. Not someone he recognized.

"Hi, Max! Hi Phoebe!" the girl called out, and she and the dog ran over and the girl gave his brother a hug, which he returned. The whole thing looked kind of awkward to Will, because Max and the girl had the dogs' leashes all wrapped around each other.

Who was she, anyway?

"So you didn't bring the guitar this time?" the girl asked. The two of them and the two dogs headed up the path, having untangled the leashes, Will following a safe distance behind.

"No, I couldn't really because my mom and my stepmom and my brother were kind of on my case about it, so, yeah."

On his case? What?

"My mom wants my brother to walk Phoebe more of the time, and he kind of wants to, so I snuck out of the house," Max continued.

"Oh, wow," the girl said. "Yeah, I know what you mean. Most of the time Ricardo doesn't want to walk Shirley, anyway, but every so often he's been saying he wants to and I have to talk him into not coming along."

"Yeah," Max said, and the two of them were silent for a while, just walking along with the dogs.

Who was this girl? It sounded like Max and the girl knew each other pretty well. Like they'd been walking their dogs together for a while. Was she his girlfriend or something? The thought of Max having a girlfriend was sort of a lot to think about, so Will took a deep breath. They weren't holding hands or anything, so maybe not.

"Like, thanks again for introducing me to your dad," Max said. "I mean, I just, like, totally appreciate the opportunity."

"Yeah, of course," the girl said. "He really liked you. He said you have a lot of talent."

Who was her dad? And what kind of opportunity was Max talking about? A lot of talent? This must have something to do with music. That's what Max was talented at. Something to do with the guitar. Maybe he was bringing the guitar to the park so this girl's dad could hear him play. But who was the girl's dad, anyway? And why would they all be meeting at the park at night to play the guitar and walk dogs? It didn't make a whole lot of sense.

"No, not really," Max said.

"Oh, come on," the girl said. "He doesn't say that about just anyone. He really thinks you have a gift."

"Really?" Max asked, sounding, like, sort of uncertain. Why didn't his brother have any self-confidence, Will wondered, feeling a little pissed off at Max. Everyone knew Max was really good at the guitar. Even this girl's dad, whoever he was, seemed to think so. Everyone, apparently, except Max.

Will wished he could hook his brother up to some kind of self-confidence machine that would pump it into him so he'd be able to realize he was good at music. Some kids were way too self-confident. The opposite of Max. Like this kid Andreas on Will's soccer team, who thought he was like the best player ever. And he was okay, but he wasn't really that good. He was always boasting, and telling everyone that he was the best player on the team, when he wasn't. And sometimes Mr. Shapiro would have to tell Andreas to shut up and stop boasting because it was so annoying to everyone else. Not that Mr. Shapiro said it quite like that. He said things in a really nice way, even if he was being kind of strict.

He remembered at the beginning of last year, when Mr. Shapiro was new, and everyone was hoping they'd get Lucy for sixth-grade English because she was such a good teacher and all the kids with older siblings had heard about her, and he knew he wouldn't get Lucy because she was his aunt, but he was kind of disappointed anyway when he saw Mr. Shapiro's name on his class listing. He had no idea who he was. And all these kids were complaining and saying they had wanted Ms. Pinsky and was she related to Will, and he had felt kind of proud and said yes. But by a couple of days into the school year, everyone in Mr. Shapiro's classes felt totally good about having him as their teacher, because he was so cool. And Ms. Collins was good, too. He'd lucked out on his English teachers both years. He wondered who he'd have for eighth-grade English next year.

He realized Max and the girl and the dogs had progressed far ahead of him, so he ran, as quietly as possible, up the path so he could hear what they were saying.

"...come to the play? It's in two weeks," the girl was saying.

"Yeah, definitely," Max said. "Like, of course."

And the girl started talking about rehearsals for some play she was in, and Will started tuning out. Maybe he should just go home. This was getting kind of boring.

And then his phone started ringing. Not buzzing, but ringing. Loudly. The ringtone he had put on for his mom. That "Seven Nation Army" song Stephen Strasburg used for his walkup music. Will loved that song, and his mom was always calling him so he got to listen to it a lot.

He saw Max and the girl turn around and stare at him. Max, from what Will could tell in the semi-darkness, looked absolutely furious. Oh, crap.

"Hey, Mom," Will said, answering the phone and waving at Max. Why was he so angry, anyway? "Yeah, I'm out in the park with Max and Phoebs." Well, that was sort of true, wasn't it?

His mom sounded as angry as Max looked. She started yelling about how he needed to ask her if he wanted to leave the house at night, and what was he thinking, and on and on, and Will held the phone away from his ear because it was just so annoying to listen to her. Why wasn't she calling Max and yelling at him? Max had snuck out of the house too.

"And please put Max on the phone," his mom said. "Now."

"She wants to talk to you," Will said, advancing upon Max and the girl with his phone held out.

Max took the phone like it was some kind of poison and put it up to his ear. Apparently their mom was yelling at Max, too, because Will could hear her voice coming out of the phone, and the girl probably could hear it, because she waved at them and dragged her giant dog off in the other direction.

And he could hear Max trying to get a word in and his mom continuing to yell, and Max was sending him these looks like he wanted to, like, totally destroy him, and Phoebe was snuffling along in an unhurried kind of way and Will realized she was the only one who was enjoying the walk at this point.

Twenty-Four

Diana

Diana and Philippe had just returned from a visit to Dr. Patel, who seemed very enthusiastic. "Nine days till your due date," she reminded them. "Everything looks great. So this could happen at any time. Get that suitcase packed."

Of course, neither of them had done anything at all about packing a suitcase. It was another thing Diana's mother had been going on about. Philippe's mother had been calling from Brussels inquiring about the suitcase. Sarah had called and said Diana should be sure to put one of her own comfortable pillows in the suitcase. The suitcase seemed to be a big deal.

"We must begin packing the valise, now," Philippe said once they got home. But then he became distracted with a mobile a friend from the restaurant had given him to put over the crib—it featured plush pieces of food with little smiling faces—and forgot about the suitcase.

The apartment had become an adjunct of Buy Buy Baby, Diana thought, looking around. Various friends had dropped off equipment they no longer needed. A stroller. A bouncy seat. A high chair. A bassinet. A swing. A car seat. Bags and bags of baby clothes. There was no room to move around, especially for someone shaped the way she was at this point.

She realized she should discuss the bris with Philippe. They had a lot of things they needed to discuss. Like what the baby's name would be. Both first and last. "Hey, Philippe," she called. "Can you come here a second?"

He appeared immediately, holding the mobile. "I am extremely confused by this," he said, waving the mobile in her direction and pushing back the floppy piece of hair that tended to fall over his eyes. "Can you figure it out?"

"Later," Diana said. She stretched out on the sofa and beckoned him toward her. "Massage my feet, amore mio?" It felt so good when he did that. She wasn't really up for anything more sensual than a foot massage these days.

He put the mobile on the table and started massaging her feet. "I am at your disposal," he said, giving her that smile that had charmed her so completely when they'd first met, five years earlier. "Your wish is my command."

"Well, so let's talk about the name," Diana said, sighing pleasurably.

"The name of the baby?" Philippe asked.

"Exactly."

"What would you like the name to be?"

Diana had a list of names that she'd discussed with him, but she figured he probably had forgotten. "Paloma or Nadia if it's a girl, and Etienne or Luca if it's a boy." She especially liked the idea of Nadia. It was an anagram for Diana, which was kind of cool. Even though she knew it wasn't a Jewish custom to name your baby after someone who was still alive. But she kept having these incredibly vivid dreams about the baby being a boy, so it probably wouldn't be Nadia anyway.

"I like all of those," Philippe said. "Did you already tell me those names?"

Diana nodded. "A while ago."

"Ah, yes," Philippe said. He stopped massaging for a minute. "What about the last name?"

"Hyphenated," Diana said. "We talked about that, remember?"

"Of course, chérie," Philippe said. "Yes, yes. Hyphenated is fine."

"Which order?"

"Order?"

"Pinsky-Moreau, or Moreau-Pinsky?"

"It does not matter," Philippe said, smiling at her again. "Whichever you prefer is good." He put his arm around her and gave her a kiss, which she returned. "And now I must go to the restaurant, but I will be calling. Frequently. I love you." And he left.

Diana spent a few hours trying to work, but then she reached for her phone. She wanted to get some other opinions about the last name.

"Mom?"

"Diana, sweetie. Is everything okay?"

"Fine, fine," Diana said. "No baby yet. I was just thinking about the last name. We're going to hyphenate, but I can't decide on the order."

"Try it each way with the names you're considering," her mom said. "See what sounds best. I don't suppose you're going to tell me the names, are you?"

"Nope," Diana said.

"Aunt Adele came with Cat and me to the literature in exile class," her mom said.

Diana was surprised. She had the sense her mom and Aunt Adele couldn't stand each other.

"How did that go?" she asked.

"Unexpectedly well," her mom said, sounding shocked. "So

have you packed the suitcase yet?"

"I will," Diana said. "Today. I promise." She would put the pillow in, and her softest most favorite maternity clothes to wear home, because she wasn't sure she'd fit into the Blattner regalia right away, and a cute unisex outfit Sarah had given her for the baby to wear home, and her toilet kit, and all her makeup, and a book, and all would be well.

"All right, sweetie, that's good. I'll talk to you later. I need to clean up here. I love you."

No sooner had her mom hung up than the phone rang.

"Diana?" Diana barely recognized Lucy's voice. She sounded awful. Like she'd been crying.

"Luce?"

"Yeah." Diana could hear some sniffing and nose-blowing. "I don't want to bother you when you're about to have the baby, but I can't help it. It was either you or Aunt Adele, and I just couldn't deal with Aunt Adele right now."

"Are you still at school?" Diana looked at the time. Three-thirty. Lucy was finished teaching for the day. But she probably was still at school.

"I'm in the car. In the parking lot. I was about to go home but I started crying and I just couldn't drive anywhere."

And Lucy proceeded to tell a convoluted story about how Jeff had been cheating on her with Matea from his office for a long time, and how the kid issue had been just a ruse, and how three months ago Lucy had slept with this incredibly cute younger guy who had been Will's English teacher the previous year, and how she really liked him but it was all wrong, and how she'd summoned him over to her apartment last night because she'd just found out about Jeff cheating on her, and how she'd kind of wanted the guy to sleep with her again but he'd said no, that he wanted to but he didn't think it was the right thing because she was too upset and he'd just be taking advantage of her.

"So he rejected me," Lucy said, sobbing even more. "It's all just so humiliating. On top of what happened with Jeff."

Diana was blown away by this entire saga. First of all, that Jeff had been cheating on Lucy. What a douchebag. Second, that Lucy had slept with someone else. She hadn't thought Lucy was at that point yet. Third, that Lucy was telling her all of this. It had been a while since Lucy had confided in her.

"Oh, my god, Luce, what an asshole."

"Which one?" Lucy asked faintly. Diana could hear Lucy blowing her nose again.

"Jeff, of course," Diana said. "The other one actually sounds like the opposite of an asshole."

"But he didn't want me," Lucy said, sniffing. "It's because I'm too old, I know it."

"Tell me exactly what happened," Diana said. And Lucy told her that the other one had come over immediately, and had held her and comforted her, and had said he'd stay on her couch if she wanted him to, but that he wasn't going to sleep with her. Not when she was this upset. It just wasn't right.

"Wow," Diana said. "He sounds really mature. How old did you say he was?"

"Twenty-six," Lucy said miserably.

"Jeez," Diana said. "I don't remember anyone I used to go out with being that mature. And I went out with a lot of guys." Most of whom were either stoned or drunk or doing shady things with money. "This has nothing to do with you being older. I dated a lot of younger guys, and it was never an issue. It's that he respects you." Which most of her own boyfriends hadn't.

She thought back to this one guy she'd gone out with in

college, Christopher, who had respected her. At least for a while. They'd been in a student production of *Romeo and Juliet* together, and had fallen for each other. And she'd stopped sleeping around and getting high all the time, and she'd pulled herself together with her classes and her mind felt clear and she wanted to do the best she could. Because she knew he believed in her, and having someone who believed in her made her more likely to believe in herself. But then the part of her she didn't especially like had returned, and she'd gotten really drunk one night and slept with his best friend, just because she could, and Christopher had found out, and had broken up with her. She thought of him occasionally. She heard he'd gone to med school and was a doctor somewhere in California now.

"...every day at school," Lucy was saying.

"Sorry, what?" Diana said.

"I have to see him every day at school, and I don't know what to do. I mean, he teaches in the classroom right next to mine."

"Did he stay over with you?"

"Yeah, on the couch."

"And then what?"

"He drove me to work in my car because he said I seemed too upset to drive. He came over to my apartment last night on his bike, all the way from Columbia Heights. He's in incredibly good shape."

This guy was sounding better and better. "What's his name again?"

"Jonah. Jonah Shapiro."

"A nice Jewish boy. Excellent."

"I guess. But so was Jeff."

"Look, Lucy, I'm probably not the best person to give you advice, but I'd say this guy sounds amazing. Just be friends with him for a while and see what happens."

That's what had happened with her and Philippe. She'd decided that this time, she wouldn't jump right into bed with the object of her affection. She'd take it slower. See how things went.

"Yeah," Lucy said, sounding doubtful. "Well, thanks, Diana. I feel okay enough to drive now." And she sniffed and hung up.

Wow. Diana felt absolutely furious toward Jeff. How could he do that to Lucy? And the guilt that was nagging at her for having introduced Lucy and Jeff all those years ago was only getting worse. She needed to talk to someone. Someone who would be objective. Not judge her. Not assume she was some kind of scatterbrained screwup. So she dialed Aunt Adele's number.

Twenty-Five

Howard

"Right, yes, my sister Adele," Howard was shouting into the phone. Bobby Slotnick seemed to have become a little deaf since they'd last talked a year or so ago.

"No way," Bobby Slotnick shouted back at him. "Just out of the blue? On your birthday? Happy birthday, by the way, Howie. Sorry I missed it. The big seven-five. Have you told Stuart yet?"

Actually, Howard had tried calling Stuart first. Stuart was a much nicer person than Bobby. But he hadn't reached him yet. "No," he replied.

"What does she look like?" Bobby asked. "You know, I always thought she was hot, as the kids would say." And he chuckled.

Howard had a vague recollection of something like that. Of Bobby making comments about Adele's looks that were kind of embarrassing. Of course, being more than a year older than Howard, Bobby often said things that Howard couldn't imagine saying. "Pretty much the same. Good, I mean. She looks like herself. Just older."

"So what's she been up to for all these years?"

Good question. Howard wasn't really sure what to say. He'd spent more than two weeks with Adele now, and he'd certainly had opportunities to find out more about her life. In fact, she'd invited him to ask questions. But then she never really seemed to answer them. At least not to his satisfaction.

"She's been living in Hawaii. Apparently she was using the name Adelaide Montgomery, which made it harder to find her."

"Hawaii," Bobby exclaimed. "Well, you can't get too much further from Jersey than that. And the circus?"

Bobby and Stuart had helped Howard with his circus research back then. Howard remembered the three of them going to the public library, scouring books and periodicals to find as much out about circuses as they could. They'd accompanied Howard to the circus whenever it came to town.

Howard sighed. "I'm not sure," he said. "She's kind of cagey when it comes to answering questions."

"I pictured her on the high wire," Bobby said, his loud voice taking on a nostalgic tone. "In one of those skimpy outfits."

Howard wasn't sure what to say to that either. "So how's life in Boca?" he ventured.

"Good, good," Bobby bellowed. "The grandkids were down for spring break, so that was a lot of fun, and the oldest just got into Columbia, so I'm going to relive our youth." Bobby had gone to Columbia with Howard.

Howard shuddered at the thought of reliving their youth. Much of his time at Columbia had revolved around Bobby in one way or another, such as when Bobby would comment on Howard's lack of success with girls or lack of ability to hold his liquor or lack of social skills in general. Of course, once Howard met Marilyn, everything changed. But that wasn't until senior year.

"Congratulations," he said. "That's wonderful." He pondered the idea of Max going to Columbia. Would that be a good place for him? His grades were excellent. Or would he go to a music school? Well, Max was only a sophomore in high school. He had time.

"Send everyone my best," he added. He should probably wind this conversation up now.

"Give Adele my love," Bobby shouted. "And Marilyn and the family. Talk soon." And he hung up.

Howard stood up from his chair. His back was killing him. He should go to physical therapy again. Maybe after the bar mitzvah and the baby's arrival.

He found Marilyn and Adele in the family room, watching Rachel Maddow. The volume was turned way up, so he didn't feel like shouting to tell them about his conversation with Bobby Slotnick. He'd done enough shouting during the conversation.

He looked at Rachel Maddow, who was talking about the Russia investigation, and then at his wife and his sister. The two of them were seated on the sofa, and, in contrast to the way they usually sat, poised at opposite ends as if to flee at a moment's notice, they were comfortably arranged closer to the middle. Well, that was good, wasn't it? Adele had gone to the literature class with Marilyn and Cat, and that seemed to have gone well.

"She asked some excellent questions, given that she hadn't read any of the books yet," Marilyn had told him after they were back home following the class. Adele had gone off to her room, and he and Marilyn were in the kitchen drinking coffee. "She's really very smart."

Hadn't he told Marilyn that, for years? Adele was incredibly smart. No question about it.

"And she was being nice to Cat," Marilyn continued. "You know how Cat's supposed to go out tomorrow night with my old colleague Padraig? The one whose wife left him?"

Howard had no idea who Padraig was, but he knew Marilyn was always trying to fix Cat up, and it never worked out. He wasn't sure why. Cat was bright and nice-looking and pleasant. She was well rid of that asshole husband. Skip. He was one of those people who only talked about himself.

"Howie?"

"Padraig, right," Howard said.

"Well, Adele was really supportive. She gave Cat some pointers on what to wear for the dinner. I was kind of surprised by how she acted."

Howard nodded. A memory popped into his head of his sister and a couple of her girlfriends, clustered around the vanity in her bedroom trying on makeup, getting ready for their Friday night dates. Adele was offering helpful suggestions to the other girls, whose names he couldn't remember. Howard was peering through the door at them, and when Adele had seen him, she shooed him away.

He wondered if Adele was still in touch with any of those friends from West Orange. Clearly she hadn't stayed in touch with Chuck, but what about anyone else? He hadn't had a chance to ask her about that yet.

"...walking the dog," Marilyn was saying.

He had clearly missed something. "Excuse me?" he said.

"Sarah," Marilyn said. "She's all upset with the boys." And Marilyn started in with a story about how Max and Will were walking the dog at night, and something about the guitar, and something else, and he couldn't really follow all of it. "So I told her if the worst the boys do is sneak out to walk the dog and play the guitar in the park, then she should count her blessings. Given what we went through with Diana as a teenager."

That was true. Although the whole business with the dogs and the guitar still confused him. Had Max taken to busking in the park? Maybe the other neighborhood dog-walkers would throw coins in the guitar case? Max could probably make some money that way, but he'd probably do better downtown on a street corner. Not that he thought Sarah would let him do something like that.

"You're not listening to a word I'm saying," Marilyn said, and she'd picked up her coffee cup and put it into the sink. But he had been. He'd been listening enough to know that things between Adele and Marilyn seemed to be improving.

And now he saw that Rachel Maddow was finishing up, and Marilyn switched off the TV.

"I just talked to Bobby Slotnick," he told them. "He says hello to both of you."

Adele smiled. "Oh, how delightful," she said. "Little Bobby Slotnick. What a menace he was. What's he up to these days?"

And he told her, and then she asked about Stuart Bernstein, whose name she couldn't remember but he figured out who she meant, and he told her about him.

"So are you in touch with anyone from back then?" he inquired. Had she cut off fully from anyone who reminded her of her past? And if so, why?

"The strangest thing happened one time in Arizona," Adele said. "I was with Herman, at this lovely Italian restaurant, and I saw someone who looked sort of familiar. And I asked Herman if she looked familiar to him, and he said no, and all of a sudden I realized it was Edith Applebaum. Remember her, Howie? The one with the bright pink car?"

Howard conjured up a hazy image of Adele, wearing a sweater and a plaid skirt and saddle shoes, running down the front steps of their house in West Orange, waving goodbye and getting into a bright pink car. "Yes," he said. "At least, I remember the car."

"Well, she recognized me too. Adele Pinsky? she said. And I said, Yes, but I go by Adelaide Montgomery now. And she looked at Herman and asked if he was Mr. Montgomery, and I said, no, he was Mr. Weinstein, and that thoroughly confused her."

"Well, I don't blame her," Marilyn said, a puzzled look on her face. "That's incredibly confusing. Did you change your name at all, or did you just keep Adelaide Montgomery each time you got married?"

"Changing one's name is a bother," Adele said. "Especially four separate times. Montgomery I was and Montgomery I remained. Except that I never officially changed it to Montgomery at all."

"You didn't?" Howard said, taken aback. "So you were officially Adele Pinsky all along?" Then how had it been so difficult to find her?

"One retains a certain fondness for one's youth," Adele said, twirling her scarf around.

Howard was speechless. If she was fond enough of her youth to keep her name, why wasn't she fond enough of it to contact him for all these years? He'd been a huge part of her youth, after all. At least, he assumed so. She'd certainly been a big part of his. Until she left.

"What are you talking about?" Marilyn jumped in, turning angrily toward Adele. "How could you be so fond of your youth if you abandoned him?" And she gestured at Howard.

And Adele gave Howard a smile. A sad sort of smile. "You were one of the best parts," she said. "Of my youth, I mean. But I felt I was somehow miscast. And that I'd do better elsewhere. And I feel I did."

And although Howard hoped she'd say more, she didn't. Instead, she retreated to her room.

Twenty-Six

Sarah

"She's my age, right? So it could be a health issue. Or it could be that she's lonely." Caroline Martino smiled at Sarah. "Family is a comfort when you get older and you feel alone."

Sarah was standing with Caroline in Caroline's packed-up living room, a place Sarah had visited many times before. It looked so empty. The entire house was bereft of furniture. The early afternoon sun poured into the room through the curtainless windows. Everything had gone into storage, except for a few things Caroline was having shipped to New Zealand. She was leaving the next day.

Sarah never really thought of Caroline as having a particular age, but yes, that was true. She was a contemporary of Aunt Adele's. Although they couldn't have been more different, Aunt Adele with her evasiveness and her high heels and her floaty scarves and Caroline with her trustworthiness and her understated elegance. Sarah had told Caroline all about Aunt Adele years ago, and had been filling her in on the visit as it went along.

"Why else would I pack up my entire life and move to the other end of the earth?" Caroline said. "Family. Of course, I've left Arts Alliance in the best possible hands."

Sarah tried to smile, but it was difficult. How could she keep everything going?

"You're like a daughter to me, Sarah, you know that. Even if I'm moving far away from you. And I have faith in you. You can do this. And if you need to talk to me, we can Skype or something. It's just the time difference that's a problem."

Sarah nodded.

"So tell me about those wonderful boys of yours. And about Vilma. I'm so sorry to miss the bar mitzvah."

And Sarah gave her an overview, leaving out the episode of the dog walking and the guitar, and then the conversation turned to Caroline's plans for her life in New Zealand, and then they discussed the office. And finally it was time for Sarah to get back to work, and she gave Caroline a huge embrace, which Caroline returned, and Sarah could tell they were both about to start crying. So she gave Caroline one last hug and rushed out the door.

Of course, her phone rang the minute she got into the car, and it was the caterer for the Kiddush lunch telling her that they were discontinuing the spanakopita and would she be okay with blintzes instead, and she dealt with that, and only then did she start the car, because she really didn't like to drive and talk, even though it was hands-free, and when she parked the car near the office and started walking over, her phone rang again, and it was the temple asking when she was planning to drop off the special yarmulkes with Will's name and bar mitzvah date printed inside, and then she got to her desk and her phone rang again and it was her mother.

"Do you have a minute?"

And of course, Sarah felt guilty saying no, I don't have a single second, and I'm about to implode, and my mentor is moving to the other end of the earth, so she said yes. She sat down and pulled her shoes off.

"So what do you know about Mr. Shapiro?" her mother asked.

Mr. Shapiro? Will's soccer coach? His sixth-grade English

teacher? "Why?" she asked. She reflected on the custom whereby she called these teachers, who in some cases were young enough to be her children, Mr. or Mrs. or Ms. Whoever, when everything else in life was so informal. It was interesting.

"Oh, Will said something to Dad about Mr. Shapiro and Lucy, so I've been trying to find out more about him."

"Mr. Shapiro and Lucy?" Sarah didn't know what her mother was getting at, exactly. "I think her classroom's next to his. What did Will say?"

"He thinks Mr. Shapiro really likes Lucy."

Sarah thought about this. Wasn't Mr. Shapiro a lot younger than Lucy? Not that age should matter. Jeff had been a decade older than Lucy, and that certainly hadn't worked out in the end, although Sarah wasn't entirely sure what had gone wrong. Vilma was two years older than Sarah, which seemed good, but then everyone was different, right?

"So what do you think?" her mom asked.

Sarah pondered some more. Mr. Shapiro did seem quite mature for his age. He was obviously a talented teacher, and also an inspiring soccer coach. Will loved him. Could this be a question of Will wanting something to happen between his beloved teacher and his even more beloved aunt, rather than something that actually was happening?

Her mind floated to the sixth-grade back-to-school night, more than a year and a half ago, the first time she'd met Mr. Shapiro. He'd stood up at the front of the classroom, so young and good-looking in his white button-down shirt and khaki pants, and all the mothers were fluttering and giggling and blushing. Not that he was flirting with them or anything. He was completely professional. It was just something about him. Even Sarah, who often missed these kinds of signals, had felt it.

"I don't know," she said. "He does have a certain charisma. But this could be wishful thinking on Will's part, don't you think?"

And she and her mother debated the issue for a few minutes, and then Monique was at the door, so Sarah got off the phone, and she told Monique about her farewell visit with Caroline, and Monique reassured Sarah that Arts Alliance would be fine even though Caroline would be in New Zealand, and of course Sarah had to act like that was absolutely right and all would be well. Because she couldn't let on to anyone else in the office that she was terrified.

"So we're thinking of a Nigerian name for the baby," Monique said, changing the subject. Her husband was originally from Nigeria. "We have a whole list of names. How did you pick the boys' names?"

And Sarah remembered how she'd agonized over the whole thing. How the choice had seemed overwhelming. It was one of the many times she'd wished for a partner, someone to help her work it through. She'd ended up naming Max after her mother's father, who had died many years earlier, and Will after her father's father, whose death had been more recent. And it all had worked out fine, hadn't it? So maybe this office situation would too.

So Sarah told Monique about how she'd picked Max's and Will's names, and then she'd given Monique Diana's contact information, which she'd meant to do for a while—she figured it was good for Diana to have another pregnant woman to talk to--and then Monique returned to her office, and Sarah was about to start reading some articles she'd bookmarked, when Vilma called.

"Max was asking if he could go to that guitar lesson on Monday and I said we'd all talk about it later," Vilma said. "And he still isn't home from school. I know we told him he had to come home right away. I texted him, but he hasn't replied, even though I know he read the message."

Great. Sarah immediately texted Max, but also got no reply. She thought back to Wednesday night, two nights ago, when Will had sneaked out of the house and Max hadn't seemed to keep an eye on him in the park. She wasn't one hundred percent sure exactly what had happened, and neither was Vilma, because each boy had told a completely different version of the events in question, but she'd been furious with both of them. Will had mentioned a girl who was also walking her dog in the park, and Sarah had asked Max who the girl was, and he'd said she was the daughter of the famous guitarist Logan MacLeish, who had offered to give Max lessons every Monday.

This all seemed rather unbelievable to Sarah and to Vilma. They'd both heard of Logan MacLeish. Sarah even had a couple of his CDs stuffed away in a box somewhere with a bunch of other music she hadn't listened to in years. But they'd had no idea he was living in their neighborhood, which generally wasn't known for housing aging rock guitarists. And while Sarah was aware that Max had musical talent—something that must have come from the donor—she hadn't realized her son had the kind of talent that Logan MacLeish would notice. It was sort of overwhelming. But of course she'd told both boys that they were grounded, which meant that Vilma had taken over the dog-walking last night and probably tonight too.

Her mother had downplayed the whole thing, saying it was nothing compared to how Diana had behaved at that age. Which of course was true. But did that mean she, Sarah, should let Will slip out of the house and wander around in the dark by himself without telling her? Of course not.

"My mom thinks it's not a big deal," Sarah mused out loud to Vilma. "She started talking about Diana as a teenager. How irresponsible she was. How we were always bailing her out of trouble."

"Oh," Vilma said. "Like the coming-out story?"

The coming-out story was something Sarah had stewed over for years, although she now thought it was kind of funny. After trying half-heartedly to embark on romantic relationships with boys in high school but knowing deep down that the whole thing wasn't right for her, she'd met Alina Shaw her first week at Harvard, and everything fell into place.

And when she was home for Thanksgiving break that freshman year, she'd mustered all her courage and, on a night when Diana was out, who knows where, and Lucy had already gone to bed, she'd asked her parents if they could come into the family room with her. She had no idea how her parents would react to her news, so she was nervous. Her parents sat down on the family room sofa, and she was pacing around in front of them.

"What is it, sweetheart?" her mom had asked, looking worried. "Is everything okay at school?"

"I have something to tell you guys," Sarah had said, her voice shaking. She stopped pacing and took a deep breath. "So I met this really great girl, I mean, woman, at school, and it turns out, well, I'm in a romantic..."

She had been about to say "relationship," but then the phone had rung.

"Hang on just a second, sweetie, okay?" her mom said, reaching for the phone. "I just have to make sure..." and she had picked it up. "Who?" she had said. A long pause. "Officer who? And she's where?" There was a longer pause. "We'll be right there." And she hung up, and turned back to Howard and Sarah, looking furious. "Diana and some other kids have been arrested for spray-painting graffiti all over the front of the school building," she said, "and this

Officer Wilson says we should come down to the station right now. Howie, come on. Sarah, you can stay here with Lucy."

And her parents had rushed out the door, leaving Sarah in the family room. Of course, she'd managed to continue the conversation the next day, and her parents had been great about the whole thing—they'd joined PFLAG the following week--but it still rankled. Diana got all the attention. And Sarah was left picking up the pieces. It just wasn't fair.

Twenty-Seven

Max

His mom and Vilma had been calling and texting him nonstop, but Max wasn't answering. He knew he was supposed to come home from school right away, because he and Will were being punished for something he, Max, had nothing to do with. How was it his fault that Will had snuck out of the house and followed him to the park? But he was supposed to be more responsible, his mom said. Just like she always did. You're older than Will. You're the responsible one. Why did it follow that he was the responsible one just because he happened to be two years and eight months older than Will? It was so insane.

So he was kind of mad at his mom, and he was furious at Will. Sneaking around behind him and Isla like some stupid spy? What did Will think he was doing, anyway? And it wasn't as if his mom and Vilma were saying Will had to miss all his sports practices. He didn't have to come home right away after school, the way Max had to, which was completely unfair.

But Max hadn't gone home right away after school this afternoon, because the jazz band auditions were this afternoon and he wasn't going to miss that for anything. Plus, he knew Vilma was home and would walk Phoebe. So he'd gone to the audition, having finally turned off his phone, and he thought maybe it went okay, even though he hadn't had that magical kind of feeling he'd had in Logan MacLeish's guitar-filled lair, and after the audition he'd come out of the band room and Isla was there waiting for him, sitting on the floor in the hallway reading a book.

"So how did it go?" she asked, looking up at him and putting her book back into her backpack. It was a book about acting, he noticed.

"I don't know," he said, and he really didn't know. Maybe it went okay. He hoped so. But maybe it hadn't. And maybe even if it had gone okay, there were lots of other kids who were better than he was.

"Come on, let's walk around for a while," she said, standing up. "I don't have any rehearsals until tonight."

And they ended up sitting in a Starbucks and she was telling him about the book she was reading, and about how she was getting a little nervous about the play she was in, and suddenly something occurred to Max.

"You know, my aunt's an actor," he said. "Maybe you could talk to her about acting."

And Isla's face lit up, and she seemed all excited, and she grabbed his hand and squeezed it. And he squeezed her hand back, and it was as if a current of electricity had shot through him. But then he thought, oh, well, maybe his hand was all sweaty, and in that case maybe this wasn't something that should continue, and so he reluctantly let her hand go.

"I can text her right now," he said, feeling a little dizzy. He pulled his phone out of his pocket and texted Diana, who replied immediately.

"Am home, why don't u and friend stop by now? Busy nesting," she wrote.

Nesting? What the heck did that mean? He showed the phone

to Isla, who also seemed confused, but even more excited. "Can we really?" she said. "That's just so cool."

So the two of them took the Metro to Tenleytown and then walked over to Diana's building. Max was still lugging his backpack and his guitar, but that was okay because Isla seemed so happy. And Diana buzzed them up, and there she was, looking huger than ever.

"Oh!" Isla said, apparently startled by Diana's appearance. "You're about to have a baby. Is that what you meant about nesting?"

"Exactly," Diana said. "I keep cleaning things, which I don't usually do, and straightening things, and putting things away. It's all very strange." And Diana hugged Max and he introduced her to Isla, and Diana brought everyone some glasses of water and these really good soft chocolate chip cookies, and they all sat down in the living room.

Max glanced around and wondered what exactly Diana had been straightening and cleaning, because everything looked, like, really awful. There was all this baby equipment all over the place. He'd banged his foot on some kind of baby chair when he'd first come in, and it still sort of hurt.

"Did you make these?" Isla asked, her eyes wide, gesturing at her half-eaten cookie. "They're so good."

"No, our friend André did," Diana said. "He's a pastry chef. I told him I was craving soft chocolate chip cookies, so he whipped them up."

And then Diana and Isla started talking about acting, and Diana told them all these incredibly funny stories about these plays she'd been in, and they were all laughing, and Philippe called to check in on Diana, and Max got on the phone too and was joking around with Philippe about what if the baby turns out to be a picky eater, which was something Max had been wondering about. The child of a chef, not wanting to eat anything except Cheerios? He remembered Will being like that when he was little.

And then Isla's phone started ringing, and she pulled it out and looked at it. "My mom," she said, and she got up and went into the kitchen area and answered it.

And Max realized he still hadn't turned his own phone back on since the jazz band audition, and he turned it on and there were like a dozen missed calls from his mom and another bunch from Vilma, and all these texts. Oh crap. And it was six-thirty already.

"What's wrong?" Diana asked.

"My mom and Vilma. They're calling and texting nonstop. Like, I'm sort of supposed to be at home, but I turned the phone off."

"Oh," Diana said. She hoisted herself to a standing position. "Well, you guys should probably go home now, then, okay? Tell your mom and Vilma that you're on your way."

Max hesitated.

"Come on," she said. "Or I will."

Would she really? Diana had been, like, totally badass when she was a teenager. He'd heard bits and pieces of various stories over the years. You'd think she'd understand.

"Look, I get it," Diana said. "But if you're supposed to be home, you should go home, okay?"

"Oh, all right," Max grumbled, and he gave her a hug and he and Isla headed back to their neighborhood. And he sneaked into the house and tiptoed up the stairs to his room with his backpack and the guitar. So far so good. He really didn't feel like interacting with anyone.

But then there was a knock on his door.

"It's me," Will said. "Can I come in?"

And Max didn't want to create some kind of scene and involve

186

his mom and Vilma, so he opened the door a crack and Will slipped inside.

"Look, I'm sorry about the other night, okay?" Will said, an apologetic look on his face. "I didn't mean to get you in trouble. I've been feeling kind of bad about it."

He had? Maybe Will was finally growing up a little.

"Like, I want to make it up to you. Mom and Vilma are totally mad at you right now. So maybe I can, like, distract them with other topics when they start yelling at you?"

Max sighed. "Like what other topics?"

"Like something about my soccer practice, or my baseball game, or my bar mitzvah."

Max nodded. It was worth a try. So the two of them went downstairs and Vilma was putting the dinner on the table, some kind of pasta that smelled really good, and Max set the table and poured everyone some water.

And they all sat down.

"So where were you this afternoon?" his mom said, her eyes shooting daggers at him. "Vilma and I tried to reach you over and over."

"Hey, Mom, you know that section in my Torah portion about God telling the Israelites..." Will interrupted.

His mom switched her furious gaze to Will. "Will, I'm talking to your brother now, all right? We can discuss your portion later."

Will shrugged and started helping himself to some pasta. "Yum," he said. "Delicious."

Max didn't have much of an appetite, but he took some too. "Jazz band audition," he mumbled, and ate a little of the pasta.

His mom and Vilma exchanged glances. "And why didn't you tell us about this?" his mom said.

"I figured you wouldn't let me go, and I really wanted to go.

And then I was over at Diana's."

"At Diana's?" his mom repeated, sounding angrier than ever. "Wouldn't you know it."

What? What did she mean by that?

"I got a hundred on my science quiz," Will piped up. "I was the only one in the class who did that well on it. Even Benjamin only got a ninety-five, and he's a total genius. Most people thought it was kind of a hard quiz, but I thought it was easy."

He was really trying, Max thought, sending Will what he hoped was an appreciative look.

"That's great, Will," Vilma said.

"Wonderful, sweetheart, we'll talk about it later," his mom said.

And she was about to focus on Max again, when, fortunately, the phone rang, and his mom got into some conversation about something relating to the bar mitzvah, and Max put his plate and glass into the sink and escaped upstairs to his room. Maybe this would all just blow over. He put his earphones on and lay back on his bed and cranked up one of Logan MacLeish's guitar solos, and his mom and Vilma and Will and even Isla receded from his mind. It was all about the music, wasn't it?

Twenty-Eight

Lucy

Lucy was at that point in her run when all her aches and pains seemed to vanish and she was almost floating down the Capital Crescent Trail and she was passing some other runners and she turned Amy Winehouse's "Back to Black" up even louder. Tears were flowing down her face but she didn't want to break her rhythm to get a tissue out of her shorts pocket and she figured she'd just ignore it.

How could he have cheated on her with Matea? Was she, Lucy, just too boring? Not good in bed? Not attractive enough? All of the above? Her legs were moving even faster but she couldn't really feel them. And all her thoughts faded away and she was lost in the sensation of rapidity and the trail and the music.

And by the time she got back to her apartment and stripped out of her sweaty running gear and took a shower, she was feeling a little better. She got dressed again, pulling on a pair of jeans—she noticed that they were kind of loose, which normally would make her happy but didn't right now--and her most comfortable t-shirt, and she flopped down on the sofa and took out her phone. Jeff had emailed and texted several times since their conversation. The messages had been apologetic, saying he was sorry she had to find out like this, and it wasn't her, it was him, and they were right to have gone their separate ways, and a lot of other bullshit that she just didn't feel like replying to.

She remembered a time, a couple of years ago, when she'd been chaperoning the sixth-grade dance with Natalia, and Jeff had texted her that he'd be late at work, and when he finally got home, after midnight, she'd noticed he smelled different. Nothing obvious, just really subtle. And she'd mentioned something to him, and he'd said, oh, he tried out a new soap at the gym, and she, of course, had believed him.

And then there was the time when he'd been on a work trip to Florida with Matea, and Lucy had called him late at night, just because she missed him and wanted to talk, and Matea had picked up his phone and said something about a late meeting and Jeff was in the bathroom and would call her back in a few minutes.

Lucy could come up with all kinds of suspicious incidents at this point. She'd spent the last three days doing just that. She really didn't want to talk to anyone about Jeff's betrayal, so she'd been regurgitating the information around and around in her head, like a cow chewing its cud. Her therapist was away for a week, so she was no help.

She probably should tell Stacy and Kathleen, but she didn't feel like it, and she certainly didn't want to tell her parents or Sarah. They wouldn't understand at all. Everything was so perfect for her parents, and for Sarah too. Nothing like this would ever happen to them. That's why she had confided in Diana. Diana was the only one who would understand. Except maybe Aunt Adele, but there was only so much of Aunt Adele that Lucy could take.

And on top of all her awful thoughts about Jeff, there were her awful thoughts about Wednesday night. When Jonah Shapiro had basically rejected her. Diana had said all this stuff about how he'd acted that way because he respected her, but Lucy found that theory ridiculous. He had rejected her because she was older and because she was so messed up. And after he'd driven her to school Thursday morning, she'd avoided him.

Of course, he'd texted her repeatedly to make sure she was okay, and she'd replied that she was, even though she wasn't, and he'd offered to stay on her sofa again Thursday night, but that was the last thing she needed, a reminder of the whole fiasco of Wednesday, so she declined. And last night, Friday, he'd texted to see if she wanted to get dinner, but she'd said no. She didn't really feel like eating anything. She just wanted to run and run until she got tired enough to fall asleep.

She'd always been into running, ever since high school when she was on the cross-country team, but over the past year it had become the only thing she enjoyed. Except hanging out with her nephews. She still liked that. And teaching her students. But the rest of her life felt as hollow as a drum, not that she was sure what a drum actually felt like.

Her mind drifted back to the summer she'd graduated from Penn. She'd moved back from Philly into a rundown group house in Adams-Morgan with Stacy and a couple of other girls and one guy from their graduating class. She was planning to start grad school at Maryland in the fall, a master's in education, and she was working as a camp counselor and earning some extra money scooping ice cream at a place on Columbia Road. So she didn't have a whole lot of time for family drama, although it was lurking in the background. Her dad was busy at the firm most of the time, and her mom—who wanted to discuss educational philosophies with Lucy—was helping Sarah with Max and Will, and Sarah was gearing up to return to her office after her second maternity leave.

Meanwhile, Diana had broken up with her on-again-off-again boyfriend Zeke, who had just been convicted of drug dealing. "It's over for good this time, Luce," Diana had said, as she sprawled out on the uncomfortable sofa in Lucy's living room. The window unit air conditioner was broken, and Diana, clad in a low-cut tank top and short shorts, was fanning herself with an antique fan one of her admirers had given her. Lucy was wearing a similar outfit, but somehow it didn't create the same effect on her as it did on Diana. Lucy often felt she was merely a pallid reflection of her vibrant sister. Diana was the shortest of the three Pinsky sisters, but somehow she seemed to take up the most space. Larger than life. "I can't put up with him any more."

"Well, that's good," Lucy said. She couldn't imagine having a boyfriend who was about to go to jail. Her own boyfriend--well, ex-boyfriend at this point--was about to go to law school. In California, which meant that he had just ended things with her. She'd been kind of upset, but she also agreed that a long-distance relationship at this point didn't make sense.

"So, you know, Zeke's going to start serving his time next week, and we're being evicted from the apartment. So I need somewhere to live, ASAP."

What? Evicted?

"I thought he was paying the rent, but apparently he wasn't," Diana said. "Not that I could have contributed all that much, since I'm between jobs, but I could have done something about it. And I don't want to go to Mom and Dad or Sarah, because they'd just go ballistic about what a failure I am. So I need to crash for a while on your sofa, okay?"

Lucy sighed. It amazed her that Diana was nine years older than she, Lucy, was. Diana was thirty-one years old. And she had absolutely no idea how to manage her life. "Yeah, okay," Lucy said. "Just for a week or so, all right?" She was sure she could work it out with her housemates. Stacy and the other girls thought Diana was fascinating, and Brian had a total crush on her.

And that weekend, Diana had thrown a party at Lucy's place. It was one of those hot, muggy summer nights, and Diana had invited all kinds of actors and other creative types, and all Lucy's housemates were enthralled, and Lucy found herself wandering around listening to scraps of conversations about Brecht and Pinter and the party spilled out into the courtyard in back of the house, and the music, some old Talking Heads album, was blaring in the background, and Diana had approached Lucy, dragging a guy in her wake. He probably was around Diana's age, but he was kind of cute, with curly light brown hair and glasses.

"This is Jeff," Diana said. "He just moved here from Chicago to work for a political consulting firm. Jeff, this is my little sister Lucy."

And Jeff had smiled at Lucy—his teeth, she noticed, were extraordinarily white, which she later learned was due to his brushing five times a day with whitening toothpaste—and said it was great to meet her, and was she an actor too?

And Lucy had said no, that she was going to be a teacher, and he said that was refreshing, and he told her he'd gone to college with Diana but hadn't seen her in a long time and he'd tried acting for a while and it hadn't worked out.

And they'd started talking about acting, and about politics, and about teaching, and it turned out they both were reading the new Harry Potter book which had just come out so they talked about that for a while, and before Lucy knew it the party was winding down and she and Jeff were still sitting outside on the patio deep in conversation. So he asked for her number and her email address, and she gave them to him, and he emailed her the next day and asked her out.

Diana, still camping out on the living room sofa, was thrilled.

"He's a really nice guy," she told Lucy. "He's a terrible actor, but I think this politics thing is working out well for him."

"What about the age difference?" Lucy asked. She'd never gone out with anyone that much older before. He was a whole decade older, which in theory sounded kind of ancient. But he hadn't seemed that old when she'd been talking with him.

"Oh, he's kind of immature for his age," Diana said. "It's not a problem."

And that was the beginning. And four months later, he'd proposed, and eight months after that, they'd gotten married, on the anniversary of the day they'd met, and even though Stacy and all Lucy's other friends were nowhere near even thinking about getting married, Lucy felt like it was the right thing for her to do. She loved Jeff so much, and she wanted to be with him, and vice versa, and this meant that she was taking a step away from her family. Toward creating something with Jeff that was their own.

Not that she changed her name. She decided she would keep Pinsky. Parker—changed from Platkow by Jeff's grandfather back in the 1940s--sounded all wrong, as if it had nothing to do with her. And Jeff just seemed so happy they were getting married that he didn't appear to mind one way or the other about whether they had the same last name.

Thinking about the whole thing now, Lucy found it incredibly ironic that Diana had said Jeff was a terrible actor. Actually, he was an amazing actor. He'd acted like he was still in love with her for all that time, when he really wasn't. He'd acted like the child issue really was the problem, when it wasn't. He'd acted like their divorce was as hard for him as it was for her. Which obviously it wasn't, because he was sleeping with Matea the whole time.

Her phone started ringing, and she looked down and saw that it was Jonah, and she didn't want to talk to him, so she didn't answer. And then a text from him popped up. "R u ok?"

"I'm fine," she replied.

She heard the sound of another incoming text, but she didn't bother to read it. There was nothing anyone could do to make her feel better. She curled up on the sofa, images of Jeff and Matea running through her head, and the tears started up again.

And then she heard a knock on her door.

"Lucy, it's me, Jonah," she heard.

She didn't really want to deal with anyone right now, but she found herself staggering over to the door and opening it.

"Someone let me into the building. I'm sorry to startle you. I tried calling and texting to let you know I was here, but you didn't see it, I guess." He was holding a bag from Harris Teeter, which he put down on the kitchen counter. "I got some salad and other stuff," he said. "I thought you might be hungry."

She shook her head. She wasn't hungry. Snot was dripping down her face and she just couldn't stop crying. The idea flitted through her head that she must look even more unappealing than ever. And she really couldn't face Jonah, and she went over to her bed and pulled the covers over herself and kept sobbing. And then she felt the mattress shifting, and she felt his arms going around her and hugging her, and he was whispering things in her ear about how beautiful she was and how amazing she was and how she'd get through this and everything would be okay. And she realized that she was so glad he was there, even if she didn't believe a word of what he was saying.

Twenty-Nine

Diana

"So here we are," Aunt Adele said, sitting down in one of Diana's chairs. "This was from my parents' living room. And that one over there was from the guest room. It's like coming home again!" She seemed very excited, Diana thought. She probably should have invited Aunt Adele over to the apartment sooner.

"I like vintage furniture," Diana said, bringing two cups of tea in from the kitchen and placing one in front of Aunt Adele. "It's fun to mix and match it, you know?"

Aunt Adele nodded. "I have all kinds of mid-century things in my apartment in Honolulu," she said. "I just don't know how much of it I'll bring with me, though."

Diana hadn't been aware that Aunt Adele was definitely planning to move to D.C. She certainly hadn't found a place that measured up to her standards, from what Diana's parents had said. "So are you actually..."

"Oh, Diana, you know how it is," Aunt Adele said, sipping her tea. "You make plans, and then things don't work out exactly how you think they will, and then you make more plans, and you take it one day at a time."

Diana thought about what Aunt Adele was saying. "Like when I wasn't getting such great parts all the time any more? And I made plans to be a ghostwriter as kind of a backup?"

"Exactly," Aunt Adele said. "Smart girl. I'm told you and I are very much alike."

Diana nodded. She'd known about the similarities between her and Aunt Adele for her entire life. She remembered conversations between her parents that she and Sarah weren't supposed to hear but she'd eavesdropped.

"So much like my sister," her dad would say frequently, a mournful tone in his voice. And then the word "circus" would be bandied about between her parents.

Sarah, of course, was nothing like Aunt Adele. Following Sarah through school, and through life in general, had been challenging.

"So you're Sarah's sister," Diana's teachers would say eagerly at the beginning of the school year, but after a few weeks they'd start frowning and muttering about how she was nothing like Sarah and how could two sisters be so different?

She remembered her mom going to a parent-teacher conference when Diana was in third grade, and Diana was supposed to wait out in the hallway, but she was restless so she cracked the classroom door open a little, and Mrs. Linton was saying something to Diana's mom about how Diana really was nothing like Sarah at all, was she, and how Diana was so high-spirited, and that was wonderful, but she needed to keep her focus on what was going on in the classroom, and how she'd had to send Diana to the principal's office twice already this week. And Diana's mom was murmuring something in response, and then Diana had pushed the door further open by mistake, and both of them looked startled to see her.

And in the car on the way home, her mom had seemed upset. "Oh, sweetheart, did you hear some of that?" she'd asked. "It's fine that you and Sarah are different from each other, okay? You each have such special qualities. You're so imaginative, and so much fun to be around, and you're such a great actress."

Diana, from her place in the back seat of the car, considered this. She loved her acting classes, that was true. She'd been taking them since she was in kindergarten. Last week she'd played Princess Leia in this *Star Wars* skit and the acting teachers had said what a fantastic job she'd done. But she wasn't sure what to do about the rest of it. She wanted to be better behaved, like Sarah, and get the best grades, like Sarah, and not get sent to the principal's office. But no matter how hard she tried, she couldn't be like Sarah.

And as she got older, it became even more difficult. Sarah always seemed so perfect, and she always was placed in the highest-level classes, and Diana pretty much never was, except sometimes for English, but then she wouldn't do her homework and she'd be dropped down to the lower track again.

There was one time, sophomore year of high school, when Diana had gotten really into this paper on Romeo and Juliet, and she'd worked incredibly hard on it, and she handed it in with a feeling of excitement, like, maybe now her teachers would like her, and take her seriously. The way they did with Sarah.

And Mrs. Hannigan had asked Diana to stay after class, and Diana thought maybe Mrs. Hannigan would tell her how great her paper was. But instead, Mrs. Hannigan had frowned at her. That teacher-frown Diana was so used to by now. "Did you really write this paper, Diana? Or did you have help with it?"

And Diana had felt like crying, but she pulled herself together and called on all the training she'd gotten in her acting classes— really the only place where she felt at home—and drew herself up to her full five-foot-four and said of course she had written it herself.

And Mrs. Hannigan had given her a skeptical look but said it was an excellent paper and maybe Diana could apply herself to her work going forward and turn things around.

But then Diana had discovered sex. It was intoxicating. She could wear really tight low-cut shirts and jeans that were practically painted onto her body, and suddenly she was getting all kinds of attention that her perfect older sister wasn't getting at all. Diana slept with a guy on the football team, and a guy who was constantly stoned, and a guy who wrote poems to her, and a guy who, like her, was into acting. And Sarah told her she was getting a reputation, and Diana told Sarah she was just jealous because she was still a virgin. And Diana's grades plummeted further.

Diana told a version of this whole saga to Aunt Adele, who sat and listened.

"And then I almost flunked physics the last quarter of senior year, and Emerson would have rescinded my acceptance if I'd failed, and the physics teacher was this total lech, and he'd already tried some stuff with me, like standing way too close to me, or making inappropriate comments, or sort of hugging me in the hallway, you know."

Aunt Adele nodded, frowning.

"So I put on all this makeup and my tightest shirt and this really short skirt, and I went in there and did what I had to do. Just like another role. Like I was acting. Because I needed to go to Emerson. It was the best place for me."

Aunt Adele's eyes were wide. "You slept with your physics teacher?"

"Well, no, actually. There was no sex involved, of any kind. It didn't go that far. But I was desperate. And I had absolutely no self-respect by that point."

Aunt Adele nodded again. "I know exactly what you mean," she said. "I was accepted to Barnard, you know, but then I left home, and it was years later when I decided that it was time to go to college. That I was far too intelligent not to pursue a degree. I was living in California, so Barnard wasn't an option, and I was divorced from Lionel, my first husband, and he was paying alimony, but money was tight. So I was involved in a similar situation, and the dean let me in. It's horrible, you know. All this #MeToo business should have happened years ago." She paused. "Of course, I didn't engage in sexual relations with the dean. I just convinced him that I needed to attend his school without paying any tuition."

"Yeah," Diana said. She remembered how surprised her parents and Sarah had been when she, Diana, got into Emerson. Her grades were, for the most part, terrible. But her verbal SAT scores were off-the-charts good and her math scores were perfectly fine, and she'd written this essay about how acting made her feel as if maybe she could change the world, and she hadn't shown the essay to any of them. She'd just handed it in along with the other application materials. And once she got in, her parents and Sarah figured it would be okay for Diana to go up to Boston, given that Sarah was at Harvard and could keep an eye on her.

And then Sarah ended up attending Harvard Law School—their father was so pleased that Sarah was interested in the law--and thus was nearby the entire four years of Diana's college career. Helping Diana out of all kinds of self-inflicted disasters.

"So Sarah followed in my dad's footsteps, even though she didn't really end up practicing law, and Lucy followed in our mom's footsteps, teaching English, and I'm like this fish out of water. And speaking of Lucy, you know I'm the one who introduced her to Jeff. So I'm feeling all guilty about that."

Aunt Adele tilted her head to the side. "But you meant well," she said. "It's not your fault that a dozen years later Jeff turned out to be an asshole, right?"

And Diana was about to say that she thought introducing

Lucy and Jeff was yet another thing on the long list of bad situations her family blamed her for, but then her phone rang, and it was Philippe, checking up on her, and she started to feel better.

"He seems very devoted," Aunt Adele said, once Diana was off the phone. "And such a charming accent. I never had a Belgian lover, but I did have one who was French. Pierre. So attentive. You're very fortunate."

Diana nodded. Philippe was indeed devoted, charming, and attentive.

"Tell me about this ghostwriting," Aunt Adele said, and Diana told her about the actors' books she'd ghostwritten, and her current Blattner project.

"I have an idea for a memoir. Would you be able to help me?"

Really? She'd get to hear all Aunt Adele's secrets? The ones no one else in the family had uncovered? "Yeah, I mean, definitely," Diana said. "Once I get this Blattner thing out of the way." She hadn't made any progress the past week, but she felt as if she'd get a lot done once the baby was born. No matter what her mom said.

"Wonderful," Aunt Adele said. "So let me ask you a question, Diana. If you feel like a fish out of water, why did you come back here after college? Why did you stay here all this time?"

It was something Diana had been pondering, ever since Nick had pointed out the same thing a few weeks earlier. "A friend of mine asked me about that too," she said. "I mean, everyone thinks I'm just like you, but maybe deep down I'm not."

Aunt Adele smiled. "Or maybe deep down you're just like you. And maybe a little bit like me, too. At least, I hope so, because I really like you. I'd like you even if you weren't my niece."

And Diana smiled back. "I like you, too. Even if you weren't my aunt."

And the baby decided at that moment to whack Diana in the

ribs, and Diana yelped in pain, and Aunt Adele looked alarmed.

"It's just the baby kicking me," Diana said. "No big deal."

"My great-niece or nephew," Aunt Adele said. "Definitely a big deal."

And they both sipped their tea and Diana reflected that if Aunt Adele had been there all along, maybe her own life would have been incredibly different. Maybe having someone to talk to who understood would have saved her from some of her mistakes when she was younger. But what if she'd pulled herself together sooner, and what if she'd ended up with someone else and had other kids, and then she wouldn't have married Philippe, and she wouldn't have this particular very amazing baby, who she couldn't wait to meet, and that would be terrible. So maybe things had worked out just the way they were supposed to.

Thirty

Howard

"Well, she's not going to stay here indefinitely." Marilyn crossed her arms over her chest and gave Howard a look that he knew meant business. They were in the kitchen, snacking on some cheese and crackers. Adele was over at Diana's.

"No, but it doesn't seem as if she wants to go back to Hawaii. And she hates all the places I've taken her to see." Howard was at his wit's end at this point. He really couldn't have Adele stay with them too much longer, could he? Marilyn would go insane.

"Cat suggested this place in Tenleytown. A nice new building. She'd be right near Diana and Philippe and the baby, and maybe she'd like that. You could take her over there tomorrow." Marilyn popped a cracker into her mouth.

Howard nodded. "Okay." He wondered if it was true that Adele couldn't drive, as she claimed, or if it was some kind of ruse to get him or Marilyn or the girls to take her everywhere. Hadn't she been learning to drive when she ran away? And living in places like Arizona and California, you'd think you'd need a car, right? It wasn't as if she'd been in Manhattan all these years. He really wasn't sure about Hawaii. Did everyone drive in Honolulu? His only clues came from *Hawaii Five-O*, where McGarrett seemed to drive everywhere. But was that really accurate? Of course, Adele wasn't a police officer. He sliced another piece of Brie and placed it on a sesame cracker.

"...teaching a class," Marilyn was saying. "Maybe she's right."

"Who's right?" he asked. The next thing she'd say is that he wasn't listening again. Which was probably true.

"Adele, of course, and if you ever listened you'd know that."

Marilyn was saying Adele was right about something? "What is she right about?"

Marilyn sighed. "Teaching, Howie, teaching. She said I shouldn't just be taking these literature classes, I should be teaching them. And I'm thinking she's right. I'm going to call the community center on Monday and see if they need me to teach anything. Maybe you should teach something too. I feel as if we've gotten into a rut lately."

She did? Since when? Howard didn't really feel as if he were in a rut. He was enjoying his retirement. And he did some pro-bono work, so that kept his mind active. Plus he was taking a fascinating course with the rabbi about the Talmud. And he needed some free time to help with the boys and drive Adele around.

"Speaking of teaching, she told me she taught Pilates until recently. She's really very flexible. She wants to come to yoga with me and Cat."

The image of Adele doing cartwheels across the lawn in West Orange flashed into Howard's head again. You needed to be flexible to be a circus performer, didn't you?

"I wonder how things are going over at Diana's," Marilyn said.

"Fine," Howard said. "I'm sure they're going fine." He knew Adele was excited to spend more time with all her nieces, but especially with Diana, given that she'd heard how much like her Diana was. Maybe if Adele stayed in D.C., that would be good for both Adele and Diana. Sometimes Howard felt Diana needed someone in the family who was more like her. More wild and crazy. He felt he and Marilyn had done the best they could with their beloved middle daughter, but over the years he'd often wondered what impact it might have had on Diana if her aunt had been there too.

"...Logan MacLeish," Marilyn was saying. "I just can't believe it."

"Who?" Howard asked.

"I told you. The famous guitarist. He wants to give Max lessons. Apparently Max knows his daughter."

Logan MacLeish. Howard rolled the name around in his brain without it gaining any traction.

"Remember? We heard him perform in the Village when he was just starting out? He probably was only around nineteen or twenty? It was when you were doing your clerkship and I was in grad school."

Howard had no memory of this whatsoever. He did remember Marilyn dragging him to various clubs in the Village when they were dating, and then once they were married. She loved all those guitarists and singer-songwriters. He preferred classical music. It was far more soothing.

"He played with Bob Dylan and Joni Mitchell and Bruce Springsteen," Marilyn said. "All the greats. And he has a new album out. Max downloaded it for me. It's really quite good."

And she kept talking about Logan MacLeish while Howard recalled those days going to clubs in the Village. Sometimes they'd meet up with Bobby Slotnick and his wife, Andrea, or with Stuart Bernstein and whoever he was dating at the time. Or with some of Marilyn's friends. And then he and Marilyn would go back to their tiny apartment and make love in the creaky bed. He wondered how time had passed so rapidly. How could it be that he was now a half-century older than that younger version of himself?

"...and she ran into Jeff," Marilyn was saying. She got up to put the cheese and crackers away, as neither of them had eaten anything for a while. "I completely forgot to tell you."

"Jeff?"

"Lucy's ex-husband," Marilyn said, an expression of supreme patience settling over her face. "Our ex-son-in-law. Jeff. Elaine Milstein said she was at that Mexican restaurant in Bethesda, you know the one I'm talking about. She was with her grandson. And she ran into Jeff. He was there with a blonde woman and three little kids."

"Elaine Milstein is a gossipy busybody," Howard said. He didn't want to hear anything about what Jeff was doing. He was furious with Jeff. All those years, and then it had ended. He had a feeling there was more to the story than what Lucy had told them. But Lucy had always been one to keep her own counsel. Not like the other two.

"I know," Marilyn said. "But I kind of wondered if it was that Matea Barker from his office. You know, his business partner. Parker-Barker. She's blonde, and she has three young kids."

"Well, maybe it was just a business thing, then," Howard said. Although he doubted it. Parker-Barker my foot. He'd like to meet Jeff in a back alley, and then he'd...

"Elaine said they were holding hands," Marilyn said. She was looking furious too. "Do you think this was going on for a while and that's why things ended? It's not like Lucy would ever tell us, but..." and her voice trailed off. "Poor Lucy. I wish we could help her, but she just keeps everything in."

Howard felt his insides crumpling. His little Lucy. How horrible. He remembered how happy she'd been on her wedding day. How happy Jeff had seemed. How beautiful she'd looked in her dress. She'd grown up so quickly. Sometimes he still thought of her as the toddler running as fast as she could after her two big sisters. The little girl who'd ask him to lift her up on his shoulders so she could see far, far away. The teenager who won all those cross-country meets, racing gazelle-like along the path. He loved her so much.

Marilyn shook her head. "If I could give that Jeff a piece of my mind, I'd ream him out."

Howard nodded. "I know."

"What do you think about this Mr. Shapiro situation?"

Howard thought about it. "If there actually is a situation, I'm all in favor. He seems very nice." Sometimes Marilyn built non-situations into situations, and he'd get all worked up, and then he'd find out the whole thing had been for naught. He didn't want to fall into that trap again.

"I'll find out more at Will's game on Tuesday," Marilyn said. "In a subtle way, of course."

And then Howard's phone rang, and it was Adele, asking to be picked up from Diana's, so he retrieved his keys from the dish by the front door and left, wondering about Jeff and about Mr. Shapiro and why everything always had to be so complicated.

Thirty-One

Will

He was on deck, so Will grabbed his bat and his helmet and took a few practice swings. Will Z. was on third, and Jayson was on first, and there were two outs and Carson was up. He was a great fielder but he struck out a lot.

"Come on, Carson," Will Z. shouted from third. "Get me home." And the pitcher threw a few wild pitches, and Carson didn't swing at them for once, and he ended up walking, which meant that Will was up with two outs, bases loaded. His team was trailing by one run, and it was the bottom of the sixth, which was the last inning in his baseball league.

And Will positioned himself in the batter's box.

"Grand slam! Grand slam!" his teammates chanted from the bench.

"Come on, Will!" he could hear Vilma calling from the area on the lawn where all the parents and other relatives were watching from their portable chairs.

"Go for it, Will!" Arjun's dad, their coach, said.

Will was pretty good at hitting. But he wasn't sure what would happen given that the entire game was on the line.

The first pitch came at him. High.

"Good eye, Will," Arjun's dad called.

The second pitch seemed hittable, but at the last minute it curved off, just as Will took a massive hack at it.

"Strike one!" the ump said.

And he missed the third pitch too.

"One and two," the ump said.

Will twirled his bat around a couple of times and assumed his position. Focus, he told himself. Focus.

The ball came toward him, just as he heard Aunt Adele shout out, "You can do it, William!" And it threw him off, but he somehow managed to get a piece of the ball, and it was enough of a piece that the ball was flying out of reach of any of the opposing outfielders, and Will flung down his bat and took off running for first base, and two runs scored, and he was mobbed by his teammates, who were jumping up and down, and chanting "Walk off! Walk off!" and this felt like the best day ever.

And his team shook hands with the other team, and he packed up his gear, and Aunt Adele clopped over to the dugout in her high heels, not seeming to care that it was all muddy, and gave him a big hug.

"William, how exciting! My own great-nephew saves the day!"

He hugged her back. It was nice of her to come to the game. And he introduced her to Will Z. and some of the other guys, and she started asking them questions about what positions they liked to play. She seemed to know a lot about baseball.

"You seem to know a lot about baseball," Will said, not realizing he was saying it out loud.

"Of course," Aunt Adele said. "I managed a women's softball team for several years."

Cool. Will wondered if that was while she was employed by the circus, but Aunt Adele was listening to something Arjun was saying, so Will couldn't ask her. He didn't think circuses had softball teams, but maybe back in her day they did. He wasn't sure.

And everyone started heading over to the chairs where all the other adults besides Aunt Adele were waiting, and his mom and Vilma were there and they both hugged him and congratulated him on his big hit, and then the four of them got into the car.

"Pizza?" Will inquired, it being almost seven in the evening. There was a pizza place right down the street.

"You have homework," his mom said. "And Vilma already made some lasagna."

"Okay," Will said. Vilma's lasagna was amazing. And his mom and Vilma started talking about something that was happening at Vilma's office, so he tuned them out.

"When I managed the softball team," Aunt Adele said from her seat next to Will in the back, "I was something of a player-manager. I was recruited by the owner. I often inserted myself into the game when my team needed a good hitter at the plate."

"So you were pretty good, then," Will said.

"I was excellent, William," Aunt Adele said. "As a girl, I often played baseball in the vacant lot down the street with the boys."

"What about Gramps?" Will asked.

"He was adequate," Aunt Adele said. "But he was very little at the time that I'm referring to. Maybe six or seven. I believe he improved somewhat as he matured."

Will pictured his grandfather as a six-year-old, playing baseball in a vacant lot. In books, kids were always playing baseball in vacant lots. He tried to picture a vacant lot down the street from the house where his grandfather and Aunt Adele had grown up. He'd seen old black-and-white photos of the house. It was nice, sort of like Will's own house. Symmetrical.

"William, I've been meaning to say that I'm honored to be here for your bar mitzvah," Aunt Adele said. "I'm sorry I missed everyone else's, but at least I'm here for yours."

"Yeah, thanks, cool," Will said. He was glad she'd be here for his bar mitzvah.

"You know, I never had a bat mitzvah," Aunt Adele told him. "Girls didn't have them back then. At least not in West Orange."

"My grandma didn't have one either," Will said. "But then she had an adult bat mitzvah a few years ago." It had been fun. The Kiddush lunch after the service was excellent. Lots of cakes and pastries.

"Interesting," Aunt Adele said, her eyes lighting up. "Perhaps I'll look into that, William. I'd love to have an adult bat mitzvah."

And then Aunt Adele's phone rang, and it turned out to be Grandma, and Will heard Aunt Adele talking about something to do with Grandma's friend Cat and a purple dress she'd worn on her date. Did people that old really go on dates?

"Wonderful," Aunt Adele was saying. "I'm delighted. Perhaps she'll go on another date with Padraig, then?"

And after a few more minutes she hung up.

"Was that my mom?" Will's mom asked from the driver's seat.

"Yes, apparently Cat had a delightful time on her date," Aunt Adele said.

"Well, that's good," Will's mom said, and she and Vilma went back to discussing Vilma's office.

"Do people your age really go on dates?" Will asked.

"Of course we do, William," Aunt Adele said, waving her scarf at him. "I go on dates frequently. Do you think only young people seek companionship?"

Will thought about it. Well, no, probably everyone wanted companionship, right? But dates? "Well," he began.

"William, do you go on dates?"

Will could tell he was turning bright red. "No," he said, the image of Katelin C. popping into his head for some reason. Maybe one day he could see if she wanted to go to a movie. Maybe the new Han Solo movie, or the new Avengers movie. He really wanted to see both of those. But the idea of asking her was terrifying. Maybe he could go with Carson and Arjun instead.

"Does your brother?"

Aunt Adele could be kind of nosy. He had no idea if Max went on dates. Did walking around the park with a girl and two dogs count as a date? Or bringing the guitar to the park for the girl's father to hear Max play count as a date? Assuming Max even liked this girl. "I don't know," he said. That was a safe answer.

And then they pulled up in the driveway, and they all went in and had dinner, and Will told Max about his game-winning hit, and the idea of dates went completely out of his head.

Thirty-Two

Marilyn

Marilyn wasn't sure why she was suddenly obsessed with the idea of going back to teaching. It must be the kind of thing where a thought lies dormant in one's head, and then it's brought to the surface, and all of a sudden, it's all one can think about. She was slightly annoyed that Adele, of all people, had been the catalyst for this transformation in her thought process, but so be it. Her mind was racing. Should she offer to teach a Shakespeare class? A class on the Victorian novel? A class on Jewish-American literature? Maybe the temple would be interested.

She needed to talk to Lucy. Lucy would understand. So she dialed her number.

"Hi, Mom," Lucy said. "Wait, hang on just a second, okay?"

It sounded as if she was talking to someone else, with her hand over the phone, and then she got back on.

"Where are you?" Marilyn asked. "Are you in the middle of something?"

"No," Lucy said. "What's up?"

"Teaching," Marilyn said. "I'm just so excited, and I wanted to talk to you."

And she told Lucy everything she was thinking about teaching, and Lucy got all excited too, and she came up with more ideas for Marilyn, like maybe she could teach at OLLI or Osher or one of those other adult-ed programs connected to universities, and Marilyn was scribbling down all the ideas on a piece of scrap paper.

"You know, Mom, I've told you that for a long time now, that you should teach a course. Ever since Cat was okay again. So what made you change your mind?"

"I don't know," Marilyn said. And she didn't. Sometimes an idea had to appear at exactly the right moment. Maybe if Adele had said something to her about teaching a week earlier, it wouldn't have had the same impact.

"Okay," Lucy said. "Cool."

Lucy sounded a little better than she had lately, Marilyn thought. When she'd talked to her a couple of days ago, she'd sounded absolutely awful. "You sound good, sweetie. Is everything okay?" Not that she thought she'd get much of an answer from Lucy. The more Marilyn thought about it, the more convinced she was that the woman at the Mexican restaurant had been Matea Barker, and that Jeff had been involved with her for a while. It all made sense. But Marilyn was determined to keep her mouth shut.

"Yeah," Lucy said. "I'm doing fine."

Which of course meant nothing.

"Do you want to come over for dinner? Aunt Adele's over at Sarah's with Sarah and Vilma and the boys. She went to Will's baseball game. So it's just me and Dad."

"No, well, actually I have plans," Lucy said. "Sorry, Mom."

And of course she wouldn't let slip what those plans were. And Marilyn was not going to ask. Even though she really, really wanted to.

"Good, sweetheart. Enjoy yourself. I love you." And Marilyn hung up.

Howie wandered into the family room. "Who were you

talking to?" he inquired.

"Lucy," she said. "She's just so private. But I had a great discussion with her about teaching." She paused. "So did I tell you about Cat?"

"No," he said. He seemed as if he wasn't listening again, but she started to tell him about how well things had gone with Padraig, and Cat hoped they'd go out again, and she told Marilyn to thank Adele for all her advice, so Marilyn had. And this was really unusual, because Marilyn must have fixed Cat up with a dozen men over the years, and Cat hadn't liked any of them. Until now.

"Uh-huh," Howie said.

Honestly, he wasn't paying any attention at all. She thought back to earlier times, when he hung on her every word. He complimented her all the time. He sent her bouquets of flowers. Of course, that was fifty years ago. Things changed.

Her phone rang. "Hey, Mom." It was Diana. "I have Poppy here from my writing group, and she's really freaking out about a lot of things, and I'm just not up for making dinner for her, so can I bring her over? Philippe left me some food, but she's vegan so she can't eat it."

"Of course," Marilyn said. With Adele in the house, she had a lot of vegan-appropriate food. She could put together a nice stir-fry. Howie would probably eat that too.

"Diana's bringing Poppy over," she told Howie.

"Oy vey," he said.

Marilyn nodded. Diana had brought Poppy over a couple of other times. She was like the young Diana to the tenth power. She seemed to view Diana as a mentor of sorts, which Marilyn figured was a good experience for Diana, but Poppy was a real handful.

Marilyn pulled a bunch of vegetables out of the refrigerator—carrots, peppers, an onion—and started peeling the carrots. The thought of mentors reminded her of Caroline Martino, Sarah's mentor. Marilyn had always harbored a vague jealousy when it came to Caroline Martino. Sarah used to joke that Caroline Martino was her work mom. Why did Sarah need a work mom, anyway? Wasn't one mom—Marilyn—good enough? But now Caroline Martino had moved to New Zealand. Which probably was difficult for Sarah. On top of the whole Vilma situation. Howie had cautioned that there might not be a Vilma situation, that maybe everything between Sarah and Vilma was fine, but she knew he was worried too.

She took out her frustration on the vegetables, chopping them into pieces and throwing them into the nonstick pan with some olive oil and spices, and then she started the rice.

And a half-hour later, the door opened and Diana came in, Poppy trailing behind her. Diana was draped in a tight-fitting batik maternity dress, and Poppy was wearing black cargo pants, black combat boots, and a black t-shirt that said FUCK EVERYTHING. Nice.

"Diana! And Poppy! So good to see you again!" Marilyn hugged her daughter and patted Poppy on the back. She was kind of scared to hug her.

Howie had retreated into his office. She wondered if he would come out at all.

"How are you feeling?" Marilyn asked Diana.

"The baby's been moving around a lot, but nothing major's going on," Diana said.

"And how are you, Poppy?"

"Life sucks, and then you die," Poppy said, sitting down at the kitchen table and resting her chin in one hand. "I'm great."

Oh boy. Marilyn had taught a lot of kids like Poppy, and sometimes they were absolutely brilliant, but their attitude just drove her crazy.

"Where's Aunt Adele?" Diana said, collapsing into a chair and looking around as if Marilyn had hidden Adele under a piece of furniture or something.

"At Sarah's," Marilyn said, sitting down too.

"Oh," Diana said. She sounded disappointed. "I thought she'd be a good person for Poppy to talk to."

Marilyn agreed. Adele would be the perfect person for Poppy to talk to. But she didn't think Adele would be back for a while, and she wasn't eager for Poppy to stay here for longer than necessary.

"So, Poppy, what's troubling you?" Marilyn asked.

"Pretty much everything," Poppy said. "So first Pietro, who was my boyfriend, was hooking up with my supposed best friend, Giselle, so I dumped him, and I'm not speaking to either one of them, and then it turns out this girl at my office, Viveca, is trying to sabotage my work. She told my boss I wrote this tweet that went out by mistake about whales, and it had some incorrect information, and I didn't come up with the idea for that tweet at all. It was Viveca. She came up with it. Not me." Poppy was getting more and more worked up as this tale of woe continued, and her voice was getting louder and louder.

Marilyn tried to remember what office Poppy worked in. Something to do with whales, obviously, but she couldn't recall any specifics. "That's awful," she said, getting up to pour some glasses of water. "I'm sorry."

Poppy nodded. "And then to put the icing on the cake, my Twitter account got hacked, and instead of retweeting things about saving animals, it started retweeting all this MAGA stuff that I would, like, never ever retweet."

Marilyn sat down again and handed the water glasses to Poppy and Diana.

"So I had to shut down my Twitter, and that pissed my boss off even more, because he wants us to tweet like twenty times a day, and I need to set up a new account, but I haven't had time because I've been dealing with the fallout from the whole Pietro-Giselle thing, and..."

"She's all stressed out," Diana said. "So I've been trying to calm her down, but as you can tell I haven't been too successful."

Food usually helped, Marilyn thought, so she brought out the stir-fry. She hadn't been able to find all that many interesting spices, so she wasn't sure how it would taste.

"Yum," Poppy said, after helping herself to a huge serving. "That smells, like, so good. Thanks, Mrs. Pinsky."

"You're very welcome, Poppy." Marilyn smiled at her. Poppy did have some manners, after all. Marilyn excused herself and went to find Howie, who reluctantly followed her back to the kitchen for dinner.

"Poppy, hello," he said, nodding at her. Marilyn could see him doing a double-take at Poppy's shirt.

"Hey, Mr. Pinsky," Poppy said.

"Hi, Dad," Diana said, as Howie leaned over to give her a hug. "So everyone, you want to feel her or him? I think he or she is trying to do flips right now, but there isn't enough room."

And everyone clustered around, waiting their turn. Marilyn knew she'd probably get all emotional, because she always did when she felt her future grandchild moving around, and she sensed the tears coming to her eyes, and she hugged Diana again.

Poppy started crying too. "It's just so cool, Diana," she said. "Don't you think so, Mrs. Pinsky?" Makeup was running down Poppy's face, and Marilyn handed her a paper napkin. "Oh, thanks," Poppy said, wiping her eyes.

And everyone was smiling by this point, including Poppy and Howie, which was good, and Marilyn tried the stir-fry and found to her surprise that it was delicious.

Thirty-three

Sarah

"So you always knew." Aunt Adele was peering at Sarah from across the table at the Thai restaurant.

Well, not necessarily. She'd let it cross her mind in high school. But it wasn't until she'd met Alina Shaw, that first week at Harvard, that she'd known. It was way too complicated to explain to Aunt Adele, though. Especially here in this Thai restaurant where the tables were incredibly close together and she could hear the women at the next table boasting about their kids' athletic accomplishments.

"I dabbled in lesbianism," Aunt Adele said loudly, taking a bite of her Pad Thai. "From time to time. But I decided it wasn't for me."

Dabbled? Sarah wondered why she'd agreed to this lunch anyway. But somehow, in the car the previous night when she'd been dropping Aunt Adele back at her parents' house after dinner, she'd said yes when Aunt Adele suggested it.

"You know, Sarah, you remind me of my mother."

This was intriguing, but perhaps not something Sarah wanted to hear. "Really? Why?" Sarah recalled her grandmother as a perpetually worried person who cried frequently.

"She was the oldest of three, just like you. And she took the weight of the world on her shoulders. She helped run that shoe store, and she took care of us, and she was the one who cared for my grandparents. And then I don't suppose it helped when I left."

No, probably not. Sarah remembered trying to engage her grandmother on the subject of Aunt Adele, but her grandmother would just start crying. Her grandfather was a little more open. "She wanted other things, so she left," he'd tell Sarah, sounding wistful. "I just wish I could see her again." And then he'd turn the conversation to something involving Sarah's schoolwork or, later, her job.

"Was she the responsible one?" Sarah asked. She twirled a noodle around on her fork.

"Exactly," Aunt Adele said. "Her brothers were charming but feckless. I would say to her, Don't you ever want to just throw your hands up and say to hell with it all?" And she threw her hands up, practically hitting one of the boasting women at the next table.

"Sorry," Sarah said automatically.

The woman glared at them, and went back to discussing her daughter's basketball prowess.

Aunt Adele finished the one last noodle remaining on her plate, ignoring the woman's angry expression.

"So what would Grandma Pinsky say when you said that to her?"

"What would you say if I said that to you?" Aunt Adele parried.

Sarah thought about that. What would happen if she threw her hands up and said to hell with it all? Her parents would completely fall apart. Diana would completely fall apart. Max would spend all his time in the park with Phoebe and the guitar. Will would spend all his time playing video games and fail out of school. Phoebe would starve. Vilma, well, Vilma would be okay. So would Lucy, probably, although lately Sarah wasn't so sure. But the office would definitely fall apart. And then Caroline would be devastated and she would fall apart. "No, I couldn't do that," Sarah said. "Absolutely not." It would be a total disaster if she did that.

Aunt Adele gave Sarah a triumphant smile. "And that's what your grandmother would say when I'd ask her."

Great. So Sarah was destined to turn into another Grandma Pinsky? She'd loved Grandma Pinsky, but being around her was often stressful and somewhat depressing.

"You have a lovely family," Aunt Adele said. "You and Vilma and the boys, I mean. Just try to enjoy them."

She did enjoy them, didn't she? But with the bar mitzvah coming up in five days now, and Vilma being in Helsinki most of the past six months, and Caroline moving to New Zealand, and Lucy getting divorced, and Diana having a baby, things had been at a fever pitch. It was difficult to slow down enough to actually enjoy anything.

She needed to change the subject. "So did you and my dad go see the apartments in Tenleytown this morning?"

Aunt Adele's face lit up. "Yes! I found them quite delightful. We saw a one-bedroom-with-den and a two-bedroom. And then I was taking a look at the common room, and I got into a fascinating conversation with a gentleman who was sitting there reading the paper. Your father was taking a walk around the outside of the building at the time, and the real estate agent was on the phone, so I had no one to talk to. And that's how I met Georges." She pronounced it with the full French flair.

"Georges?"

"The gentleman I was conversing with," Aunt Adele said. "Yes. Georges. He's a retired French diplomat, and he's been living in that building for several years, since his wife passed away. And wouldn't you know it, we're planning to have dinner together."

Wow. Aunt Adele was really something. It did sort of remind Sarah of Diana, before she met Philippe. Some people had it, and some people—like Sarah—didn't.

"That's great," Sarah said, impressed. "Where are you going?"

"I thought I'd take him to Philippe's restaurant, as I haven't been there yet. Apparently it's impossible to get in, but Philippe said he'd reserve a table for us."

That reminded Sarah of Will's actual birthday. It was on Wednesday, three days before the bar mitzvah, and he'd requested that the whole family go to Philippe's restaurant, so Sarah had organized it.

"So you'll get to go twice in one week," Sarah said.

"Ah, yes, William's birthday," Aunt Adele said, smiling. "I am quite fond of William."

Sarah thought about the fact that Will, her baby, was turning thirteen. A teenager. It was unfathomable. How had it all gone by so fast?

"Do you ever think about how fast time goes by?" Sarah asked Aunt Adele. "I mean, one minute Will's a baby, and now he's about to have his bar mitzvah?"

A pensive expression came over Aunt Adele's face. "When I saw your father at the airport three weeks ago, I almost fainted. Sixty-four years gone by, like that." And she snapped her fingers. "There he was, and part of me felt I'd just seen him yesterday, and part of me felt confused by how so much time could have passed."

It passed because you never chose to contact him until now, Sarah thought, but she didn't say it. "So what made you finally get back in touch?" she asked instead. "Had something happened to change your mind?"

Aunt Adele tilted her head to one side. She was silent for a moment. "One gets lonely," she finally said. "That's why. After

Rudy died, I thought I'd continue on in the house in Honolulu, but two years passed and I found I couldn't concentrate any more, despite all my volunteer activities and my occasional romances."

"So you started thinking about my dad?" Sarah felt a surprising pang of sympathy for Aunt Adele.

"I never stopped thinking about him, Sarah. I started thinking about how I was about to turn eighty, and what was I waiting for? So that was that."

Sarah nodded. It made sense. "You're okay, aren't you? Health-wise, I mean?"

"Of course," Aunt Adele said. "My health is fine. This has nothing to do with my health." Well, that was good. "It was quite a blow when Rudy died, but of course Rudy wasn't the true love of my life. Herman was. I assume Vilma is the true love of your life?"

Sarah assumed so, yes. Her thoughts flicked back to the day she'd met Vilma, at a mutual friend's dinner party. The boys had been at her parents' house, and it was the first time she'd been to a party in months, and she thought she'd probably forgotten how to talk to anyone except the boys and her parents and her sisters and everyone at work. But then Vilma had struck up a conversation with her, and Sarah was amazed that this self-possessed, incredibly attractive woman was interested in talking to her at all, and they discovered that they'd both been wanting to join a book club, and Vilma suggested the two of them start one and invite some friends, and that was how it started. The relationship, and their still-ongoing book club.

And the waiter came by with the check, and then Sarah asked Aunt Adele if she'd like to see Sarah's office, which was just down Wisconsin Avenue, before she went home, and Aunt Adele said of course, and Sarah realized she probably wasn't going to get a whole lot of work done that day.

Thirty-Four

Max

The list was posted on the wall outside the band room, and Max was feeling kind of queasy as he made his way over to it. He could see a bunch of other kids peering at the list and either fist-bumping each other triumphantly or skulking away in disappointment. Which would it be for him? He held his breath. He sort of wanted to wait until everyone else had cleared out, but it was his lunch period and he didn't have all that much time if he wanted to go get a sandwich with Isla. He edged his way closer and squinted at the piece of paper. He probably did need glasses. His mom had taken him to an eye doctor a few months ago, who'd said Max was getting nearsighted and was on the verge of needing glasses and his mom should bring him back in a year.

Trumpets, piano, saxophones, percussion, with various names listed, some of whom he knew. But where was the listing for guitar? Another kid's head was right in front of him, blocking part of the piece of paper. It would be okay if he didn't make it, he reassured himself. He'd have another year to improve and then try again. The kid's head moved, giving Max a glimpse of the entire piece of paper. And there it was! Max Pinsky, guitar. Holy shit, he'd done it! This was incredible!

The jazz band teacher, Mr. Wiggins, was on his way out of the band room and he gave Max a high-five. "Great audition, Max," he said. "I'm really looking forward to next year. I'll give you some stuff to work on, okay?"

Max nodded. "Yeah, thanks, I'm looking forward to it too." He couldn't believe it.

Mr. Wiggins started talking to some other kids, and Max moved away from the wall and reached for his phone. His hands were shaking as he texted Isla. "I got in! Lunch?"

"OMG, congrats! I knew you would!" she texted back, with tons of smiling emojis. "Meet you outside?"

"OK, thx!!!" he wrote back. The band room was at the other end of the school from where he was going to meet her, and all these visions were floating through his head of how cool this was and how maybe Isla would want to come over to his house some time and hear him practice and maybe if no one else was around he could sneak her up to his room and then maybe...and he realized he had just banged into someone.

"Dude! Watch where you're going!" It was Seb. But he didn't seem mad. He was actually sort of smiling. This was the most Seb had said to Max in weeks, so Max was a little taken aback.

"Hey, sorry, man," Max mumbled. It was unusual to see Seb without the group of guys he tended to hang with lately. He wondered where they all were.

"So you want to get lunch?" Seb asked.

What? He and Seb used to eat together every single day, from kindergarten all the way through to the beginning of this school year. But now Seb always ate with a group of popular kids. "I can't," Max said. "I'm already eating with someone else."

"Oh, that girl you've been hanging out with?" Seb asked. "From the bus stop?"

Max nodded, surprised. Seb had actually been paying attention to what he, Max, was doing?

"She's hot," Seb said. "What's her name again?"

Max told him.

"Isn't her dad, like, someone famous? I heard somebody say that."

"Yeah," Max said. "He's a guitarist." Should he tell Seb about the lessons, which, amazingly, were supposed to start this afternoon? Should he tell him about getting into jazz band? He would have told him if it had been a few months ago. But he didn't really feel like getting into it now.

"So I can't believe Will's bar mitzvah is this weekend," Seb said. "Like, I can't believe he's that old already."

Max couldn't believe it either. His little brother, a teenager? And then he remembered that Seb and his family were supposed to be at the bar mitzvah. This was kind of awkward.

And then one of Seb's buddies, this dude Bruno, appeared, and Seb and Bruno started goofing off and elbowing each other and then they headed off down a different hallway. "Later," Seb called to Max.

"Yeah," Max said. A memory hit him. It had been in, like fifth grade or something, and this douchebag kid had started in with all this homophobic shit, and Max had punched him, and he and the other kid had gotten into this huge fight, and it was the one and only time in his life that Max had ever ended up going to the principal's office. But the other kid was the one who ended up getting in trouble. And the next day at school, when the kid started another round of taunting, Seb had stepped in and told the kid that if he ever said anything like that again to Max, who was his very best friend, no one in the entire fifth grade would speak to him. Ever. And the kid shut up after that. Soon thereafter, he'd moved away. But Max had never forgotten the whole episode. He missed Seb. Isla was amazing, but not having your best guy friend any more really sucked.

He remembered something Aunt Adele had told him last night. She'd been over for dinner, and once they'd all finished eating, she'd taken him by the hand again and led him off into the living room. His mom and Vilma were cleaning up, and Will had been sent upstairs to practice the trumpet, which tended to produce an ear-splitting cacophony as far as Max was concerned.

"Max," Aunt Adele had said. "I really haven't had that much of a chance to talk to you. Cousin Morty hijacked the conversation the other day, and I believe he was trying to convince you to be an attorney."

Max nodded. He remembered.

"Let me guess, that's not what you have in mind," Aunt Adele said. She was still clutching onto his hand. "But let's not talk about that. Let's talk about what you do for fun. Do you have friends?"

"Well, there's one," he said. Isla was probably his only friend at this point. "And another one in Argentina."

"So tell me about this friend. The one who's here."

And Max started telling Aunt Adele all about Isla, and about Logan MacLeish, and about how he was going to have a lesson tomorrow, and how he couldn't believe it.

"I played the ukulele," Aunt Adele said, a dreamy look crossing her face. "During my first stint in Hawaii. I was asked to play with a number of famous musicians. A delightful instrument."

She was that good that she was asked to play with a number of famous musicians? "How many years did you play it?" Max inquired.

Aunt Adele waved the end of her scarf around. "Oh, a number of years," she said vaguely. "I plan to have the ukulele shipped out here once I find somewhere to move. Perhaps we could play a duet."

And she talked about the ukulele for a while, and then she focused back on Max. "Your mother mentioned a friend, a male friend, who lives nearby who's coming to the bar mitzvah?"

Seb. "Well, she probably doesn't know, but Seb and I kind of aren't friends any more."

Aunt Adele looked sad. "Oh dear," she said. "And why not?"

So Max went into the whole story, about Seb hanging out with the popular kids, and how he barely saw Seb any more, and when they did Seb ignored him, and what was the point?

"And do you think Seb cares about your friendship at all?"

Max thought about this. Probably not. "I don't know."

"I'd give it another try. Old friendships are worth keeping. I should have done better with that myself." And then she let go of Max's hand and pointed upstairs. "Your brother is an excellent baseball player, but his skills on the trumpet could use some work."

And that seemed to be the end of the conversation.

Max snapped back into the present. He had reached the front steps of the school. He looked around. And there was Isla, and she ran over and threw her arms around him right in front of everyone and she wasn't letting go, and he was hugging her back and it just felt really good to be this close to her, and she was whispering in his ear that she was so proud of him, and once again he wondered if there was more he should be doing and if she was expecting something else, but just holding her was more than enough for him right now, so he kept doing that. And finally she broke away from him and grabbed onto his hand and they were walking hand in hand up East-West Highway and he had never felt better in his entire life.

Thirty-Five

Diana

Diana had awakened that morning unable to see. It was as if a dark circle had descended upon her right eye, which happened to be her only eye that actually saw well. Her left eye had always been a total disaster. She had worn glasses for her entire life, except that she had started wearing contacts in middle school, so most people had no idea that her vision was so bad.

"Philippe, I can't see very well," she said, nudging him in the side. She blinked a few times to see if somehow the dark circle could be dislodged. Maybe it was some kind of particle that had gotten into her eye. Maybe it was an eyelash. But nothing changed. Once she'd had an ocular migraine, so she wondered if perhaps that's what this was. She reached for her glasses, on the night table, but they didn't really help either.

"What is it, chérie?" Philippe asked, half-asleep. She looked at him. He appeared quite blurry, an indistinct shape under the covers.

"Oh, nothing," Diana said. She maneuvered herself out of bed. This thing would resolve itself after a while, she was sure. So she went over to her computer and turned it on. See if she could get a little work done. She yawned. She really was feeling tired. But when she got into her Blattner manuscript, she realized it was completely illegible. The dark circle was making it absolutely impossible to read anything. How frustrating. How could she get any work done this way? She squinted at the screen, and was able to make out a few words. Enlarging the text helped a bit, but actually editing and rewriting in a coherent way seemed an insurmountable task.

So she went into the baby's future room, which used to be her office. She had organized everything in the dresser, and she pulled out the outfit Sarah had given her for the baby to wear home. She still hadn't packed the suitcase. She really needed to do that. The outfit was yellow, and depicted little animals playing happily with various types of toys. But right now Diana couldn't really make out the little animals on the outfit. Was this something to worry about? Probably not. She didn't need to get everyone all stressed out.

Maybe the best thing to do would be to go back to sleep. So she got back into bed. Philippe, still half-asleep, curled himself around her. The baby was moving to and fro, and Diana felt as if she were sandwiched between her husband and her baby. The filling in the middle. It was nice. And the next thing she knew, the sun was streaming in through the windows and she was alone in the bed. She blinked a few times. But that circle was still there. She still couldn't really see that much. She peered over at the clock. What did it say? There were four digits, so it must be past ten.

Philippe came in with a tray of blurry but beautifully displayed food for her. Toast, eggs, juice. All very healthy.

"Thanks, my love," Diana said. He was just so thoughtful. She stretched and felt that annoying pull in the area under her stomach on her right side. The thing Sarah had thought was probably a ligament. Should she ask Sarah about this eye thing? No, Sarah would just tell their parents and they'd all freak out and what would be the point? She wouldn't tell anyone. Even Philippe. He would worry too.

Philippe set the tray on a table next to the bed. "Breakfast in bed for the very best future mom in the whole world," he said, and kissed her. His face seemed indistinct. She thought he was smiling, but she wasn't sure.

"Oh, this is fantastic," she said. "Thank you." She reached for the fork and took the plate with the egg and balanced it on her stomach. She couldn't see the egg very well, but she managed to get it into her mouth, bite by bite, without dropping it on the bed. "Delicious." Being married to a chef was perhaps the most wonderful thing that could ever happen to anyone. "I love you so much." And for a second she forgot that she couldn't see, and she set the fork and the plate back on the tray and she pulled her blurry husband toward her, onto the bed, and kissed him passionately. He was kissing her back, and starting to do more, and it felt really amazing, but then he stopped.

"I think it is probably not the best thing right now," he said. He gave her one more kiss. "With only a few days to go."

She really wasn't sure. She hadn't wanted to have sex for a while now, but for some reason right at this moment it seemed like a possibility. Maybe to keep her mind off her eye? And then the thought of her eye, paradoxically, made her stop thinking about sex. "Yeah, you're probably right," she said.

"You are so sexy," Philippe said, kissing her again. "You always have been and you always will be." And he put his arm around her, and she finished her breakfast and leaned against him and decided maybe she should go back to sleep.

And when she woke up the next time, he was gone. She looked at the clock. Everything was still blurry. She thought there were only three numbers on the clock, which meant it was probably after one in the afternoon. Monday was usually his day off, but she knew he had a meeting with an investor.

This was ridiculous. She should go about her business, vision or no vision. So she got up, took a shower, and tried to get some work done. But it was impossible. She really couldn't see anything well enough to edit it. She could get a sense of a couple of words, and then the rest of it would be too indistinct to figure out.

She probably shouldn't put in her contacts, given what was going on, so she put on her prescription sunglasses, threw her maternity bathing suit and a towel into a bag, and walked over to the Wilson pool. It had become her favorite source of exercise during her pregnancy. In the water, she felt buoyant. Un-whale-like. Energetic. She lowered herself down the ladder into the pool and started doing her laps. It didn't matter as much in the water that she couldn't see clearly.

And when she got out and showered and dressed, she took a look at her phone. She could see that the text icon had a little red dot next to it, so she clicked on it, and yes, there must be new texts, but she couldn't read any of them. She wondered what she was missing. She saw that she'd missed some phone calls too, so she listened to them. Three from Philippe, one from her mom, and one from Sarah, all asking how she was doing. And one from Dr. Patel's office confirming her appointment for tomorrow morning.

It was a beautiful day, so she walked around for a while. She called Philippe back and told him she was doing fine, and she called her mom and Sarah and told them she was doing fine, and then she went home and fell asleep again, and then she got up and squinted at the clock and realized it must be almost time for her writing group.

So she ate the dinner Philippe had left her—a very tasty pasta and vegetable dish—and rushed over to the Starbucks, wearing her glasses, and everyone was already there except Nick.

"Diana!" Marcia said. "We thought maybe you'd gone into labor!" Marcia's face looked blurry too. Her freckles were all merging into one another. "I like your glasses. I haven't seen you wear them before."

"Yeah, no, still here," Diana said. "Still waiting. Thanks." She patted her stomach, and the baby kicked her. The baby didn't seem to mind that its mom couldn't see anything. She had a horrible thought. What if she couldn't see the baby once it was born? What if it would be a blur forever? What would she do? But that was absurd. This problem would go away. It would have to.

"Thanks for last night," Poppy said. "I feel better after that dinner. Your mom's a great cook." Diana couldn't really tell, because Poppy was a blur of blue hair and black clothing, but she thought Poppy looked happier than she had lately.

"I'd like to talk about my revised chapter," Gideon said. He was another blur. "It's about what happened to my great-great-great grandfather right before the Civil War. Or the fictionalized version of him, that is. But it's all historically accurate. I found some new documents, so I was able to rewrite that section. Is that okay, or did you have other plans for us tonight?"

He seemed to be looking at Diana, so she nodded. "No, that's great, Gideon, yeah."

He passed out copies of his chapter, and Diana thought she saw Marcia and Poppy pulling out their pens and getting to work. She looked at Gideon's chapter but she couldn't see anything much. The print was fairly small and she could only make out a few words here and there. If it was anything like Gideon's usual writing, it was incredibly well researched, but a little dry. He needed to work on his dialogue.

"Hey, everyone, sorry I'm late again." It was Nick. He pulled up a chair, and Gideon handed him the chapter. "Cool," Nick said, and took out a pen.

There was silence for a while. Diana tried again to read the first page of Gideon's chapter, but she just couldn't see anything well enough. So she gave up.

"Diana, aren't you reading it?" Gideon said. He sounded kind of hurt.

"Oh, god, you guys, I can't see," Diana blurted out. "I have this huge circle thing right in the middle of the field of vision in my good eye, and my other eye doesn't see very much, and I can't read anything."

They all looked up from their reading. She imagined that their expressions were probably horrified, although she had no idea.

"Oh my god, Diana," Marcia said. "I mean, I'm sure everything will be fine, but you should go to the doctor and get this checked out! When did this happen?"

"This morning," Diana said. "I slept a lot today, and I thought it would go away, but it hasn't."

"It could be an ocular migraine," Gideon said. "I had that once, and it was like a curtain had dropped over my eye. Go get it checked out, Marcia's right."

Diana nodded. An ocular migraine. That sounded right.

"What did Philippe say?" Nick inquired. "Didn't he think you should go to the doctor? If I were him, I would have."

"Oh, I didn't tell him," Diana said. "You know. I didn't want to worry him. Or my family. They'd freak out."

"Holy shit, Diana, you need to go to the doctor," Poppy said. "You need to tell Philippe. This is fucking crazy."

And Diana realized that if even Poppy was giving her responsible advice, she probably should listen. She'd make an appointment with her eye doctor tomorrow morning. Maybe they could squeeze her in this week. Unless the baby arrived first.

Thirty-Six

Howard

"So you don't feel any anger toward her?" Stuart Bernstein asked. They'd been on the phone for half an hour already, discussing Adele's reappearance and how Howard was feeling about it. Stuart was one of the few people to whom Howard felt he could unburden himself. Bobby Slotnick and Cousin Morty were more inclined to go on about themselves and not listen to anything Howard said. But Stuart had always been a good listener.

Howard had wondered himself about anger. Why wasn't he angry with Adele? Of course, he'd had phases over the years when he'd been furious with her. At various life cycle events, when her absence was especially bitter. When their parents were elderly and infirm and he wished she were there to help him and Marilyn care for them. Over the years, he'd been tortured by the same questions, again and again. Why had Adele left? Had he done something wrong? Why did she only call their parents, not him? What was he supposed to say when people asked if he had a sibling? He'd say yes, he did, he had a sister but he hadn't seen her for a long time. And as time went on it became less of an issue to say they were estranged. There were similar stories in other people's families too.

But since Adele's return, with the exception of that one outburst during her first phone call, he'd mostly just been glad to have her back in his life. "No," he told Stuart. "At least not right now." Maybe as he had gotten older, all the anger had been leached out of him. Or maybe he would go into an angry phase at some later point? Did that make sense?

Stuart wasn't a therapist, he was a retired high school science teacher, but Howard supposed he'd had to listen to various tales of woe from students over the years. He knew Marilyn had experienced that. And probably Lucy, too, although she'd never mentioned anything about it.

"Well, that's good," Stuart said. "And she's planning to move right near you?"

Howard replied in the affirmative. He'd taken Adele to see a new condo building yesterday and she'd warmed to it immediately. She'd also met a man in the common room. Howard had left for a brief walk, and he'd returned to find Adele in the process of accepting a dinner date from a dapper Frenchman named Georges.

He told Stuart all of this, and Stuart started laughing.

"She really hasn't changed, has she," Stuart said. "I can't wait to see her."

Stuart and his wife, Clea, were coming down from New York for the bar mitzvah. Bobby Slotnick and Andrea were flying up from Boca. With Cousin Morty there too, plus Adele, it would be like West Orange all over again. A giant reunion.

And Stuart asked about Lucy and whether she was still enjoying teaching and how she was doing in the wake of the divorce, and Howard inquired about Stuart's son, Jon, who had just started a new job, and they were in the middle of talking about Diana and the baby when Marilyn rushed into the room.

"It's Diana!" she exclaimed. "Philippe just called."

"Oh, my god, I think Diana's having the baby right now," Howard told Stuart, who said mazel tov, and they ended the call.

"She's in labor?" Howard asked. He found that he was having trouble breathing. Did he feel like this when Sarah was having her boys? Or when Marilyn was giving birth to their three girls? Probably. But he just couldn't remember. All he could think about was that he was feeling kind of dizzy. He put his head down on his desk.

"Her eye, Howie, her eye!" Marilyn was saying. "She's not in labor."

Howard picked up his head. "What do you mean, her eye?"

Adele, rousted out of her room by the commotion, appeared in the doorway of Howard's study. "She's having the baby?"

"No, no, no," Marilyn said, apparently about to lose control. "Her eye! Her eye!" And she pointed at her own eye. "Let's go, Howie. Now."

"What's going on with her eye?" Howard and Adele said in unison. He looked at Adele. "Jinx," he would have called as a kid, and Adele would have crossed her arms exasperatedly and frowned at him.

"She can't see out of her good eye," Marilyn said. She appeared to be literally wringing her hands, which, Howard recalled, was something she tended to do when situations came up with Diana. "And you know her other eye is pretty much useless. Come on! We need to go to the retina specialist. That's where they are."

"Retina specialist?" Howard repeated, confused.

"I think Philippe's English deserted him because he was so stressed out, and I can't remember my French all that well, so I have absolutely no idea what's going on. Just that it's something involving her eye, and she can't see."

"I could have helped with that," Adele said, twirling her scarf around. "My French is excellent. As I proved with Georges."

"Come on, Howie. Now." Marilyn seemed insistent, so

Howard trailed behind her to the front door and retrieved the car keys. Adele followed in their wake, and the three of them got into the Avalon. "It's that first medical building on Wisconsin. You know the one I mean. Where Dr. Goldstein's office is."

Howard nodded and backed the car carefully out of the driveway.

"Why exactly are we doing this?" Adele inquired from the back seat. "Philippe is with her, isn't he?"

"Yes, but Philippe is very absent-minded, and I know neither of them will be taking notes, and someone needs to be there to keep them organized," Marilyn said, turning back to face Adele. "And what if Diana goes into labor right then and there? And then what?"

"Ah," Adele said. "I see. Well, I assume Philippe must be possessed of some sort of common sense to pull off a successful restaurant."

"Anything to do with food, yes," Marilyn said. "Everything else, no."

And there was silence the rest of the way to the medical building, where Howard parked the car and the three of them made their way to the retina doctor's office. Diana was sitting in the waiting room. She looked quite glamorous, Howard thought, in her sunglasses and her black maternity dress. Philippe, on the other hand, looked like a nervous wreck. He was pushing his hair back from his forehead and pacing around the room.

"Hey, Dad. Mom. Aunt Adele," Diana said, unfazed. Everyone sat down, except Philippe. "So this is my third doctor's office waiting room today. And it's not even afternoon yet." And she laughed.

"First we were at Dr. Patel's office," Philippe said, stopping in front of Howard's chair. "And she said you must call your eye doctor immediately, and so I called Dr. Bloomfield, and then his office said to come in at once, and we did, and then Dr. Bloomfield said it was a problem with Diana's retina so here we are."

He seemed to be speaking English perfectly well, Howard thought. What was Marilyn talking about?

"What kind of problem with her retina?" Marilyn said. She was pulling out a piece of paper and a pen, obviously preparing to take notes.

"They don't know, Mom," Diana said. "That's why we're here, okay?"

"I had a problem with my retina a few years back," Adele chimed in. "A detached retina. Perhaps that's what you have, Diana?"

"We'll see," Diana said. She put her hands on her stomach, which seemed to be undulating.

"Diana Pinsky?" A young woman in black scrubs was standing in front of a doorway.

And they all got up.

"We can't fit all of you back here," the young woman said, sounding somewhat alarmed.

"Okay, can my husband come with me?" Diana said, and the woman nodded, and Diana and Philippe disappeared down the hallway behind her.

"Oh, dear," Marilyn said, wringing her hands again as they sat back down. "Neither of them will be able to remember anything the doctor tells them."

Howard thought about this. "Well, they did manage to organize the whole IVF thing, which was kind of a big deal, logistically speaking."

Marilyn was pulling out her phone. "I need to call Sarah and let her know what's happening." And she started dialing.

"Do you remember when you had your tonsils out?" Adele said, turning to Howard. "And Ma was beside herself, and Pop was pacing around, and Aunt Ida and Uncle Louie and Cousin Morty were there too? We were all waiting in the hospital. Everyone. For hours."

No, of course he didn't remember that. He'd been under anesthesia at the time.

"Well, this reminds me of that." And Adele nodded at him and Marilyn, and she stood up. "I'm going for a walk." And she departed, leaving Howard to wonder exactly what her point was.

Thirty-Seven

Lucy

"Her eye?" Lucy was confused. She'd thought Sarah was calling to tell her Diana was having the baby. But no.

"Mom and Dad and Aunt Adele are on their way back to the house now. They all went to the retina specialist with Diana and Philippe. No one wanted to bother you while you were in class, but I figured you were done now, right? So I could tell you. This isn't the day you have the creative writing club, is it?"

"No, that's tomorrow," Lucy said. She was the faculty sponsor for the creative writing club, which consisted of six girls who were all writing dystopian YA fiction and one boy who wrote stories about Fortnite. "But what's going on with her eye?"

"It's always something," Sarah said, and Lucy could hear her sighing. "So she woke up yesterday and she couldn't see out of her good eye, which meant she basically couldn't see at all, but for some strange Diana-like reason she didn't tell Philippe or anyone else, and then she and Philippe were at Dr. Patel's this morning and she told them to go to Dr. Bloomfield's immediately. And then he sent them to this retina person, who said Diana has something called central serous retinopathy."

"Oh my god." Lucy felt a pulse of dread run through her. This sounded serious. Serous. Serious. "What's that? Central what?"

"Some kind of fluid leaking onto her retina, and it happens to be in this one particular spot where she does all her seeing. They said it tends to happen to type A personalities and people who are stressed out all the time. Neither of which would fit Diana, so I don't really understand. But they think it's going to resolve itself eventually."

"They think? Do they know?"

"Not for certain. But the odds are really good that it's going to go away. Of course, they also said it could come back at some point. But the doctor told them by six weeks from now it should be gone."

Lucy heaved a sigh of relief. "Well, that's good. Maybe I'll stop over later and see her."

"Yeah, I'm going over after work, so maybe I'll see you there."

There was a pause.

"So Lucy, how are things going?" Sarah asked. "I mean, how are you doing? I feel as if we haven't really talked for a while, and I know you're going through a lot right now, and..."

"Yeah," Lucy said. They really hadn't. She just hadn't wanted to get into the whole confused mess her life had turned into, with Sarah of all people. Sarah would never let her own life devolve into chaos like this. Diana would, but never Sarah. And even Diana seemed to be pulling things together lately. Maybe she, Lucy, was the new fuckup in the family. Orange is the new black. Forty is the new thirty. Lucy is the new Diana. Great.

"So let's make a plan, okay? We'll get together, just the two of us? As soon as the bar mitzvah's over?"

"Okay," Lucy said. And they hung up.

Lucy pulled out her phone and looked at the latest email missive from Jeff. "Lucy, we really should talk in person. I feel terrible. I was trying to protect you, but I guess it all backfired, didn't it.

Matea feels awful too. This was all my fault, not yours."

Matea feels awful too? Poor Matea. Lucy deleted the email. There was no way she'd answer it.

Her phone buzzed. It was Stacy. Lucy hadn't told Stacy anything that was going on. Not about Jeff and Matea. Not about whatever was going on with Jonah Shapiro. She really couldn't figure out what was happening.

"Dinner one day soon? Let's catch up!" Stacy had texted.

"Okay, great!" Lucy replied. It actually wasn't great, because she wasn't sure what to tell Stacy. She had alluded to the fact that there had been a romantic interlude with a colleague a few months back, but she hadn't wanted to say more, despite Stacy's obvious curiosity.

"Next Wednesday?"

"Sounds good!" She'd have more than a week to figure out what to tell Stacy, then. That would be okay.

And then there was Kathleen, who seemed to have picked up that there was something going on. It was hard to keep anything secret at school.

Kathleen had come into Lucy's classroom a few minutes ago, closed the door, and plopped herself down in a chair.

"So what's going on with you lately?" she had asked.

"Nothing much," Lucy had said. Apart from the fact that her ex-husband had been cheating on her for months, possibly years, with his colleague, and the fact that she had been getting more and more involved with her own—and Kathleen's—colleague. It was too much to get into.

"You seem, well, sort of distracted. There's something going on, isn't there?" Kathleen had said. And she'd given Lucy a look. "Listen, you're both totally great people, and I hope it all works out. And I get it that you don't want to talk about it right now, and that's absolutely fine. But if you do feel like talking, I'm right here." And she'd given Lucy a hug, opened the door, and left.

Lucy was sure Kathleen wouldn't say anything to anyone else. She was an incredibly loyal friend. But she knew that if Kathleen was starting to pick something up, it was only a short time before other people would, too. And she hated being the subject of gossip. It had been bad enough when everyone found out about her and Jeff splitting up. She'd walk into the teacher's lounge and sense that people had been in the process of discussing her. It felt terrible.

Jonah had said not to worry about it. That people were too wrapped up in their own lives to care that much about what other people were doing. He'd said that when they were postcoitally entwined in her bed at three that morning. He'd been twisting one of her curls around his finger and she had been just sort of admiring him. He was so incredibly good-looking. What did he see in her, anyway?

He'd arrived the previous Saturday evening with the food from Harris Teeter, and she hadn't been in the frame of mind to see him at all, but then he'd been so sweet and so caring, and they'd ended up both sleeping in her bed that night.

"But platonically," he'd said, after they'd eaten some of the salads he'd brought with him and they'd discussed the whole Jeff and Matea issue. "I really, really want to do more, but I still don't feel right about it given how upset you are."

And he'd curled himself around her and they'd both fallen asleep. And then they'd spent the whole day together Sunday, going for a run and then driving to the Billy Goat Trail and hiking around, and talking about school and books and movies—they seemed to share similar tastes--and their families. He was an only child and he'd grown up in New Jersey and then gone to Georgetown and ended up staying in D.C. She tried not to think about what year he'd graduated from Georgetown, and what year he'd gotten his master's, and how when she was in college he would have been in elementary and middle school.

And then Sunday night they'd gone out for dinner at an Indian restaurant near her apartment, and he'd said would it be okay if he stayed over again? And she'd said yes, and then he'd asked if she wanted to come back to his place instead, and she'd said all right, and she'd wondered what a twenty-six-year-old guy's apartment would look like, and would it be a total pit, and maybe he even had a roommate?

But when he opened the door to his apartment, she was impressed. It was a tiny studio, even smaller than hers, in Columbia Heights, but it was really clean and featured tons of books, which she immediately started inspecting, and he actually had more food in his refrigerator than she did. And that night they'd followed the same protocol, and had slept in the same bed more or less platonically. Although it ended up being slightly less platonic than the previous night. And then they'd tried not to smile at each other too much at school on Monday, but it was kind of difficult.

And then last night he'd been back at her apartment, and they'd been in her bed, and they'd been holding onto each other, and he had taken a deep breath and said this was all just too difficult, and he knew it was wrong to actually sleep with her because he knew how upset she was about Jeff and Matea and he didn't want to be taking advantage of her, but he couldn't keep sleeping in the same bed with her and yet not actually sleeping with her because he was just too attracted to her, and what should they do?

And she'd said she didn't know. And she felt as if everything was falling apart again, and she'd turned away from him and buried her head in her pillow, and she couldn't help it but she started crying. And he'd said, oh, my god, Lucy, no, I don't want you to think

I'm rejecting you, that's the last thing I would want to do, and he started kissing her, and she was kissing him back, and then things became decidedly unplatonic, in fact they became as unplatonic as you could possibly get, and it all turned out to be as amazing as it had been three months earlier. And then everything happened again in the middle of the night, and she couldn't remember the last time she'd felt that passionate and emotional-in-a-good-way and alive. And that morning before school he'd been looking at her with this dazed but joyful expression, and she probably was looking at him the same way, and she felt as if she couldn't stop smiling, and he kept smiling every time she looked at him. And she couldn't wait until she'd see him again that night.

And how was she supposed to tell Stacy or Kathleen or Sarah about any of this? Stacy would probably say something about how incredible it was that Lucy was sleeping with this hot younger guy, and Kathleen would probably say something about how fond she was of both Lucy and Jonah but they needed to be careful to avoid being the subject of too much gossip, and Sarah would probably worry that Lucy was going to get hurt again.

Which, of course, Lucy was worried about too. This couldn't really last, could it? And if it did, it probably wouldn't last too long, because what kind of guy Jonah's age would want to be saddled with someone Lucy's age's biological clock issues? Aunt Adele would probably tell her to just enjoy it for now, and not worry about the future. Which was a good approach for Aunt Adele, but Lucy wasn't sure she could manage it. But maybe she could try?

Thirty-eight

Marilyn

Given the situation with Diana's eye, Marilyn had almost forgotten that it was Tuesday and she was supposed to go to Will's soccer game and subtly find out what she could about Mr. Shapiro. She and Howie and Adele had returned from the retina doctor's office, somewhat shaken. At least she and Howie were shaken. Adele seemed fine.

Marilyn had been on the phone with Cat, describing the eye situation, and Cat had been exclaiming in sympathy, and then Howie had interrupted.

"Aren't you supposed to go to Will's soccer game and pick him up?" he asked.

"Oh, of course, how forgetful of me," Marilyn said. And she'd explained the whole thing to Cat, who had asked if she could come along, and Marilyn had said of course.

And she'd left shortly thereafter, having instructed Howie to stop over and make sure Diana was okay, as Philippe was probably leaving for the restaurant soon.

Cat spent most of the drive exclaiming over how Padraig had called her every night since their date, and how they were planning to go out again Friday night, and Marilyn was feeling sort of happy about that, and she was also feeling sort of happy about the temple's interest in her teaching a Jewish-American literature class next fall, but she couldn't stop thinking about Diana's eye. She wondered if this had anything to do with Diana being pregnant in her mid-forties. Everything had gone so well until this point, knock wood. The retina doctor and the obstetrician had both told Diana that although hormonal changes related to her pregnancy might be involved, her age was not a factor. But Marilyn couldn't help worrying.

And before she knew it, she and Cat were pulling up in the parking lot of a middle school further out in Bethesda. She could hear the yelling of adolescent boys, and she and Cat found themselves in front of a soccer field.

"Where's Will?" Cat asked, peering out at the boys who were running up and down, passing the ball back and forth.

Marilyn squinted at the field. Dr. Bloomfield had said she needed a cataract operation, but she'd been postponing until after the bar mitzvah. Was that Will? She just couldn't tell. "I think he's over there," she said, gesturing vaguely toward the field. Let it not be said that she couldn't recognize her own grandchild.

"So is that Mr. Shapiro?" Cat asked. "The young guy over there, across the field?"

Marilyn could see a distant figure on the opposite sidelines. "Good pass, Will!" the figure was shouting. So Will was out there somewhere. "Mohammed, go to the left! Will Z., pass the ball!"

"Oh my god, he's really cute," Cat said. "That's who Lucy might be involved with? He's much better-looking than Jeff." Marilyn had told Cat her suspicions about Jeff and Matea Barker, and Cat had launched into a rant about Skip and how he'd done the same thing with the woman who ended up being his second wife.

Now, listening to Cat gush about Mr. Shapiro, Marilyn glanced around. As a teacher herself, she knew that Lucy would not appreciate having her personal life bandied about with other interested parties—parents, students, who knows who—in the vicinity.

"Shhhh," she counseled Cat. Fortunately, no one seemed to be within earshot.

"Oh, sorry," Cat whispered. "Is that who Lucy might be involved with?"

"I can't really see him very well from here," Marilyn whispered back. "And I actually have never met him, so I don't know. But Sarah said he had charisma. And it does seem as if he's the coach, so I assume that must be Mr. Shapiro." She cursed her cataracts. Enough with all these eye problems in her family. She really wanted to get a better look at him. "Maybe we should walk around the outside of the field. As if we're taking a stroll. And then we'll casually walk past him."

Cat was game to try it, so the two of them set out around one side of the field. As they got a little closer, Marilyn spotted Will. "There's Will. See?" she told Cat, who nodded.

"Take it up the field!" the coach was shouting to the boys. "Go get it, Will!"

And Marilyn saw the ball fly through the air and into the goal. What had just happened?

"Great goal, Will!" the coach called. "Good job!" She could see Will high-fiving some of his teammates.

"Did he just do something?" Cat inquired. She was not a sports fan.

"He scored a goal!" Marilyn said, feeling proud of her grandson despite her dislike of familial boasting.

They had passed one of the ends of the field by now, and were heading toward the side where Mr. Shapiro was pacing around. Marilyn could see him coming into closer focus, and she was dumbstruck. Mr. Shapiro was a dead ringer for Dick Schwartz, the best-looking boy in her high school class in Flushing, Queens. Except Mr. Shapiro looked somewhat older than Dick Schwartz had looked back then, which of course made sense.

Marilyn had no idea where Dick Schwartz was now, and she hadn't thought about him in decades, but all these memories were suddenly flooding into her head. Dick Schwartz had been going out with Peggy Edelman, and then they'd broken up right before the junior prom, and Dick had asked Marilyn to go to the prom with him, and of course she'd said yes, even though she knew Harold Miller had been planning to ask her, and she and Dick had dated all summer and into the fall, and then he'd dumped her and gotten back together with Peggy Edelman. She had been devastated. Would Mr. Shapiro do something like that to Lucy? That would be awful. Especially on top of the Jeff situation.

She recounted the story to Cat, who listened in fascination. "But just because he has some vague resemblance to someone who treated you badly almost sixty years ago doesn't mean he has the same personality," Cat scolded her. "That's magical thinking."

Still, these very good-looking guys could be too cocky, Marilyn thought. Too sure of themselves. Not that Howie wasn't good-looking. Of course he was. She'd been completely smitten that first night, when they'd eaten those omelettes in that diner and he'd gone on about his crazy sister. But men who looked like Dick Schwartz and Mr. Shapiro were, she had to admit, in another league entirely.

They had passed Mr. Shapiro and were making their way toward the other end, and she saw the ref blow his whistle and apparently the game was over.

"Hi, Grandma," Will said, waving to her. He and his teammates high-fived their opponents and ran off the field toward Mr.

Shapiro.

Marilyn waved back. She wondered if they'd won.

"Who won?" Cat asked, as the two of them continued marching around the field and back toward their original position closer to the parking lot.

Marilyn shrugged. "I don't know," she said.

"So I really want to talk to Adele again before Friday night," Cat said. "I want to get her sense of what I should wear. Maybe you and Adele can stop by and look at a couple of things I was considering."

"Okay," Marilyn said. Adele really had been helpful, she had to admit. And then she realized she probably should call Diana and check in. Maybe Howie had forgotten to go over there. "Excuse me for a second," she told Cat, and she pulled her phone out.

"Diana?"

"Hi, Mom." Diana sounded tired. As if Marilyn had woken her up.

"Hi, sweetheart. Did I wake you?"

"Yeah," Diana said. "I convinced Philippe to go to the restaurant, and then I convinced Dad and Aunt Adele to go home, and I was getting a little sleep. You know, now that I know what's wrong with my eye, and that it's most likely going to be fine in six weeks, I feel mostly okay. But then...but then..." and Marilyn could hear Diana start to cry. Which didn't happen often.

"What is it, sweet girl?" She wished she were there to hug Diana and make everything all right. The way she had tried to do when the girls were little. But it was more difficult now.

"It's just that I won't be able to see the baby all that well at first, and I'll miss these really special moments because of this stupid eye thing, and..." She sobbed some more.

"It's all going to be okay," Marilyn said. "Your eye's going to get better, and we'll take lots of pictures, and…"

She heard Diana blowing her nose. "I know, Mom. It's okay. It's just that lately I'm so hormonal, and I'm crying all the time, and I'm kind of ready for this baby to come out."

"I know, sweetie, I know," Marilyn said. "I love you."

"I love you too, Mom. Now I'm going to go back to sleep," Diana said, and she hung up.

Marilyn was almost crying herself. She told Cat what Diana had said.

"Oh, poor Diana," Cat said, shaking her head. "But at least it's all going to be okay."

And Marilyn nodded, and she pulled a tissue out of her bag and blew her nose.

"What's wrong, Grandma?" It was Will, toting a large gym bag and a bottle of water. He looked all sweaty. He reached over and gave her a hug. She hugged him back. He smelled of adolescent boy. She was used to that, with Max. It had been different with the girls. "Are you okay? You know, we won the game, four-two. I scored a goal."

"I'm fine, Will, sweetie," Marilyn said. "And that's wonderful. Look who's here!" And she gestured toward Cat.

"Will, we saw the goal," Cat said enthusiastically. "Congratulations! And I can't wait to come to your bar mitzvah. Only a few days now."

"Yeah," Will said, smiling at her. "Thanks, Cat. Hey, Mr. Shapiro!" Will had turned and was beckoning toward his coach, who had been talking to another boy and his mother.

Mr. Shapiro made his way over. He was carrying a bag full of soccer balls and other equipment, which he plopped down on the ground. "Will. Great game," he said.

"Thanks," Will said. "You want to meet my grandma and her

friend?" And he pointed at Marilyn and Cat.

Marilyn smiled at Mr. Shapiro, observing him closely. She could see him blush a little and try to smile back. He really did look just like Dick Schwartz. It was uncanny. The same dark curly hair and dark eyes and ridiculously long eyelashes and expressive face. "Hi, I'm Marilyn Pinsky. It's so nice to meet you," Marilyn said, extending her hand. "And this is my friend Catalina Thompson."

Mr. Shapiro shook hands with both of them.

"You know, Mr. Shapiro was my English teacher last year," Will piped up. "He's like the best teacher in the school, well, besides Lucy, of course." And he beamed at Mr. Shapiro and then at Marilyn.

Mr. Shapiro had turned bright red. He looked down and scuffed at the ground with his running shoe. Then he seemed to compose himself and he mumbled something about how Lucy was definitely the best teacher, by far. "Well, gotta run now," he said, and picked up the bag with the soccer balls. "Bye, Will. Nice to meet you both." And he left.

Well. Something was definitely going on. She'd need to discuss this further with Cat at some point when Will wasn't around. Mr. Shapiro really did seem very nice, though. And not all puffed up and pleased with himself the way Dick Schwartz had been much of the time. She hoped for Lucy's sake that whatever was going on would make her youngest daughter happy. She deserved only the best, not another cheating scoundrel like Jeff.

Thirty-Nine

Will

Part of Will couldn't believe he was actually thirteen. And part of him thought it was no big deal, because most of his friends had already turned thirteen and also because the bar mitzvah was the actual big deal. And it was only three days away.

He had to admit that the whole thing was starting to stress him out. Everyone was asking him about it, and talking about it, and he knew that all these people like Cousin Morty and Lucretia and a bunch of family friends were flying in for it, and he'd have to stand there in front of all of them and not mess up.

He actually wasn't all that hungry, even though the food at Philippe's restaurant was incredible and he'd asked to come here for dinner, and he'd ordered his absolute favorite, this chicken thing Philippe made that was amazing, and it was sitting there on his plate.

"Are you okay, Will?" his mom asked from across the table. She looked worried, as usual. He wondered if after this weekend she'd calm down a little. Had she been this stressed out before Max's bar mitzvah? He hadn't really been paying attention at the time. He'd have to check with Max later.

"Yeah, I'm fine," he said, and he took a big bite of the chicken. It actually was so good, he was starting to get his appetite back.

Maybe there was some way to just not think about the bar mitzvah for a while. He took another bite.

"...just talking to the moving company," Aunt Adele was saying. She was sitting on one side of Will, with Vilma on his other side. "It costs a fortune to ship everything from Hawaii, and I suppose I'll be staying with you for a while more until everything gets here." She looked at his grandparents and raised her eyebrows.

Will noticed his grandma taking a deep breath, and Gramps taking Grandma's hand and squeezing it.

"We'll work it out," Gramps said, and he nodded at both Grandma and Aunt Adele.

Grandma was looking all skeptical, but then she switched her gaze to Will and smiled at him from her seat diagonally across from him. "Let's just focus on how proud we are of Will," she said. "It's his thirteenth birthday, and he's about to have his bar mitzvah, and we're all delighted to be here, together, at Philippe's wonderful restaurant on this very special occasion." And she started going on about what a great kid Will was, and some more sort of embarrassing stuff, and Will felt really happy even though he thought it was all too much. But it was kind of a tradition for Grandma to make a speech on people's birthdays, so overall he was fine with it.

"And Gramps was at home with Max, and I rushed over to the hospital with your mom, and I was right there in the room when you were born," Grandma said, beaming at him. "Such a beautiful baby. And so good."

This was part of the family tradition too, talking about the day the birthday person was born. Will had been thinking maybe Diana would have the baby on his birthday, and he thought that might be cool, to share a birthday with his little cousin, but now it seemed unlikely, because Diana was right there at the table with everyone else. He and the baby could each have their own separate birthday, which probably was better anyway. Maybe the baby would be one of those, like, possessive little kids who didn't want to share.

"...in labor for eighteen hours," his mom was saying. "You always forget that part, Mom." She was laughing, which was a relief. His mom needed to chill more often. "But it was more than worth it in the end." And she gave Will a huge smile and reached her hand across the table and squeezed his hand. "Happy birthday, sweetheart. I love you."

"Thanks, Mom," he said. "I love you too."

"And I was displaced," Max contributed from down at the other end of the table. "Completely forgotten about." And he grinned at Will. "It's good to have a fellow teenager in the house."

Will grinned back. And then he listened as Vilma and Aunt Adele and Gramps all said nice things about him, and Gramps talked how he was babysitting Max and watching all these *Sesame Street* videos the day Will was born, and everyone was laughing.

"My turn," Lucy said, tapping on her glass. "I was away at school, and I got the call that Sarah was going into labor, and I was running around shouting to everyone that I was about to be an aunt again." She paused for a second. "Here's to the coolest kid in the whole seventh grade. And I should know. No one else even comes close." Lucy looked really happy, Will thought. He'd noticed her and Mr. Shapiro talking in the hallway outside their classrooms as he'd passed by between classes, and she was actually being nice to Mr. Shapiro for once.

"I was playing the Stage Manager in *Our Town* at this theater near Baltimore, and Dad called and said Sarah and Mom had gone to the hospital, and I was so excited I almost forgot all my lines that night," Diana said. She stopped, and took a deep breath. "I just want to say that I'm so happy the baby will have Will and

Max around. The way everybody's always been there for me." She seemed like she was about to cry, for some reason. Maybe that's what happened to people when they were about to have babies. They got all emotional. "Happy birthday, Will. I love you. And Max, I love you too." And she blew him and Max each a kiss.

Will saw Grandma also looking like she was about to cry. What was going on with everyone lately, anyway?

And then Philippe showed up in his chef's outfit, and all the other people in the restaurant were staring at him and saying all this stuff about what an amazing chef he was, and Will was impressed, because Philippe was just, like, Will's uncle, but apparently he was kind of famous.

"You're just in time for the toasts and reminiscences," Diana said, as he leaned over and kissed her, and then he went around the table hugging everyone, and everyone was saying how great the food was, and then he got to Will, and he stopped and put one hand on Will's shoulder.

"When I met Diana, and I began to know the entire family, and I realized that marrying Diana meant marrying this entire family"—everyone started laughing, even Will, although he wasn't totally sure what Philippe meant—"I was very content because I love you all very much. And I am glad the baby will be part of this wonderful family, and especially the two cousins, Will and Max." And he seemed sort of as if he might cry, too, and he gave Will a huge hug, and wished him a happy birthday, and went over and hugged Max again too, and then he said he needed to get back into the kitchen to make sure the birthday cake was ready. And he left.

And then everyone started talking, and Will took the opportunity to glance down at his phone. He'd been getting birthday texts all day. There were a few new ones. One was from Marco, of an out-of-tune marching band playing Happy Birthday. Another one was from Will Z., of a bunch of cartoon baseball players singing Happy Birthday. And then there was one from Katelin C., of a cartoon basset hound singing Happy Birthday. He must have told her about Phoebe at some point. Cool. He replied to them all and put the phone away. And he was starting to feel like being thirteen would actually be okay, and he realized he still had some of the chicken left on his plate, and why waste it? It was way too good.

Forty

Sarah

Sarah had left work early, right after lunch, because she had so much to do with the bar mitzvah only two days away. She'd barely slept the night before. She'd had a vivid dream that she had somehow turned into Grandma Pinsky, and she was in the house in West Orange overcome with despair over Aunt Adele's departure for the circus, and then that turned into another dream that she was sitting up on the bimah at Will's bar mitzvah wearing her pajamas, and then she woke up shaking. Vilma had tried to calm her down but she still hadn't been able to go back to sleep.

So she was in the car heading home to take care of some last-minute bar mitzvah things, yawning every so often, when her phone started ringing. Damn. She'd need to get it because it might be someone from work, or it might be something about Diana and the baby, or it might be something relating to the bar mitzvah.

So she pulled over and saw that it was her mother.

"Hi, Mom, is it the baby?"

"No, no, it's not the baby," her mother said. "Do you have a minute?"

"I'm still in the car," Sarah said. "Can I call you back in a few minutes once I get home?"

And her mother agreed, and Sarah had a feeling she knew what her mother was calling about. It was what her mother had started referring to as "the Vilma situation." Sarah had done her best to tell her mother that there was no Vilma situation, that things between her and Vilma were fine, but her mother didn't seem to believe her. Ever since Lucy's divorce, her mother had been in paroxysms of worry over the states of Sarah's and Diana's marriages.

The other day on the phone, her mother had gone into these suspicions she had that Jeff had been cheating on Lucy with Matea from his office for a long time, and while Sarah actually thought her mother might be right, her mother took it one step further.

"That Lillian at the restaurant, I mean, there Philippe is, working with her almost every day, and who knows what might be going on, and there are all these things in the news about chefs, and..."

Sarah had cut her off. "First of all, Lillian's a lesbian, and second of all, just because Jeff might have been cheating, that doesn't mean Philippe is, okay? People can work together and have meetings together and spend time together without being tempted into things they shouldn't be, all right?"

And that had shut her mother up for a while. But later that day, she'd called and started asking Sarah why Vilma couldn't just move back for good now, and why were the two of them never in the same city, and then Sarah had lost it and had yelled at her mother, which she hardly ever did because it always upset both of them too much. And then she'd spent the next half hour apologizing. And then her mother had apologized too, and they'd both decided they were way too stressed out and needed to calm down.

So it was a pleasant surprise when, after arriving home, she called back and her mother didn't say anything about Vilma. Instead, she said Diana had just told her she'd had a short story accepted for publication in what sounded like a very prestigious literary journal. "It's supposed to appear in their fall issue," her mother said. "I'm so proud of her. You know, I remember when Diana was little, and she'd ask me to buy her those black and white notebooks and she'd write novels in them. Do you remember that?"

Sarah thought back. And yes, she had an image of Diana sitting on the floor of her room scribbling away, and protectively shielding the notebook with her arm when Sarah came anywhere near her. She wondered why Diana had stopped writing for all those years. Or had she? Maybe she'd kept on with it and just not told anyone.

And after she finished the call with her mother, and fielded a bunch of calls and emails and texts from people with last-minute issues relating to the bar mitzvah, her thoughts returned to Diana. She'd been kind of scatterbrained as a kid, except when it came to her writing and her acting, but something had started shifting when Diana entered middle school.

Before that, Diana had followed her around like a small pet. She'd wanted to wear matching outfits with Sarah, and tag along with Sarah and her friends, and read the same books Sarah was reading. She'd ask Sarah for help with her homework, and seek Sarah's advice when someone was mean to her at school.

But then, gradually, she'd started withdrawing. Avoiding Sarah. And when they did interact, it often resulted in arguments.

"I'm not like you, okay?" Diana had screamed at her one day. It was right after Diana's bat mitzvah, and Sarah had been telling Diana about what she had done with her own bat mitzvah money--put most of it in the bank--and suggesting that maybe Diana could do something similar. "I can't be like you, and I don't want to be like you."

And Sarah had tried to explain that she didn't want Diana to be like her, and that Diana was great the way she was, and why couldn't they ever get along any more? But it was like talking to a wall. A dissatisfied, angry wall.

And by the time they were in high school, they lived in two separate worlds. A memory flashed into her mind. Her parents had gone to an all-day gathering at the weekend cabin of another partner in her dad's firm. It had been a late spring Saturday, right before Sarah's high school graduation, and her parents had left her and Diana in charge of Lucy. But she and her parents all knew Diana was pretty useless as a babysitter and Sarah would really be doing everything.

Sarah had set up the sprinkler in the back yard because it was a hot day, and Lucy was in her pink flowered bathing suit running around, and Sarah was supervising her, and Diana was lying on an outdoor chair in a bikini top and really short cutoff jeans shorts, and she had brought the kitchen phone, on its long cord, outside and was whispering to someone. Probably one of her various boyfriends. She slathered on some more baby oil as she talked.

Sarah loved playing with Lucy, but sometimes she wondered. Why couldn't she be the one on the phone talking to someone and slathering baby oil all over herself as she lounged in a chair? Why couldn't Diana be the one watching Lucy for once? But that would pretty much never happen, and someone had to watch Lucy, and that someone was her, Sarah.

And then this guy showed up, Ricky Fulton, who was a senior like Sarah but he and Sarah had little to do with each other. Ricky Fulton was on the football team and hung out with an entirely different group of people. But there he was in their back yard, having come around through the side gate, and Diana ran over to him and they started making out, right there, with Lucy watching in fascination and giggling.

And then Ricky Fulton seemed to notice Sarah and Lucy's presence, and he muttered, "Hey, Sarah," and said hi to Lucy, and then Diana pulled him over to the chair, and somehow they both fit into it, and didn't Diana have any common sense at all? It just wasn't appropriate to be engaging in quite such passionate displays of affection in front of a first grader. Sarah knew Diana was sleeping with Ricky, and had slept with a few other guys too, and she'd tried to warn her that maybe it was too much and she was only a sophomore and wasn't it better to wait? Or at least sleep with only one guy per month rather than two or three? And was she on the pill and was she making sure the guys were using condoms because she didn't want to end up pregnant or with some sexually transmitted disease? And Diana had snapped at her that of course she was, why did everyone think she was so stupid, and that Sarah was just jealous because she hadn't slept with anyone yet. Which of course was true. But Sarah hadn't found anyone she wanted to sleep with. Nothing seemed quite right.

So Sarah had brought Lucy inside, after shutting off the hose, and they'd made up various games with Lucy's stuffed animals, and then they'd gone for a bike ride in the neighborhood, Lucy careening around on her training wheels, and then they'd baked chocolate chip cookies. And by then their parents were home, and Diana had disappeared somewhere with Ricky, maybe to his house, and that had been that. Sarah had gone up to her room and finished her homework.

But throughout this whole time, Sarah's parents had been deputizing her, as their emissary into the teenage world, to help keep an eye on Diana. To help her make it through her classes without failing. To help her make better choices. Sarah sensed that this had something to do with her long-absent Aunt Adele. Aunt Adele had run off, possibly to join a circus, and Sarah was sure her parents thought Diana would do the same thing if not properly tended to. In fact, Sarah thought her parents had probably had Lucy to provide another sibling for Sarah in case Diana departed.

Sarah had tried to help out when it came to Diana, because Diana was totally circus and Sarah didn't want her to run off, but it often felt as if the whole effort was in vain. Diana had been picked up several times for shoplifting, and she'd participated in some kind of streaking incident after which she'd almost been expelled, and on and on.

So it had been a relief for Sarah to escape up to Harvard. But then Diana had somehow gotten into Emerson, and Sarah had been drawn right back into it. Diana had taken to calling Sarah at all hours with tales of woe about these awful relationships she seemed to be prone to, and asking Sarah to come over right then and there because she needed someone to talk to, and while Sarah was thrilled that her sister was confiding in her again, she was tired of being awakened, heart pounding, by these three a.m. phone calls.

And Sarah had the sense over the years that maybe there were even more stories that Diana wasn't telling her, stories that Diana was embarrassed to tell her.

But then, about five years ago, after decades of falling for the absolutely wrong guys, Diana had met Philippe, who was perfect for her. And she seemed as happy with Philippe as Sarah was with Vilma, which was saying a lot.

And here they all were, in their forties, and Diana was about to have a baby, and she'd just had another story published in a literary magazine, and she was doing well with the ghostwriting, and was still acting a little when she found the right parts, and it suddenly hit Sarah that maybe she didn't need to worry so much about Diana. Maybe Diana actually was doing okay. Maybe, as Aunt Adele might say, she, Sarah, could throw up her hands. Not saying to hell with Diana, but letting Diana go a little bit. Not hovering so much. Maybe Diana wouldn't fall apart after all

Forty-One

Max

Living in a house with two moms was great most of the time, but sometimes Max needed male advice. Usually he went to his grandfather, but this time he kind of doubted Gramps would be the best person to talk to. The thing is, he thought Isla was mad at him, and he had absolutely no idea why.

He'd been allowed back on nighttime walk duty with Phoebe, and they'd been walking around in the park with Isla and Shirley last night, and he and Isla had kind of been holding hands, which felt really good, and he was going through his usual worrying about whether she wanted him to do more but not getting up the nerve to try. Although in his mind he was trying all kinds of things.

Instead, he'd started talking to her about how amazing the lesson with her dad had been. Because Logan MacLeish was officially the absolute coolest person Max had ever met in his entire life. He'd given Max all these suggestions and taught him these new approaches to jazz guitar, and Max had been practicing even more than ever, if that was possible. He'd dug through these boxes of old clothes no one ever wore that were down in the basement, and he'd turned up this leather jacket that was kind of similar to Logan MacLeish's leather jacket, and even though the weather was getting all warm out, he'd started wearing it everywhere. His mom said she thought it had belonged to this old boyfriend of Diana's who had given it to Diana, and somehow it had ended up at Max's house because Diana didn't want to be reminded of him but it was a really nice jacket so she didn't want to completely give it away.

So anyway, after a while of Max talking about how cool her dad was, Isla had seemed a little mad, and she'd said she needed to get home and finish her French homework, and then she'd left. And he'd messaged her a bunch of times, and she'd sent these totally monosyllabic messages back, and then on the bus this morning she'd seemed all withdrawn, and she had play rehearsals after school so she hadn't taken the bus home with him.

And after walking Phoebe once he got home from school, he decided to text Philippe. Philippe probably would be the best person to consult about this whole thing with Isla. Gramps's experiences were from more than half a century ago, from before he'd met Grandma, so anything he'd say on the whole subject would be kind of useless because Max was sure people had acted completely differently back then. But Philippe, Max knew, had more relevant experience. He'd been married in his twenties, back in Belgium, but that hadn't worked out, and then he'd come to New York like fifteen years ago and hadn't met Diana until about five years ago when he'd moved to D.C., so he must have some idea about why Isla was acting like this.

Of course, Max could have consulted with his friends, but nothing more had transpired with Seb since their interaction the other day, and he barely ever had a chance to talk to Lucas, and Facetiming with Ernesto about this kind of thing could be totally awkward.

So Philippe was the best option. Having Philippe as his uncle was really great. Jeff, their former uncle, had never seemed to like him and Will all that much. Jeff and Lucy would come to family dinners and Lucy would be all about spending time with him and Will and hanging out with them, but Jeff barely talked to them. It seemed like a chore for him to have a conversation with them, like they were totally boring or something. So he and Will didn't really miss Jeff, to tell the truth.

It had been an entirely different story once Philippe appeared on the scene. Max had an idea, from overhearing conversations between his mom and Vilma that he probably wasn't supposed to hear, that Diana's boyfriends were awful. He and Will didn't get to meet any of them, even though Diana was around all the time, taking them to plays at Adventure Theater and Imagination Stage, and, when they got older, to Arena Stage and other places.

So it was a surprise when Diana showed up with this guy to take him and Will, who were about ten and eight at the time, to a Marx Brothers play. The guy, who turned out to be Philippe, was on the thin side and had straight brown-with-a-little-gray-in-it hair that he kept pushing off his forehead, and this cool accent, and Diana said he was a chef, which had surprised Max because he thought chefs were probably kind of overweight from eating all the time. And Philippe was incredibly nice, and he seemed, unlike Jeff, to really enjoy being with Max and Will, and Max was confused as to why his mom said Diana's boyfriends were awful because Philippe was, like, the opposite of awful.

And Philippe had always been encouraging to Max about his music, and told him he'd been the same way when he was younger, practicing new recipes the way Max was practicing the guitar, and so Max had been incredibly excited when it turned out Diana and Philippe were getting married. It had been a couple of years ago, a few months after Max's bar mitzvah, and he and Will got to be the two groomsmen and wear tuxedos. It was the second wedding Max had been to, the first one being his mom and Vilma's, back when

Max was in fifth grade, which had been totally cool. He and Will had been the attendants in that wedding, too.

So he texted Philippe, and Philippe actually texted right back and said why didn't Max come down to the restaurant and they could talk a little bit before everything got really crazy again. So Max figured that would be okay—his mom and Vilma were over at the temple checking on some stuff for the bar mitzvah—so he took the Metro down and walked over to the restaurant.

And Philippe came out of the kitchen and introduced Max to some of the other people who worked there, and then he suggested that Max sit down with him at one of the tables. The whole place was empty except for the staff, who were frantically rushing around, and it was kind of bizarre because Max had only ever been there when it was totally bustling with customers.

"So what is on your mind?" Philippe asked, leaning back in his chair and smiling at Max. "Everything is all right?"

"Like, some things are great," Max said, thinking of Logan MacLeish. "But then there's this girl."

"Ah, yes," Philippe said. "A girl." And he seemed to go off into one of those absent-minded states he got into, and Max figured he was probably remembering being fifteen and being in a similar situation.

"And I think she's mad at me," Max said, and he described the entire thing, the guitar lessons, and walking the dogs, and how all they'd done is hold hands and maybe he should have done more but he'd been too nervous, and how he'd talked a lot to Isla about how great her dad was. "So what did I do to make her mad?" he asked. "Was it that I didn't do more than just hold hands?"

Philippe was frowning. "And you talked a lot about her dad and how great he is?" he said.

"Well, yeah," Max said. "Her dad's totally cool. I mean, he's

Logan MacLeish."

"But did you say anything about how great this girl, Isla, is? Or just about her dad?"

Max tried to remember. He must have said some things about how great Isla was, right? He thought about how great she was all the time. And she was always saying all these, like, complimentary things to Max that kind of made him feel embarrassed. Like they couldn't really be true and she couldn't really be thinking stuff like that about him. So he must have said similar things back. But he couldn't remember anything. Oh no. What if Isla thought he was just hanging out with her to get to know her dad? When actually it was just an incredible coincidence that he had met Isla and really liked her and then her dad turned out to be Logan MacLeish?

He put his head in his hands. What an idiot he was.

"So this could be the problem?"

Max reluctantly lifted his head up. "Yeah," he said. "So what do I do?"

"This happened to me once with the daughter of a chef," Philippe said. "Seriously, the same thing." And he got all absent-minded again, and Max figured it would take a while before Philippe focused back on Max's dilemma. He checked his phone to see if Isla had texted, but she hadn't. So he started reading an article about jazz guitarists that Logan MacLeish had suggested he look at.

"You must talk to her at once and apologize," Philippe eventually said. Max looked up, startled. "And some desserts will help. I will have someone wrap up a box of them and you can bring them over to her house. But you should not feel so bad about this. You are far from an idiot, Max." And he smiled at Max. "It is true what I said last night, that I am delighted the baby will have you and Will to look up to."

And Max was starting to feel a little more optimistic about things, like maybe he could explain everything to Isla in a satisfactory manner and she'd be less mad at him.

But then something else popped into his head, something troubling: Once Diana and Philippe had the baby, would Philippe still have time to talk like this with Max? Or would he just be all busy with his own kid?

"And I will always be there for you, Max, even once this baby has finally arrived," Philippe said, as if he was reading Max's mind. He got up and so did Max, and Philippe slung an arm around Max's shoulders and started moving toward the kitchen. "And now you must come back to the kitchen with me and we will get some desserts for you to take to Isla, and some for you to bring home for you and Will, and then I must get back to work. But all will be well, do not worry."

And as Max headed back to the Metro with his desserts, he started practicing what he'd say to Isla. Maybe by the time he returned to his neighborhood, he'd finally get it right.

Forty-Two

Marilyn

Marilyn hadn't meant to invite Adele along to the hairdresser's, but Adele had been making noises about how she'd been here for three weeks and her hair looked terrible and she should make an appointment at the beauty parlor.

And Marilyn had made the mistake of mentioning that she was getting her hair cut that afternoon in preparation for the bar mitzvah, and Adele had somehow ended up joining her. Marilyn was in her usual chair, with Trish, her usual hairdresser, and Adele was in the chair right next to her, with Ming, one of Trish's colleagues.

Trish was going on about her son, who was in his eighth year of college, and how she wondered if he'd ever graduate, and how she wanted to kick him out of the house but she just couldn't bring herself to do it, and how his girlfriend and their baby had also moved in, and how Trish and her husband were beside themselves. The girlfriend had a degree from the University of Maryland and an excellent job as a paralegal, and Trish had no idea why she couldn't get an apartment for herself and Trish's grandson and hopefully Trish's son as well.

Marilyn was half-listening, as she usually did, and trying to boost Trish's spirits by recounting success stories about some of her own former students who had taken years and years to finish college. She was also trying to eavesdrop on the conversation between Adele and Ming, which was quite intriguing.

Adele was telling Ming all about her fourth husband, Rudy, and how devastated she'd been when Rudy died, although Rudy was not the love of her life, and how she just couldn't be alone in Honolulu any more, and how she was getting older and for once in her life was actually feeling kind of lonely.

And Ming asked who had been the love of Adele's life, and Adele said it was her third husband, Herman, and Ming started talking about the love of her own life, and Adele asked how many times Ming had been married, and Ming said only once, but not to the love of her life.

And Adele said, well, she'd been divorced from her first two husbands, and then her second two had died, and here she was, eighty years old.

And Ming had expressed shock that Adele was eighty. "You look seventy at most!" she exclaimed. "And your hair is just beautiful!"

Which annoyed Marilyn, because Ming had never said anything like that to Marilyn on the occasions when Trish had been away and Ming had done Marilyn's hair. Ming was more likely to tell Marilyn that she needed to come in more often because she didn't want her roots showing, did she?

"...my daughter," Trish was saying. "I'm just so proud of her."

And Marilyn felt terrible because she hadn't been listening to Trish at all, and she had no idea what Trish's daughter had done to make Trish so proud.

"That's wonderful!" Marilyn said enthusiastically, hoping Trish would say more.

"I know," Trish said, snipping away at Marilyn's hair.

Oh dear. Now Marilyn would be expected to remember what

Trish's daughter had done that was wonderful, and she had no clue. She knew Trish's daughter was at the top of her high school class, so she assumed it was something to do with college plans.

"Yes, I'm staying with my brother," Adele was saying to Ming.

And who else are you staying with? Marilyn wanted to say, but she didn't. She was feeling somewhat sorry for Adele after hearing her admit that she was lonely in Honolulu. It was hardly surprising, but sad nonetheless. She had thought Adele must be running away from something in Hawaii, and now she had an answer. Loneliness.

"You look great," Trish was saying, pulling the cape off from around Marilyn's shoulders. "See?"

Marilyn surveyed herself. Definitely an improvement from her pre-haircut appearance. "Thanks, Trish. You do such a good job."

Trish smiled. "Awww, thanks. And congratulations on the bar mitzvah, and send my love to Will. I remember when he was just a baby. And tell Sarah I'm looking forward to seeing her tomorrow. Maybe I can talk her into another highlighting."

Marilyn nodded. "I hope so."

"We're not quite done here," Ming said, gesturing at Adele, whose hair was in rollers.

So Marilyn paid, and tipped Trish, and went and sat up front to wait for Adele. She pulled out her phone. She needed to check in with Diana.

"Hi Mom. I'm feeling really tired," Diana said. Her voice sounded weak, Marilyn thought. "I was all energetic for a while last week, but now I'm just totally worn out. I've been lying here listening to some audiobooks, since I can't work and I can't read."

Marilyn tried to remember if she had felt really tired right before she gave birth, but it was all a blur in her mind. She wondered what would happen if Diana went into labor before the bar mitzvah. Or during the bar mitzvah. How would they manage if it all happened at once?

"...remember that?" Diana was saying. "At my bat mitzvah?"

"I'm sorry, sweetie," Marilyn said. "My mind was wandering. What did you say?"

"Cousin Morty and Jocelyn. Remember? They got in this huge fight at the Kiddush lunch? And Dad was trying to get them to be quiet, and she screamed at Cousin Morty that she wanted a divorce?"

Marilyn did remember. It was one of the reasons she didn't especially like Cousin Morty. Who behaved like that at their cousin's daughter's bat mitzvah? Lucretia was an improvement over Jocelyn, who had been Cousin Morty's first wife, and Sybilla, his second.

"Let's hope he and Lucretia are getting along," Diana said, and she started laughing.

And Marilyn couldn't help it, and she started laughing too, and the two of them were on the phone in total hysterics, and then Diana said this was all too much for her bladder and she had to get off the phone and she'd talk to Marilyn soon.

And a few minutes later, Adele appeared, and for some reason Marilyn asked her if she wanted to get a cup of coffee at the Starbucks next door, and Adele agreed, and they each got a cappuccino and Marilyn got a couple of biscotti and she and Adele sat down at a table.

And Marilyn decided it was now or never. She'd meant to do this for weeks. She took a deep breath.

"So why were you so rude to me?" she inquired. "Especially at first?"

"Rude?" Adele said, looking surprised. "Was I?"

Marilyn sighed. The woman was impossible. "Yes," Marilyn

said. "You were."

"You know, I imagined Howie as a little boy," Adele said, a thoughtful look on her face. She took a sip of her cappuccino. "Eleven years old, playing baseball and building those Erector sets, and then I saw him at the airport, and I was just overwhelmed."

Marilyn nodded. That was understandable.

"And I suppose when I arrived at your house, I was just unable to process your existence, even though I knew you existed. I was unable to process that Howie was married, and had a family. And thus it was easier to simply ignore you."

Oh.

"And then after a while I decided I actually liked you, so I stopped ignoring you and decided to give you advice instead."

Give you advice instead? Marilyn could feel all these words boiling up inside of her, and she knew she needed to hold her tongue but she just couldn't. "Maybe I go too far in one direction, and I hover over my family too much, but you've gone way overboard in the other direction. You've just run away your whole life. If you want to be part of a family, part of this family, going forward, you have to act like it. And that's my advice to you." She realized she was shaking. Had she really meant to say that? She wasn't sure.

Adele was silent. She took another sip of her cappuccino and twisted her scarf around in her fingers.

Marilyn could hear everyone around her talking and scraping their chairs on the floor and the baristas were calling people's names and it all sounded sort of hollow. Like she was in a vacuum. What had she done? Maybe she should have just kept quiet.

"You're right," Adele finally said. "I've been trying, but I have a long way to go. I think we both do."

And Marilyn nodded. They did. And then something else struck her from their conversation, something Adele had said that had surprised her. "You like me?"

And Adele nodded. "Despite myself." And she smiled at Marilyn. A somewhat wry smile.

And Marilyn smiled back. Despite herself. "Same here," she said, realizing it was true. "You're growing on me." She took a sip of her cappuccino. "Biscotti?" she asked, offering one to Adele.

"Biscotto," Adele said. "Singular. But yes, I'd like that."

So Marilyn, after involuntarily rolling her eyes, handed the cookie over. Biscotto. Who actually called it that? And they sat back in their chairs and dipped their respective biscotto into their cappuccinos and Marilyn felt a sort of contentment seeping into her. She wasn't sure it would last, but it felt good for now.

Forty-Three

Diana

"Monday?" her mother said. Diana could feel her excitement bursting through the phone. "Oh, Diana, how wonderful! Three more days? So I guess you really do have to pack the suitcase now."

"I know," Diana said. She couldn't believe it. Three days from now, all things being equal, the baby would be out in the world. Dr. Patel had told her that morning that she was scheduling Diana for an induction Monday, assuming the baby hadn't made his or her appearance before then. Diana had felt for days that she was more than ready for the baby to be born, but now that she had an actual date, she felt uneasy. What if she just couldn't handle being someone's mother? What if she screwed the whole thing up, just like she'd screwed up so many things over the course of her life? Her own mom and Sarah made it all look sort of easy, but she knew it wasn't. What if the baby acted the way she, Diana, had when she was younger? What would she do? And then there was the fact that she wouldn't be able to see the baby very well, at least not at first. Whenever she thought about that, she started to cry, so she was trying to banish the whole eye thing from her mind.

"You will be incredible," Philippe had said, giving her what seemed, through her impaired vision, like a reassuring smile. "This baby will be so fortunate." He was starting his paternity leave that night—they were going to the temple for the pre-bar mitzvah Shabbat service that evening, and then the bar mitzvah was the next day--but he needed to stop by the restaurant to make sure everything was okay. So he had reluctantly left her in the apartment.

"...induction Monday," she could hear her mom saying now. "No, not her eye, Howie. The baby. The baby." And she could hear conversation in the background. "Your father and Aunt Adele are so excited. They both send their love."

"Do you think everything's going to be okay?" Diana asked her mom.

"Of course, sweetheart. It's going to be more than okay. You'll be such an amazing mother," her mom said.

And Diana had thanked her and they'd talked for a while about other things and once they'd ended the call, the phone rang again. Various friends had been checking in on her, including everyone from the writing group, who were aware she couldn't really read emails and texts given her eye situation. So they were all calling her. Poppy had offered to come and read to Diana, which was thoughtful of her, and Marcia had offered to do any last-minute errands Diana needed, and Gideon had said his kids were eager to babysit, and Nick had given Diana his sister's contact information.

So yesterday, Diana had talked to Nick's sister, Hannah, and to Sarah's co-worker, Monique, both of whom were due in a few months. They seemed really nice, and the three of them had decided to get together for dinner at some point in the near future. Well, the four of them, given that Diana probably would be bringing the baby along. It struck Diana that both Hannah and Monique were like a decade younger than she was. But that was okay. She'd deal with it. She looked like she was still in her thirties. Maybe she just wouldn't tell anyone exactly how old she was. Or maybe she would. It wasn't like having your first baby at forty-something was so unusual any more.

"Diana?"

It was her father. Oh no. She'd never gotten back to him about the bris. She'd talked about it with Philippe, and both of them agreed that if a bris was important to her parents, that it was fine. They'd do it. Assuming the baby was a boy. Diana had had yet another dream last night that it was indeed a boy, so the bris was a strong possibility.

"Hi, Dad."

"Mom told me about Monday. We just can't wait! How are you feeling?"

Her dad sounded just as excited as her mom had.

"Oh, fine, fine."

"I'm heading to the airport soon with Aunt Adele to pick up Stuart and Clea and Bobby and Andrea and Cousin Morty and Lucretia."

"Can all of you fit into the Avalon?" Diana pictured everyone squeezing in and then bursting out once they got back to her parents' house. Sort of like a clown car at the circus. Which, of course, was appropriate, given Aunt Adele.

"No, Vilma's coming too, with the van."

"Great," she said. "So we've decided we're going to have a bris. If it's a boy, of course."

She could hear her father sighing with relief. "Oh, good," he said. "Wonderful. I'll let your mother know. What?" A pause. "A bris. Yes. She says they're going to do it. Oh." Another pause. "I need to leave now for the airport. But we're all very excited."

And as soon as she'd gotten off the phone with her father, it rang again, and it was Philippe checking in, and after that she decided to lie down on the sofa. It had been in her mom's parents' living room. She remembered visiting them in Flushing when she was little, and they'd give her and Sarah books and paper dolls and all this other stuff every time they'd see them. And she'd lie down on this same sofa and read. Not that she could read right now, of course, and she'd never been a big fan of audiobooks. She tended to get distracted and miss part of the plot.

Perhaps she should take Poppy up on her offer to read to her. Yesterday on the phone, Poppy had discussed this guy, Ivan, who'd always been into her, and now that Pietro was out of the picture, she was wondering what to do about Ivan, and he was great but was too into drugs and drank too much. And Diana had said that sounded like a lot of her own ex-boyfriends, and maybe getting involved with Ivan wasn't the best idea.

Now, lying on the sofa, Diana reflected on those exes. Zeke, who'd been arrested and actually served time for drug dealing. The two of them had been off and on for years. And Corbin, who had been involved in what turned out to be some kind of financial swindle and had almost gone to jail too. And various other guys with various other issues. She'd been almost thirty-nine when it had clicked in. This wasn't how she wanted to spend her life. She deserved better. She'd awakened one Sunday morning in the bed of a guy named Darren, whom she'd met at a party the previous night, and she thought things had gone well, but then his phone had rung and it emerged that it was his wife—out of town for the weekend—calling, and Diana had stormed out of the apartment, more furious with herself than with Darren. Enough was enough. She'd recently finished her first ghostwriting project, for an actor friend, and everyone thought it was amazing, and various other actors had asked if she'd work with them, and she'd started to feel a little better about herself.

And then a month or so later, she'd been at another party, mostly actors but other people too, and she'd found herself talking to this really cute guy who seemed a little shy. Not her usual life-of-the-party type. He'd just moved to D.C. from New York, and the next week he'd be starting work as the chef at a French restaurant downtown, and he had this totally sexy accent and when he smiled at something she was saying about the first time she'd tried escargots, she felt something turn over inside of her. And, she'd ascertained, he was single. Divorced. Unencumbered. And normally she'd have ended up in bed with him that night--she got the sense he liked her--but instead she'd asked if he might want to go to a play with her, one that a couple of her friends were in, and he'd said yes, but he'd be working long hours starting two days from now, and so they'd started a friendship with the promise of more, and they'd gone for a lot of morning walks and breakfasts and very late-night dinners, and when they finally did end up in bed together, weeks later, she felt a sense of contentment she'd never experienced before. Contentment combined with passion, of course.

And now the phone was ringing again, breaking into her reverie, and it was Sarah, and she said their mother had told her about the induction, and she reminded Diana that she, Sarah, had been induced with Max, and how was Diana feeling, and Diana had asked her a bunch of questions about Max's birth, and then asked her how things were going with the bar mitzvah, and Sarah said there were still a few things to work out and a few people had cancelled at the last minute but overall she thought it was under control.

And once Diana had hung up with Sarah, the phone rang once more, and this time it was Lucy, who was on a break between classes and had heard about the induction, and Diana wanted to ask Lucy about Jonah Shapiro and how things were going but she knew she couldn't ask her that while Lucy was at school.

Lucy sounded a lot better than she had a few days earlier, Diana thought once the call had ended and Lucy had returned to class. She wondered if Jonah Shapiro was the reason for Lucy's improved mood, or if it was something else. And she felt that annoying guilt emerge again, about her own role in Lucy's current situation. If only she hadn't introduced Lucy and Jeff. And then there had been a phone call with Lucy, right after she and Jeff had ended things, when it had come out that one of the precipitating factors was Diana's IVF, which only made Diana feel worse. Of course, now that Jeff's heinous cheating had come to light, the child issue was probably a red herring anyway.

And Aunt Adele's advice floated into Diana's head, as the baby moved around and kicked her. Maybe she didn't need to feel so bad about her role in Lucy's divorce. Maybe Lucy would be okay, with or without Jonah Shapiro.

Forty-Four

Howard

It had become a second home, this baggage claim area at the airport. Howard and Adele were seated on the now-familiar black vinyl chairs, awaiting the onslaught of bar mitzvah guests. Marilyn was back home organizing the house. Of course, the guests were staying at the Embassy Suites, not at the house. But she'd told Howard that after the service that night—where Will would help light the candles—the guests would all come back for a late dinner. She'd bought a bunch of cold cuts and salads, nothing fancy.

"I'm just so excited!" Adele exclaimed from her seat next to Howard. "Seeing Bobby and Stuart, and being here for the bar mitzvah, and the baby coming Monday. This is just wonderful." And she leaned over and hugged him. "Howie, I'm so grateful to you. Letting me back in after all this time. Being a part of this really delightful family you've created."

And Howard felt tears spring to his eyes as he hugged her back. "I'm glad you're here," he managed to say.

And then he heard a loud voice booming into his ear, and there were Bobby Slotnick and Andrea, and Bobby was hugging Adele, and introducing her to Andrea, and the three of them were chatting away, and there was Vilma tapping Howard on the arm.

"I'm here! The traffic was terrible."

Howard heaved a sigh of relief. He'd been worried that somehow he'd have to squeeze eight people into the Avalon, and all those suitcases, and of course he could have put some of them, both people and suitcases, into a taxi. But he was glad Vilma had appeared. At the airport, and in general. He hadn't expected, with three daughters, to end up with a daughter-in-law, but he and Marilyn loved Vilma. Even though Marilyn had worked herself into a frenzy over this possible Vilma situation.

Vilma pulled Howard over to the side, away from the others. "Listen, Howard, I just wanted to reassure you about something." And she told him she and Sarah were fine, and that she'd be back for good from Finland in a couple of months, and she had a sense he and Marilyn was worried, but there was nothing to worry about.

And Howard had embraced her and exhaled. Another sigh of relief. And then the New York flight arrived, and there were Cousin Morty and Lucretia and Stuart and Clea, and they'd all piled into the Avalon and the van with the suitcases, and once the guests had been dropped off at the hotel, Vilma and Howard and Adele returned to their respective homes.

The house looked incredible. Marilyn had cleared all Adele's shoes and scarves out of the way, and she'd moved most of the piles of newspapers and magazines that always seemed to crop up into Howard's office, and the dining room table was set. And he complimented Marilyn on how nice everything looked, and she seemed pleased.

And before he knew it, they were all dressed and ready to go to the temple for the Friday night service—the main event was the following morning—and when they arrived at the temple, there everyone was, including the man of the hour, Will, looking spiffy in a blue blazer and khaki pants. Howard felt a burst of pride as he looked at Will, and then at Max, who was dressed the same way.

In what looked like an old blazer of Howard's. Maybe Marilyn had given it to Max? Sarah and Vilma both seemed happy but slightly frazzled. Cat was there too, and she and Adele and Marilyn gathered in a clump and they all started talking at once.

Soon thereafter, everyone was gravitating toward the tables of cheese and crackers and fruit and water and coffee and lemonade that were set up in the hallway outside the smaller of the temple's two sanctuaries, and after the West Orange crowd showered Will with mazel tovs and hugs, they turned toward Adele, and she was clearly basking in being the center of attention. Soaking up the adoration from Cousin Morty, Lucretia, and Bobby. Clea and Andrea were looking on in rapt fascination, while Stuart stood slightly at the edge of the group, a nostalgic expression on his face.

Lucy arrived, looking better than Howard had seen her in a while, and between greeting everyone and embracing them, she kept pulling out her phone and smiling at whatever was on her screen, except she kept covering her mouth with her hand. It was a gesture he remembered well from years past, their ever-private youngest daughter shielding her emotions from the world.

"Lucy looks good," Marilyn said, appearing beside Howard. "Don't you think? I wonder…"

Howard wondered too, but he knew they shouldn't ask Lucy anything, so he changed the subject. "You look good too," he said. And she did.

Marilyn smiled. "Thanks, and so do you." And she reached over and squeezed his hand. He smiled back at her.

She leaned over and whispered in his ear. "And I'm so relieved about Sarah and Vilma. That there's no situation."

Howard nodded, and then Diana and Philippe appeared, Diana looking radiant and Philippe looking nervous, and Diana took her turn as the center of attention, but Adele and Will didn't seem to mind, and then it was time to go into the service. And Will, flanked by Sarah, Vilma, and Max, said the blessing and lit the candles, and Howard clasped the hands of Marilyn and Adele on either side of him, and he felt that for once in his life, maybe, he had nothing to worry about.

Forty-Five

Lucy

"So how did it go?" Jonah was waiting for Lucy in her apartment when she returned from the synagogue. He was sitting at her small dining table grading papers, but he put down his pen and stood up to give her a kiss, which she returned, and then everything turned totally passionate.

"Great," she managed to say, as, entwined, they made their way to the sofa and slightly thereafter to the bed. And it was a while later before she ended up telling him about how grown-up Will looked up there saying the prayer and lighting the candles, and how proud everyone was of him, and how incredible it was to see the whole West Orange reunion. By now, Jonah had some familiarity with the entire cast of characters. And he'd asked if Will seemed nervous, and said he'd been unable to sleep the night before his own bar mitzvah, and Lucy said she'd been the same way, and that yes, Will did seem nervous but sort of self-confident, in a way that Lucy couldn't imagine being.

"But you should be," Jonah said, wrapping himself around her. "You have a lot to be confident about."

And Lucy thought about that, and even though she wasn't sure what she had to be confident about, she knew she was happier than she'd been in ages. And she wondered if Jonah was, too. So she asked him, marveling that she felt comfortable enough to talk to him about something like that.

"Do you really need to ask?" he replied, and he smiled at her, and she smiled back, and then there wasn't all that much talking for a while. And Lucy felt as if she was floating away.

And it struck her that she'd really like Jonah to come with her to the bar mitzvah. So she told him that, too. Sarah had mentioned there had been some last-minute cancellations, so there should be enough food.

"Wow," he said. "Thanks, I'd love to." But then his face took on a doubtful expression.

"What?" she asked, a pulse of worry shooting through her. Did he think she'd been too possessive in asking him to come with her? Was it too soon? Yeah, probably. She'd screwed up again.

"No, I really do want to come. It's just that the kids are going to see the two of us together, and..."

"Oh." Now she got it. Will was inviting like fifty kids to the bar mitzvah, most of whom were their former students. But there had to be some way around this dilemma, right? "Wait, let me think."

And she thought and thought, although she kept being distracted by the fact that Jonah was kissing her, and finally an idea came to her. And she texted Kathleen. And Kathleen texted right back and said that would be great.

And then she called Diana, and Diana said, yeah, good idea, because she'd need to be sitting in the back anyway in case she went into labor and had to make a quick exit. Their parents, up in the front row, would have Max and Aunt Adele and Cat and the West Orange contingent with them, so they'd be okay.

Lucy felt a surge of triumph as she hung up with Diana. "Okay, Mr. Shapiro, looks like you're going to the bar mitzvah," she told Jonah. "I think it's all going to work out."

"I can't wait, Ms. Pinsky," Jonah said, and Lucy found that she just couldn't stop smiling.

Forty-Six

Will

Will had a great view from his seat on the bimah, and he could enjoy it now that he'd chanted his Torah and Haftarah portions and given his speech and recited all the prayers he was supposed to recite, and he had a sense it had gone well. No mistakes. His mom and Vilma were indeed beaming with pride, and they both kept hugging him, right up there on the bimah, which normally would have been sort of embarrassing but he didn't care.

And as the rabbi went through some more prayers, Will looked out at the congregation. His friends were there, Will Z. and Marco and Arjun and Benjamin and the others. Katelin C. was there too, along with a bunch of other girls. She'd smiled at him a couple of times, which was cool. Grandma and Gramps and Max were sitting in the front row, along with Aunt Adele and Cat and Cousin Morty and Lucretia. Gramps's friends from New Jersey were in the second row, right behind them. Everyone looked really happy. Even Max, who'd been kind of grumpy lately. Will had seen Max talking with Seb before the service, and the two of them had been joking around, and Will wondered whether they'd stopped being friends or something, because he hadn't seen Seb in months, but the way they were talking, they did seem like friends, so that was good.

And then he'd noticed the girl from the park, whose name was apparently Isla, and she and Max were exchanging these looks all the time, like they couldn't stop looking at each other. And Isla was sitting with this older dude who looked totally lit. He was wearing a suit and a yarmulke, like all the other men--including Will himself, who was now a newly minted Jewish man, however crazy that seemed--but somehow the suit and the yarmulke looked different on this guy. Cooler. Was this Isla's dad? The one Max was taking lessons from? Will hadn't realized they were coming to the bar mitzvah, but he was glad they were there.

Diana and Philippe were way in the back, in the last row. Diana had had this kind of strange look on her face earlier, before the service started, but when Philippe asked if she was okay, she said of course she was, and she dragged him off to their seats.

Oddly enough, next to Diana and Philippe were Lucy, Mr. Shapiro, and Ms. Collins. Will also hadn't known Mr. Shapiro and Ms. Collins were planning to be there. He hadn't seen them before the service. They must have slipped in just as it was starting. Will peered more closely at Lucy and Mr. Shapiro, and, from his bird's-eye vantage point, it seemed as if they were holding hands. Wow! Maybe Mr. Shapiro would end up being his uncle after all.

And then the cantor was asking everyone to join in a song, and all of a sudden there was a commotion at the back of the room, and Diana stood up, and she waved at Will and headed for the door, followed by a stressed-out-looking Philippe. Diana didn't seem stressed out at all. She seemed like she was an actor making an exit in a play. But Will could see his mom looking alarmed, and Grandma appeared to be about to stand up and run down the aisle after Diana and Philippe, but then Gramps and Aunt Adele leaned over toward Grandma and they all seemed to be conferring, and Vilma was conferring over Will with Will's mom, and in the end

Grandma settled back in her seat, and looked up at Will and gave him a huge smile.

And Will usually didn't like to sing, but he was feeling so good and so relieved to be done with everything and so excited that maybe Diana was finally having the baby that he joined right in with the cantor. And Aunt Adele gave him a thumbs up, and he wondered for the millionth time what exactly she'd done in the circus. But in the end, maybe it didn't matter. She was back, after all, part of the family again, and that's what really counted, wasn't it?

Acknowledgments

I have so many people to thank in connection with this book! First of all, many thanks to everyone at Apprentice House Press for their willingness to publish Off to Join the Circus. Beginning with editor extraordinaire Kevin Atticks and continuing with student editors Brian Leechow, Rachel Hoos, Catherine Cusma, Claire Marino, and their colleagues, it has been a pleasure to work with you. I am most grateful.

My gratitude also goes to amazing friends and wonderful publicists Jill Bernstein and Mary Bisbee-Beek. Your generosity goes above and beyond.

Naomi Feigenbaum and Mary Grace McGeehan, what can I say to thank you for your fantastic friendship, and for your incredible support of my writing for decades now. I am beyond fortunate to know both of you.

Kevin Scott, thanks for your advice on the life of a chef. Any mistakes on that front are my own.

I'm sure I'm forgetting other people who have helped me, and I apologize in advance.

As always, my family has provided the most incredible support. Thank you, thank you, thank you to my parents, Marvin and Madeleine Kalb, who have always been there for me and for my writing. Thanks beyond words to my husband, David Levitt, who in recent years has battled health concerns with courage. And many thanks to my son, Aaron Kalb Levitt, for his humor and for his understanding of my weird working hours. Thank you to Judith Kalb, Alex Ogden, and Eloise Ogden, as well as other family members who have cheered me on. I love you all.

And no, we really are not the Pinskys!

--Deborah Kalb

About the Author

Deborah Kalb is the author of the novel *Off to Join the Circus*, her debut novel for adults. She has written fiction for kids and non-fiction for adults, and she's the host of the blog *Book Q&As with Deborah Kalb*, where she interviews an eclectic range of authors. A former longtime D.C.-based journalist covering Congress and politics, she lives in the Washington, D.C., area.

Apprentice House Press
Loyola University Maryland

Apprentice House is the country's only campus-based, student-staffed book publishing company. Directed by professors and industry professionals, it is a nonprofit activity of the Communication Department at Loyola University Maryland.

Using state-of-the-art technology and an experiential learning model of education, Apprentice House publishes books in untraditional ways. This dual responsibility as publishers and educators creates an unprecedented collaborative environment among faculty and students, while teaching tomorrow's editors, designers, and marketers.

Eclectic and provocative, Apprentice House titles intend to entertain as well as spark dialogue on a variety of topics. Financial contributions to sustain the press's work are welcomed. Contributions are tax deductible to the fullest extent allowed by the IRS.

To learn more about Apprentice House books or to obtain submission guidelines, please visit www.apprenticehouse.com.

Apprentice House
Communication Department
Loyola University Maryland
4501 N. Charles Street
Baltimore, MD 21210
Ph: 410-617-5265
info@apprenticehouse.com • www.apprenticehouse.com